NEW BEGINNINGS AT THE LITTLE CHRISTMAS INN

GEORGIA HILL

BLOODHOUND BOOKS

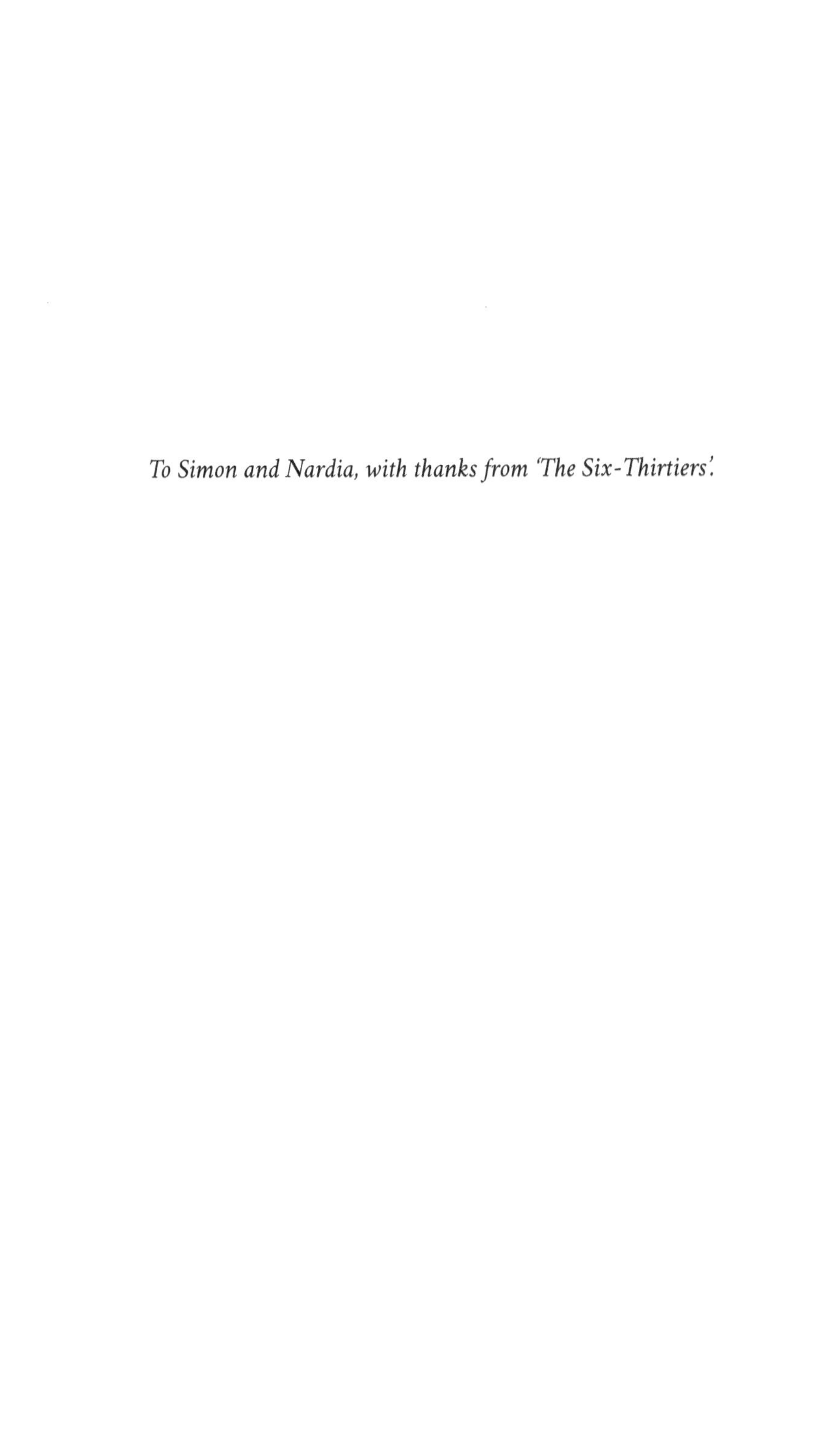

To Simon and Nardia, with thanks from 'The Six-Thirtiers'.

CHAPTER 1

West Country cider. Dry on the palate, occasionally fruity, and potent
when drunk to excess

'You our new landlady then?' The old guy wheezed as Livvy handed over his pint of cider. Nervously tucking a strand of blonde hair behind her ear, she waited for the inevitable. It came.

'Bit young, ain't you?'

Refusing to rise to the bait, she smiled and gave him his change. He shuffled off, followed by his equally ancient dog, to sit in the darkest corner of the pub.

'Welcome to Lullbury Bay and The Runaways.' It was another male voice. Younger this time, friendlier, with a twist of humour and slightly northern.

She turned to the customer who had just come in. He was waiting at the other end of the bar, a rolled-up broadsheet under his arm.

'Don't mind Old Pete. One of Dorset's most eccentric characters. He's quite friendly once you get to know him.' He nodded to the collie at the old man's feet. 'Can't say the same for Skip, though.' Grinning, he added: 'A politic biscuit works wonders there.' He stretched over a hand and she shook it. 'Mark Cavanagh. I'm in most evenings when I'm in town so I suppose I'll be another of your regulars.'

'Lovely to meet you. Olivia Smith. New owner for my sins. Call me Livvy.'

'Hello Livvy Smith. Pint of bitter when you're ready and a packet of salt and vinegar.'

Livvy busied herself pulling his pint of beer, eyeing Mark surreptitiously. Thank goodness at least one of her customers was friendly. It had been quiet since she'd taken over but then maybe seaside pubs in October were? Apart from a group of braying businessmen, hardly anyone had been in and, until tonight, no one had introduced themselves.

She overfilled Mark's pint glass with clumsy fingers and put it on the bar towel to absorb the drips before giving it to him. In his late thirties maybe, dressed in a nondescript grey sweater and jeans, he'd perched on a stool and had spread out his newspaper. She liked the way his thick red-brown hair swooped down as he bent over the small print.

'Put your glasses on, why don't you?' Pete yelled from his corner, making Skip growl.

Looking up, Mark took his pint. 'Thanks.' He flipped open a designer case and put on some tortoiseshell specs. 'Vanity is a terrible thing.' He wiggled his brows.

Livvy liked him more for admitting it. Reaching into the box of crisps behind her, she passed some over.

'Are you going to change the name?' He ripped open the packet and began to eat enthusiastically.

'Of the pub? I haven't really had time to think about it.' Livvy screwed up her face. 'I can't say The Runaways is the most traditional of names.'

'The last chain who owned the place renamed it.' He took a swig of beer and made an appreciative noise. 'Supposed to stem from back in the nineteenth century. Forbidden love.' He frowned, obviously thinking. 'Young couple met here before they ran away to be together, or so the story goes.'

'Don't you be boring the girl,' Pete shouted.

'If you're going to join in the conversation, come and do it here rather than yelling at us,' Mark called back.

'Happy here, I'll have you know. Although another cider wouldn't go amiss.'

'I'll bring it over.' Livvy began to pour it. 'What happened to them? The young couple I mean?'

'No idea. Tragedy probably. Isn't that how those stories always end? Jason might know. He's into local history. Pops in here sometimes.'

Livvy took Pete his pint, noticing how her feet stuck to the carpet. She looked down at the worn paisley pattern. That would have to go. Glancing at the dated hunting prints resplendent against the pink flock wallpaper and the cerise frilly lamp shades, the same thought occurred.

'There you go, Pete.' She put the cider down, keeping a wary eye on the collie which had bared its teeth.

'Thank you, my lovely. Put it on the tab, will you. I'll be having another before I goes.'

'I'm not doing tabs,' she said firmly.

The old man scowled. She half expected him to bare his teeth in solidarity with his dog. 'No tabs you say. What's all that about then?'

Livvy folded her arms, ready for her first battle. 'New rule of the house.'

'Where do you think I'm going to run off to, with my arthritis? And at my age too. I'm eighty-three.'

'Sorry, Pete. I can't make exceptions. One rule for everybody. Eighteen or eighty-three.'

She tensed, expecting him to put up a fight, but instead he reached into his pocket and handed over the money. 'Thanks, Pete. Give me a nod and I'll bring another over when you're ready.'

'Ar, that I'll do.' He bent down to the dog. 'Remind you of anyone, Skip? Yes, just like our Marjorie. We likes a woman with a firm hand, don't we, boy?'

'I think you've scored a hit there,' Mark said, on a laugh, as she returned to the bar.

'How so?'

'To be compared with Pete's late wife is the height of compliments and not one given lightly.'

Livvy glanced over at the old man. He was staring into space, sucking on his teeth. 'He's on his own? That's rather sad.'

'Another saddo here,' Mark said. 'Divorced,' he added as explanation. 'All very amicable, I'm relieved to say and a while ago. Speaking of which, I thought there was going to be a couple running this place? I only saw one name over the door as licensee. Is it just you? Sorry. Eye for detail. I notice these things.'

Livvy leaned her hip against the glass washer and pondered what to say. 'That's right,' she said crisply. 'There's only me.'

Mark took the hint. 'So, what are your plans for the place?'

She hesitated. 'I don't really know.' This wasn't true. She and Gavin had once had plans. Wonderful plans for a gastropub. All scrubbed pine and mismatched chairs. They'd had plans for their life together, but it seemed those had been mismatched too. Like the couple in the story, he'd run away. Only not with her. She straightened her shoulders. 'Ease into things gently, I think.'

Mark nodded. 'Well, you won't get all that much tourist trade being this far up the hill away from the beach, but the beer garden has a fine view over the bay in the summer. That's a draw. You get the builders coming in from work when they've finished a shift building those houses on the new estate.' He shrugged. 'You won't be as busy as the pubs on the front but it's steadier, more all year through trade. Helps, of course, if you do food and it's probably the only way to make money. Are you planning on doing any?'

Gavin was going to do the cooking and she was going to concentrate on front of house. A wave of loneliness engulfed her. It was all going to be so much harder on her own. She bit her lip, refusing to show weakness. 'It's something I'm thinking about.' Forcing a smile, she added, 'I'll have to find a chef though. I'm strictly a toast girl.'

Mark eyed her curiously. 'Well, there's usually someone around looking for work, even in the winter. And you've got a few months to get established before the summer season gets going.'

He was being kind, but Livvy sensed he was dying to ask more. Just as she was determined not to reveal the sorry truth. 'Thanks,' she said, coolly. 'For the advice.' To her relief, a couple walked in and she had an excuse to cut the conversation short in order to serve them.

CHAPTER 2

*L*ivvy lay in bed that night, exhausted but unable to sleep. Her brain hard-wired back to the moment when, just as they were about to enrol for the pub licence course, Gavin had turned to her in panic.

'I can't go through with it, Liv. It's too much responsibility. What if it all goes tits-up?'

She squeezed his hand. 'It won't, darling. We've talked it all through. We're going to make a go of it.' When he hesitated further, she added, 'Gavin, this is our dream. To run away to the seaside. To have our very own pub. We've worked so hard for it. Saved up, gone without. The course is the last hurdle.'

His face was ashen. 'I'm sorry. I'm so sorry.' He shook his head vigorously. 'It's not for me. I can't do it.'

As he stumbled down the steps of the town hall, she cried

after him, 'But we've nowhere to go. It's too late to back out now, the flat's been let.'

As an answer, without turning around, he'd simply put up his hand in a sad, defeated gesture.

Livvy had stood, one foot on the step above. One foot already on its way to the future.

She could back out and, like Gavin, run away. Part of her longed to do just that. And part of her acknowledged she'd known this was coming. She thought back to his shifty glances whenever she'd tried to discuss a business plan, his refusal to attend meetings at the bank. She had put in the lion's share of the money, Gavin had promised to put in the lion's share of the work. It had all been decided. And now their plans were nothing but dust and ashes.

Someone knocked into her, forcing her onto the next step up. It was a man wearing a suit and a carnation buttonhole. Probably on his way to the registry office.

Livvy hovered, thinking furiously. She had nowhere to go except to the pub she'd just bought. She had no job other than as its new landlady. The enormity of it all overwhelmed her and, for a second, tears threatened. Then anger began to lick at her. *Bloody Gavin! How dare he force me into this position?* She should be excited, looking forward to the next phase in her life. Instead, she was facing it alone.

Two more wedding guests hurried past, in flowery dresses and cheap perfume. Gavin had proposed once, but only in a horrible, jokey sort of a way, when drunk. The memory was the final straw. A pure, white-hot rage fired within her. *I'm going to do this. Even if it means doing it on my own.* She'd wasted enough time on Gavin Marshall. She'd marched after the women and had turned decisively left to the examination room.

Livvy flung herself over in bed and thumped the pillow into submission. She could do this! Even without Gavin. She was the one with the background in hospitality, with years of experience in the family business. What's more, she longed to prove to her father she could stand on her own two feet, run her own place. Her parents hadn't been happy with her decision to break away but Livvy couldn't be satisfied knowing she was thought of as the Smith-Lygott nepo child. It would have been all too easy to stay working for them and within their long-established company. The Smith-Lygott hotel chain, at its zenith, had had a worldwide reputation for luxury and excellence. All well and good but it had been built up by her father. Livvy wanted something she'd created, something of her own, no matter how lonely the path forward was going to be.

Willing herself to sleep, she closed her eyes. And opened them again at the sound. Wind buffeted at the building. Her bedroom shook and the windows rattled. The pub was set high on the main road leading east out of Lullbury Bay, on an exposed stretch of cliff. Livvy pulled the duvet over her head, tried not to think about how alone she was in this big old building and concentrated on sleep.

CHAPTER 3

Tracy's Hot Chocolate Special – proper cocoa, chocolate flakes, giant
marshmallows and maybe a tot of rum.
Best drunk with friends.

She woke to a bright morning. Puzzled and bleary-eyed, she stared at the still-closed curtains. How could it be so light? Then she realised her bedside light was still on. Freaked by the weird noises, she'd eventually drifted off to sleep with it still on. Looking around her bedroom she mustered a smile. IKEA's finest looked at odds with the ancient black beams and lime-plastered walls but it was the only furniture she had. Any refurbishment was going to be done downstairs where it mattered. Yawning, she got out of bed and drew back the curtains.

Gasping with pleasure, she rubbed off condensation and gazed out. Whatever the job threw at her it was going to be a privilege to wake up to this every day. Although not the biggest bedroom, the view was the reason she'd chosen it as her own.

The rosy-misted dawn lit the sky and the sea to the east. From here, she could see right across Lullbury Bay, to Portland stretching out as a finger in the sea. All was calm this morning. After the squally weather in the night, the sea possessed a milky tranquillity, the only thing interrupting the horizon, an enormous trawler. She could stare at this view all day. Her phone ringing out the alarm had her running for the shower. She had a busy day ahead. Reaching for her favourite shower gel, all thoughts of the weather were dismissed. She had too much on to get all meteorological.

The morning was a blur of deliveries. She desperately needed to stock up but when she signed the invoice, she blanched at the cost. To take her mind off things she drove to the local Cash and Carry and bought some bar snacks. She thought, in lieu of doing any food, she'd offer high-end crisps and nuts. The idea was to have them out on the bar for customers to help themselves. With Skip the collie in mind and wanting to be dog-friendly, she also bought some dog treats. It was going to cut into her profit margin and she might have to rethink, but she wanted to give the idea a go. No chance of breaking even until she could start offering meals.

Driving back to the pub – *to home,* she amended, she took the long way round and drove along the seafront. Having worked mostly in midlands towns and cities, the strip of golden sand with the bluey-purple sea beyond lifted her spirits and made her forget how much she'd spent that morning. She wound the window down and sucked in a lungful of fresh briny sea air. Rattling along in her van, she spotted a parking space big enough and pulled in. Getting out, she rested her arms on the railings which separated the promenade from the beach below. Spying a takeaway shack open, she treated herself to hot chocolate and, feeling childishly pleased, sat on a bench and took in her new surroundings.

It would be strange to spend Christmas by the sea. She always associated the season with pretty, snow-covered villages and fields. She'd be on her own too. No Gavin; and her parents were booked on a cruise over the holidays so there was little point taking much time off. Livvy concentrated on the view, trying not to dwell on how alone she was.

Lullbury Bay was split in two, with the harbour at one end and the shops at the other. Both had steep roads leading out which had made the van creak and groan. The town was joined by a long flat promenade and sandy beach. In the summer it would be heaving but today there were only a few dog walkers wandering around. The sky was a vivid blue, with white clouds scudding across. Lifting her face to the October sun she marvelled it still had some warmth beyond the biting sea breeze. She skidded her trainers on the concrete, feeling the sand beneath her feet. It was wonderful. Like being on holiday. Next to her the bench sagged. She opened her eyes to see an old man had joined her. Dressed for the cold wind, he wore a beige cap and a bright red scarf above which could just about be seen a bulbous, pink veined nose and kind eyes behind thick lenses.

'Morning,' he said. 'Smashing day.'

'Good morning.' She was cautious. Unless behind a bar and working she wasn't in the habit of striking up conversations with strangers. It just hadn't seemed to happen wherever she'd lived before. In fact, making eye contact and talking to someone you didn't know had been interpreted as the reserve of the desperate or those with issues. She flicked her hair over her face giving herself something to hide behind.

'You got that from The Sea Spray?' he said, nodding to her takeaway cup.

Livvy shook her head, licking a dribble of melted cream off her finger.

'Next time, take my advice, my lovely, and go there. It's over yonder towards the harbour. Tracy does the best hot chocolate this side of Weymouth. Might be so bold and say best in west

Dorset. I'm on my way there to get me one now. Marshmallows and a flake is my tipple of choice. With sprinkles. Can't beat it when there's a wind like today.' He pointed to the grey clouds bubbling up in the far west. 'Nice at the moment but, mark my words, it'll go nasty later. Reckon there's a spot of hail coming in.' He held out a hand. 'Austin Ruddick. Born and bred. You on holiday, my lovely?'

Livvy took his hand warily and shook her head again. 'Livvy Smith.'

'Pretty name. So, if you're not on your hols, what you be up to then?'

Livvy edged away slightly. 'Just enjoying the view.'

'It's grand, isn't it? Best time of the year to enjoy it an' all. Quiet. Time to take it all in, listen to the sea, breathe in the ozone. Noticed they're putting up the Christmas trees above the shops in the high street today. Can't believe Christmas is round the corner. Lullbury likes a bit of Christmas. There'll be lots going on. It's grand old town to spend the season in.'

She remained silent.

'Forgive me, my lovely, but you don't seem very chatty.'

This stung. Her behaviour had nothing to do with how any man, even one so old and gentle as Austin seemed, dictated. 'Am I supposed to be?'

'You'm sitting on a friendship bench.'

'Sorry, a what?'

'Looky here.' Austin pointed to a plaque behind Livvy's back. 'Bee from the bookshop and community café got it all sorted. Lots of folk on their own, she reckons, and don't know how to start a conversation, pass the time of day, like.' He chortled. 'Never had that problem myself. My Aggie reckons I can talk the hind legs off a donkey. But there are some folk, lonely folk, who want to chat but don't have the wherewithal to drum up a conversation with a stranger. So she got the council to put these plaques on some benches along the front here. You sit on 'em if you've a mind for a chinwag. Been ever so popular. She got a community award for them, did our Bee, because of it.'

'Oh I see,' Livvy said, not sure she actually did. 'I didn't realise. I'm new to the town and simply down here to get my bearings and enjoy the sunshine.'

'Well, that's good. Mind you, I always say, warm sun in October means snow come December. Mighty fine sight, is snow on the beach.'

'It must be.'

'Doesn't happen very often.'

'I can imagine. Where I worked last, we had snow quite a lot.'

'And where would that be?'

'The Cotswolds. Not far from Stratford.'

'Lovely part of the world. And what brings you to Lullbury Bay?'

'A job.'

Austin peered at her, brows raised questioningly, so she gave in.

'I've just bought the pub up on the hill. The old coaching inn.'

'Have you now? Well done you. Been closed awhile that has. Will be good to see the old place open again. I'll drop in and have a pint with Old Pete. He still going in, is he?'

'Oh yes.'

'That's good.' Austin nodded approvingly. 'Lifeline for him now his Marjorie has gone. Don't know what he'd do without his skittles and his cider. Not to mention that raggedly old mutt of his. Mine's gone now. Had a German Shepherd. Lovely dog she was. The best. Miss her like a limb.' Tears sprang into his age faded eyes and he stood abruptly. 'Can't stay sitting too much longer, the old legs get stiff if I do. Lovely talking to you, Livvy.' He touched a finger to his cap in a charming, old-fashioned gesture. 'You take care of yourself, and I'll be along for a pint. Bye now.'

'Goodbye.' She twisted to read the plaque she'd missed before:

"Rest awhile. Make a friend. Enjoy the view. Life's richer with a chat."

Smiling, she watched Austin as he sauntered away, limping slightly on his right leg. It had felt good to talk to a stranger. Had left a warm glow in her heart. Perhaps there was something in this friendship bench idea. Maybe, just maybe, her Christmas by the sea wouldn't be lonely after all.

CHAPTER 4

Lullbury Bay Craft Distillery Gin – smooth classic juniper flavour with a subtle bite. An acquired taste.

Opening up at eleven, she was met at the door by Pete and the collie. She sighed a little. Was she destined to be surrounded by old men today?

'What are these then?' He peered suspiciously at the chilli nuts and hand-cut crisps displayed in pretty glass dishes on the bar.

'Bar snacks.' Livvy began pulling his pint of cider.

Pete wrinkled up his nose.

'They're free,' she added, placing his full glass on the bar mat.

'In that case, I'll have me a few.' He scooped up an enormous handful, grabbed his pint and shuffled off to his corner.

'Here, Skip.' Livvy threw a dog treat which the collie caught deftly.

'You'll never make a profit that way.' Pete chuckled. 'Giving folk free stuff.'

'I won't if you're my only regular,' Livvy muttered under her breath. This wasn't her idea of how her pub would be. In her head she had sanded wooden floors, a wood burner gusting out heat, quirky artwork on the walls. She looked around at the fusion of clashing and worn patterns and huffed. Was she mad to take this on? Pete opened his newspaper and shook it hard. Sipping his pint and eating his chilli nuts one by one, he looked set for the day.

How would he feel about the changes she wanted to make? She needed to attract a different clientele, those who would spend generously and enjoy the ambience she wanted to create. But she needed to be fair to the established regulars, like Pete, too. Suppressing a smile, she couldn't help but think how different he was to the sort of customer her father's hotels dealt with. Both difficult in their way but both deserving of the very best in hospitality.

She looked around at the otherwise empty pub. Maybe it was too optimistic to expect many in on a Thursday lunchtime in October, but she'd hoped for more customers than Pete and his dog. Her heart sank. If this was going to be what it was like, there hardly seemed any point in making any changes at all.

Get a grip, Liv, she scolded. *Remember your dream.* Leaning on the bar, she grabbed a notebook and began outlining an advert for a chef. The sooner she had someone in the kitchen the better.

'Good morning.'

Livvy looked up to see a tall, slender man, maybe in his forties, standing at the bar. He had pale hair which had possibly once been blond and wore a three-piece suit with studied elegance. A pair of expensive-looking glasses with thin black frames completed the urbane effect. He must move silently, like a cat, as she hadn't heard him come in.

'Good morning.' She glanced at the ancient station clock on the wall. She liked it and had decided it would stay. 'Although I rather think it's good afternoon.' She smiled warmly. 'What can I get you?'

'A gin and tonic if I may. Local if you have it. Salcombe otherwise. Botanicals tonic.' He held out a hand. 'And perhaps we should compromise on hello. Saves all the tedious uncertainty of when it's morning and when it's afternoon. It's so good to see the old place open again. I'm Jason Lemmon.'

Livvy shook his hand, hoping her own wasn't too sticky from Pete's cider. 'Livvy Smith. Your new landlady.'

'Delighted.'

'Ice and lemon?'

Jason smiled. He had very white teeth and the smile warmed his otherwise chilly, patrician features. 'Of course.'

'Help yourself to bar snacks. Please.' Turning her back on him to make his drink, she was relieved she'd taken her gin stock seriously and had a range of local ones in. When she turned back, she was delighted to see him eating a kettle crisp. Just the one. He was nibbling it with a fastidious reserve.

'These are very good.'

'I'm afraid we're not doing any food just yet. But hopefully soon. Just as soon as I've appointed staff.'

'Ah. Not a worry. I seldom eat lunch.'

Livvy could believe it. The man was scarily lean. She gestured to the notepad in front of her. 'I was drafting out an ad just now.'

'Who do you need?'

Livvy picked up her biro and tapped it against her teeth. 'A chef who knows what he's doing, plus a sous chef and waiting staff. Eventually I'd like an experienced barman and cellarman too.' She caught herself and blushed. 'They might have to wait until things pick up.'

Jason sipped his G and T. 'You have big plans for this place, I take it?'

Livvy nodded eagerly. 'There's a function room at the back I'd like to renovate as a restaurant, and I'd really like to refurb this place too. Hoping for the gastropub vibe.' She paused. Having voiced it she wasn't sure this was still her vision. Austin's words about the place being Old Pete's lifeline returned. 'I need to take it one step at a time though,' she added.

'It sounds a very promising plan, and I for one would welcome another fine dining choice in Lullbury.'

Pete ambled up to the bar. He nodded curtly at Jason.

'What do you think of our new landlady's schemes, Pete?' Jason asked.

Livvy stiffened. She wondered if Jason was stirring things. An old man like Pete surely wouldn't welcome change to his local.

'As long as I gets a good pint of cider and Skip is still welcome, I ain't complaining.' He took the fresh pint Livvy had poured and turned to go. Then stopped and turned back. He wagged a finger, its joints thickened with arthritis. 'Don't you go messing with the skittle alley though, you hear. The lads are looking forward to the winter season. Tain't been the same without the alley being open.' He ambled back to his seat, spilling a little cider on the carpet.

Jason pursed his lips. 'There's your answer. Change is acceptable as long as there *is* no change.' He gave a short laugh. 'About sums up this town.' His eyes flickered. 'It's a lot to take on. For someone on their own. Which I assume you are?'

Livvy squared her shoulders. 'Oh, don't worry about me. My parents have been in the hotel trade all their lives. I used to work for them. I know my stuff.'

'Good. Then I wish you all the luck in the world.' Draining his glass, he put up a hand in farewell. 'And I may have someone in mind for your kitchen. I'll ask him to get in touch.'

Livvy watched Jason's departure thoughtfully. Taking a crisp, she glanced through the notes she'd made. A personal recommendation would be far better than attracting some randoms through an ad. She took another crisp. Jason was right; they were delicious. Far too nice to give away. She eyed the generously filled bowls she'd put out so optimistically. She couldn't afford this. She'd have to keep the better stuff back to sell and try to make at least a small amount of profit. She'd put out some cheaper snacks on the bar.

Glancing over at Pete, his chin nodding against his chest as he dozed off over a copy of the *Lullbury Bay Echo*, her thoughts strayed to the skittle alley. She'd had no idea pub skittles were still so popular. The alley was a long narrow building snaking along from the side of the pub held up, from what she could see, with ivy and mould. It had an ancient, corrugated tin roof that was well down on the list of renovations. A team of skittles players coming in once, maybe twice a week would bolster her takings through the winter until the tourist season began again. Might be worth keeping going.

A gout of wind threw hail at the window, the sunshine of the early morning having long gone. It made her look up and her glance took in the darts board. She'd been planning on getting rid of it as soon as possible. A mistake? Darts teams, like skittles players, liked the odd pint or three. Perhaps she'd keep it. At least for a while. Too much change too soon might not be wise. And maybe Austin Ruddick had a point about the pub being all people like Old Pete had.

CHAPTER 5

*Builder's Tea – strong, three sugars, hint of milk, best served
with biscuits*

It had been a difficult decision, but Livvy was sure it was the only way to do it. Despite what she'd said to Jason about easing the pub into change, she couldn't bear the pink chintz and hunting prints one moment longer. A refurbishment was urgently needed. The trouble was, she had to close down. The three-man team of decorators, a father and two sons, had been adamant they could get the work turned around in two weeks. Plenty of time to open up with a party for fireworks night; ease a new staffing team through November – a notoriously slow month in the pub trade – and then go all guns blazing in the run-up to Christmas and the new year. It also gave her an opportunity to actually appoint some staff.

Pete had complained vociferously so, as a compromise, Livvy had agreed to keep the skittle alley open for the first few fixtures of the season. She promised them burgers – even she could rustle up a batch of burgers and rolls – and a barrel of real ale.

Luckily, the chain which had previously owned the pub had revamped the commercial kitchen and it was, if not exactly state of art, perfectly suitable. She needed to do nothing in there for a while. The bar was a priority, but she'd also decided to attack the function room. The more food she could offer, the better her chance of a profit. She had long-term plans to let the rooms upstairs and convert the outbuildings into holiday accommodation but all that would have to wait.

The 'lads' – a group of silver-haired men all in their eighties, seemed happy with the skittles alley as it was, so that would definitely have to languish at the bottom of her list of priorities.

The handyman, painting and decorating team of Darrell, Dougie and Duncan – she couldn't distinguish who was who, they were all rotund and dark-haired – set about their task with gusto, beginning with the bar. The plan was to strip the walls back to the original plaster, see what was under the revolting sticky carpets and take off the laminate cladding from around the bar. Darrell, or it could have been Dougie, was sure the original stone bar lay underneath.

'Leave it with us, Livvy my lover,' he said, cheerfully. 'A brew on the hour, every hour is all we need. You won't recognise the old place once we've finished with it.'

Livvy fled to the kitchen, where she sought refuge. She began ringing round beer suppliers, wanting to reopen with something more exciting than the generic stuff previously on offer. Trying to overlook the ominous bumps and thumps coming from the bar, she ignored the missed call from her parents and dialled the first number on her list. It was Lullbury Bay's Micro Brewery and sounded promising.

Taking in a tray of tea and biscuits, an hour later, she gasped. The chintzy wallpaper had been stripped off, the Germoline pink lampshades had gone, and half of the revolting carpet had been torn up.

Putting the tray on the dust-sheet covered bar, she stood in amazement.

One of the Ds came up to her, stepping carefully over the rolled-up carpet. He took a mug and drank half in one go. 'Told you we'd get a shifty on.' He brushed a hand over his mouth, leaving a streak of dust. 'To be fair, the stripping out don't take too long. We'll need another skip though.'

Livvy nodded.

'You'm lucky. Walls are sound as far as we can tell. Might need a bit of re-plastering in places. You want a rough look though, don't you?' He beckoned to her. 'And come and have a look-see over here.'

Following him, Livvy looked down to where he pointed. 'Stone flags!' she exclaimed.

'Original ones, I reckon. From when the place was built.'

'Why would anyone want to cover them up?'

'Beats me.' Darrell/Dougie/Duncan scratched his head. 'Some folk reckon they feel cold but in a bar you can't do no better. Don't have to worry about mucky boots or spills, or Pete's smelly dog.'

'Do you think they'll come up with a clean?'

'Oh yeah. We'll give 'em a deep clean and shove some sealant on. Be as good as new.'

'They'll be fantastic.' She paused and hazarded a guess, 'Darrell. Just what I had in mind.'

He beamed, a blush staining his rounded features. 'Pleasure. Be nice to see the old place go back to what it was. Didn't like what that company did to it. Didn't suit the old girl.'

They returned to the bar where he drank the rest of his tea. Shoving two custard creams in at once, he said, through crumbs, 'You'll be wanting the back room done too, I reckon?'

'Do you think you'll have time?'

He nodded. 'Oh ar. We likes to get our heads down, get the inside jobs done this time of year. If you wants, we can come back in the spring and get going on the beer garden. Been fair neglected has that. Shame. Best view in Lullbury. We do a bit of landscaping too. Can't do that until the weather improves though and we go off to the family place in Lanzarote January to March, like, but we'll fit you in. Only take the jobs we wants to do.' He gave a broad wink and named the pub chain Livvy had bought The Runaways off. 'They didn't give no locals no work so it's good to get all the crap they foisted on the place out. You get back to what you'm doing. We'll be clear by eight tonight and then you can have the place to yourself again.'

Livvy returned to the kitchen. It had been a gamble to take Darrell and his sons on, but it looked to be paying off. Ringing her father to assure him all was going to plan, she was so engrossed in furniture catalogues she didn't, at first, hear the knock on the kitchen door. Opening it, she said, with genuine pleasure, 'Mark!' She hadn't seen him since the night he introduced himself.

They settled at one of the high food prep tables, on two bar stools she'd rescued before they disappeared into a skip. Livvy made yet another pot of tea. Pushing over the half empty packet of custard creams, she asked, 'What brings you here? You know I'm shut for the duration, don't you?'

He nodded. 'Saw Darrell's sign outside. And the full skip. Once he gets going, he doesn't mess about. I see all the pink is on the way out.'

'They're okay though, aren't they? Pete said they were local and reliable although Jason Lemmon said, in his opinion, they were a bit flaky.' Pete was rapidly becoming the go-to source for local knowledge. She was getting fond of him.

Mark looked up quickly at the mention of Jason's name. 'They're fine. They'll do a cracking job. So, you've been getting to know the locals then?'

Livvy pulled a face. 'Not many. Old Pete's been in every evening and Jason's popped by once or twice. I suppose it doesn't help that I've had to close.'

'Probably not,' Mark said cheerfully. 'But we're used to the place being shut. We can put up with it for another week or so. What are you having done?'

Livvy showed him her ideas folder. It was nothing more than a messy collection of photographs, but it gave an indication of how she saw the pub developing. 'The wood burner is going in the old fireplace, once Darrell has opened it up and I've booked the chimney sweep in.' She gave Mark a quick glance. 'I can't believe it was bricked up, it'll be such a super feature when it's done.'

He nodded. 'I have a wood burner in my place. You can't beat them on a winter's night. It's almost like having another person there. They're good company.' Shrugging, as if embarrassed about what he'd revealed, he added, 'Not that it often gets all that cold here, but the damp comes off the sea and gets right into your bones.'

'Darrell's promised me the stone flags are going to come up beautifully. I'm really excited about those. The walls are going to be rough rendered and the beams cleaned back. Haven't decided on lighting yet, that's a fairly crucial thing to get right and I need to source some furniture too.'

'You're on your own with the lighting, I wouldn't have a clue, but I might be able to help you with furniture. A friend runs an auction house in Bridport.' He took a biscuit and crunched into it. 'I'll give him a ring, shall I? Fancy a day out?' He looked around at the unused kitchen. 'You can't do much in the pub while the work's going ahead, can you?'

Livvy regarded his open, friendly face. 'Thanks, Mark. That would be lovely. I haven't seen much of the area since I moved here.' She smiled. 'And I have to admit I'm getting rather stir-crazy.'

'Leave it with me then. I'll give you a ring. The pub's still on the old number, I take it?'

Livvy nodded. She watched as he slid off the bar stool and let himself out. A kind man. One who would be good to have as a friend.

CHAPTER 6

Espresso – a concentrated form of coffee, small serving topped by crema.
To brighten the senses

Two days later, Mark called for her at eight in the morning. It was a fresh, breezy day with cotton wool clouds boiling up over a sea foaming with white horses. Livvy took in a great gulp of briny air as she waited for Mark to pull into the pub car park and turn around. Several gulls took off in high dudgeon at the intrusion and she watched as they wheeled and swooped expertly. Sometimes she couldn't believe she was living by the sea. Living her dream. Waving to Dougie, or possibly Duncan, who was leaning against the wall having a smoke and a mug of tea, she got into Mark's Mercedes.

'Lovely day,' she greeted him.

'It is. Proper wintry bite to that wind, though.' He turned out of the car park and concentrated on navigating the narrow hill up out of town. Livvy was happy to sit back and admire the sea on one side and the elegant Georgian houses on the other. One or two already had Christmas trees in their windows, with lights strung up outside and one house had a fine display of white reindeer in the front garden.

Austin had said Lullbury Bay went mad for Christmas and it looked like some started early. She hoped she could get the pub properly going in time for the season. Christmas could be a wonderful time in a pub. She pictured the place, warmed by the wood burner, a tree in one corner, the bar festooned with lights.

Once clear of the town and on the road to Bridport, Mark picked up the conversation. 'Craig assures me he's got some stuff in which might be of interest. A job lot of chairs and tables from a restaurant.'

'Sounds promising.'

'If we get there early, we can have a good look at it and then get some breakfast somewhere. How does that sound?'

Livvy grinned. 'Perfect.' She sighed and leaned back against the headrest. 'It's really nice to let someone else do the driving for a change. I've been so busy rushing around getting things done, I've hardly noticed where I am most of the time.'

Mark chuckled. 'Let me know when you're next on the road. You don't sound very safe.'

'I'm probably not. Too busy thinking about collecting the next order of soft drinks from the Cash and Carry.' Livvy gave a short laugh. 'If it's any consolation, my old van won't go above thirty with my foot floored, so I don't think I'm too much of a danger to anyone. And, to think, I had to sell my gorgeous Mini to buy it.' She looked around at the Mercedes' interior. 'This is a lovely car. Very luxurious.' She wriggled. 'Loving the heated seats.'

'Thank you. It's a bit of a weakness of mine. I like nice cars. And I'm in it for a fair bit of the week, travelling for work, so I consider it a necessity.' He flashed a quick grin.

'What do you do, Mark?'

'Argh, I was hoping to put off telling you the sorry truth. I'm an accountant. Not very glamorous.'

Livvy looked around at the car's interior again. 'But well-paid.'

'That's the pay-off. A grindingly boring job which pays dividends.'

Somehow Livvy thought there was more to it but didn't feel it was the time to probe. She hardly knew the man, after all. 'You don't sound as if you're from Dorset?'

'The northern accent escapes sometimes although I haven't lived there for years. Yes, Yorkshire born. Trained and worked in London and then made good my escape to Dorset.'

'After your divorce?'

Mark slowed the car as they reached the outskirts of Bridport. He paused before answering. 'It was one of the contributing factors. Gemma was very bedded in with London life; she's a real city girl. Born and bred. I wanted out.' He shrugged as he indicated and turned into an enormous car park which flanked a bland-looking square building. 'It was all very amicable in the end. We're both happy and have ended up friends. I go up to London for work quite a lot and we've got to the stage where we can have a civilised conversation over dinner.' He parked up and killed the engine. 'Here we are.'

Livvy followed him into a cavernous space full of every object she could imagine. Enormous, old-fashioned wardrobes lined the walls, paintings hung in random patterns, crammed onto any available space, sagging sofas and scruffy chairs hogged the floor and tables were littered with vases and ornaments, all decorated with tiny For Sale tags. Her heart sank. She couldn't imagine any of this having a place in her pub. She was about to say so when a voice boomed from behind them.

'Mark, you old reprobate. Good to see you!' A man the size of a small planet descended upon them. He clapped Mark on the back with such force that it moved him a couple of inches forward.

Mark coughed a little, turned and greeted his friend. 'Craig mate.' They shook hands then Mark introduced Livvy.

Craig beamed. He put an arm around her shoulders and began leading her through the warren of furniture. 'Ah, the brave soul who has taken on The Runaways. Do tell me you're going to change the name. I must pop by when you're all set up. Always a favourite hostelry of mine. Such charm. Or it had before it was covered up in corporate chintz. Now, my dear, come this way. I may have just what you seek.'

Craig took them into a side room, still an enormous space but more intimate than the main floor. 'Took delivery of it all last week. They'll fly. Good stuff. All antique pine, ready-stripped, none of your violent orange here. Have a good old look and, if you're interested, come and take a punt. Main auction is at ten. They're up fairly early on in the list so don't be late.' A voice shouted his name from somewhere distant. 'Ah, duty calls.' He pushed them both forward, thankfully more gently this time. 'Enjoy. Enjoy!'

Livvy caught Mark's eye and smothered a laugh. 'Quite an eccentric.'

'He is. But he knows his stuff. Said on the phone that he's pushed this lot in today as he knew someone was interested but couldn't bid until later in the week. If you want it, now's your chance.'

Livvy took her time. There were about twenty or so tables. All slightly different designs but the same height. None of the chairs matched either and were a collection of spindle-backed kitchen chairs, and solid more formal ones which she could use in the restaurant. Importantly, although they were of different types, they too were the same height and type of wood. Someone, when originally buying, had had a keen eye for design. The furniture, although mismatched, went together perfectly. Put in the bar and restaurant, it would create exactly the look she had in mind. Unfussy, understated and practical. Running a hand over the scrubbed pine table nearest her, she visualised it all in her pub. No table linen needed, fat sputtering candles in the restaurant, some good quality table mats, wooden maybe or slate. She shuddered as she thought of the ones with hunting scenes that had been thrown into the skip that morning. Excitement bubbled. She might, after all, achieve what she was after.

Looking up, she became aware of Mark studying her. 'Any good?'

'Perfect,' she breathed. 'Just perfect.'

CHAPTER 7

Strong English Breakfast tea – best served in a plain half pint mug and ideally accompanied by bacon and eggs.

Over the best full English she'd ever eaten, in the greasy spoon attached to the auction hall, she found out a little more about Mark. He was thirty-eight, had parents who lived in York and a younger sister who lived in London. He spent the majority of his time in Lullbury and worked remotely but went up to London about twice a month.

'I stay with sis,' he added. 'Works well. She's an actor so isn't there too much of the time.' He went on to list some of his sister's work.

'Oh, I know her! She was in that hit thriller on the BBC last year, wasn't she?' Livvy went a bit starstruck. Mark, despite his claim to be a boring accountant, and his sibling, both seemed impossibly glamorous. 'She was fantastic in it.'

'Natalie's really talented,' he agreed. 'She keeps trying the States but it's hard to break into film or TV over there.'

'So exciting.'

'As is taking over a pub and restaurant.' Mark put down his knife and fork with a satisfied sigh and slid his empty plate to one side. 'They do a good breakfast here.'

'Agreed.' Livvy took in her surroundings. It was a utilitarian place, as boxy and bland as the auction house, but it was busy, hummed with good-natured banter punctuated by a noisy coffee machine and smelled enticingly of bacon. Now and again, when there was a lull in the chatter, Bay Radio could be heard playing cheesy Christmas pop songs. The only other concession to the upcoming season was a small, decorated tree on the counter flanked by a Father Christmas figure which lit up and danced whenever anyone went by.

'I don't think I could eat another thing. Would you like the last piece of toast?' When she refused, he asked, after a pause, 'Tell me, I can't help but be curious. How does a woman like you, obviously talented, ambitious and hard-working but who openly admits to not being able to cook, want to open a restaurant?'

Livvy also put down her cutlery. Out of habit, long engrained, she stacked her plate neatly on top of Mark's, tidying the used knives and forks. She sipped her builder's tea. Putting down the plain white china mug and admiring its simple pared-back style, she began, haltingly, to tell him about Gavin and how their plans had all gone wrong.

'I've been brought up in the hotel trade. I've known it all my life. Mum and Dad only have the one place now but at one point owned a whole chain of hotels worldwide. I spent every summer working in a different one, gaining experience the hard way. Chambermaid, waiting tables, bar work. Then I wanted to break free for a while. Went off travelling, rattled around the world for a few years working in any hotel not owned by my parents, did a degree in history, rebelled a bit I suppose.' She smiled. 'As you do. And also, as you do, found out that a history degree and a passport full of stamps doesn't necessarily lead you to the career of your dreams. Fell into a rather tedious office job in Stratford, funnily enough not far from my parents' Cotswolds hotel.

'And there I met Gavin. He cooked in the office canteen, but I could see he was talented. Some of his food was wasted on the workers. They just wanted a quick salad or toasted sandwich for lunch. His *scallops au beurre* with black pudding was left untouched.' She gave another smile at the memory of Gavin's frustration. He only stayed in the job as he was asked to cater for the occasional works function when he could showcase his talents. So, we came up with a plan. I had some money released from its trust fund when I turned thirty. I had the experience in the hospitality trade, Gavin had the cheffing skills. Except–'

'Except?'

Livvy didn't speak for a moment. She wasn't sure she could bear to. Twisting a lock of hair around her finger she listened as Michael Bublé sang 'Jingle Bells' on Bay Radio. Its jollity mocked her. Staring out through the windows misted with condensation, she finally answered. 'He ran out on me at the last moment. We were about to go in and do the exam which you have to pass to obtain your publican's licence.' She gave a dry laugh at the memory. 'Can you imagine, all my experience in the trade and I didn't actually have a publican's licence? We were standing on the steps about to go into the town hall and he said he couldn't go through with it.' Livvy peered disconsolately into her empty mug. 'I'm still not sure if it was me or the pub he ran out on.'

A silence descended. A curvy, comfortable-looking woman collected their plates, replacing them with two coffees and a parcel wrapped loosely in a holly patterned serviette. 'Never too early for your first mince pie,' she said, grinning broadly. 'Make a wish on 'em, don't forget.'

Mark expressed his thanks and opened the serviette. The warm aroma of spice and nutmeg drifted up in the steam from four mince pies. 'Can you manage one?'

'It's not too long until Christmas.' Livvy smiled. 'I think we're honour bound. And it will be my first so I'm definitely going to make a wish.' Biting into one, she closed her eyes and wished her new pub success. When she opened them again, Mark was staring. 'What was your wish?'

'Don't think they come true if you tell.' Unexpectedly, he took Livvy's hand, releasing it almost immediately. Pausing, he sucked in a deep breath, but all he said was, 'You're very brave to take all this on alone. I admire you for it.' Then he added, on a more upbeat note, 'Well, you've got your pub but at the moment it's extremely empty. We'd better go and buy you some furniture then, hadn't we?'

Livvy once again sank back on the luxurious passenger seat in Mark's car. They were making the return journey to Lullbury Bay. The auction had been tense, exciting and successful.

'Happy?' Mark glanced across as he changed gear.

'Completely. The furniture is exactly what I was looking for.' Livvy grinned. 'And I can't believe we got it at such a knock-down price too.'

'I thought that bloke at the back was going to keep bidding but he chickened out.'

'All the better for me,' Livvy said smugly. 'And it's fantastic that Craig is willing to store it all until the pub is refurbed.'

'He's a good bloke. Might cost you a few white wines on the house though.'

'That I can do.' She looked across to Mark with affection. 'Thank you for today. It's really helped me out. One huge step forward with my plans.'

'No problem at all. I really enjoyed it. What's next? Step, I mean.'

'Staff,' Livvy said decisively. 'I really need to get some staff in. Otherwise, I'll run myself ragged if I get busy.'

'*When* you get busy,' Mark replied, warmly.

'Thank you for your optimism. Okay then,' Livvy laughed, 'when I get busy! Mark?'

'Yes, Livvy.'

'Is there any more to that story you told me of the runaway lovers? Do you know anything more about them?'

He shook his head. 'Sorry no. Why do you want to know?' He chuckled. 'Haven't you enough on your plate?'

'You'd think, wouldn't you! It's nice to have a sense of history of the place. I was thinking of making a feature of the story. People like that when they eat somewhere, or stay.'

'You're going to do rooms?'

'Eventually. But that's long into the future. I still have a gutted bar and restaurant to conquer.'

'You'll get there. Darrell's team are an anomaly in the tradie world. Efficient, turn up when they say they will and do the job.'

'I know. I can't believe my luck in finding them.'

'Darrell's a nephew of Pete's, I think.'

Livvy smiled. 'That makes sense. No wonder he recommended them.'

'It's how things work round here.'

'For which I'm very grateful. I might tap Pete for info about the runaways then. He seems to know everything there is to know.'

'Someone at the museum might be able to help too. Pete's tales tend to get more far-fetched the more cider he drinks.'

'I'll maybe give Jason a ring. He said he might have someone in mind for chef, so I need to speak to him anyway.'

Mark slowed to turn into the pub car park. 'About Jason,' he said stiffly.

'What?' Livvy looked at him. The bantering, reassuring, slightly flirty tone had disappeared.

'He's okay, from what I know. But he's a ruthless businessman.' He parked the car but left the engine running. 'Just be careful.'

'Consider me warned.' Livvy wanted to ask how she should be careful and indeed why but could see Darrell peering into the skip. Some wag had tied a large bunch of mistletoe and tinsel to it. Darrell tweaked it, grinned and headed her way. 'Thanks again for today, Mark.'

'My pleasure. Make sure you let me know the reopening date and I'll be there.'

'Will do.' She got out of the car and watched as it growled in a low gear up the hill out of town. His warning about Jason had left her unsettled but she couldn't deny how nice a man Mark was. Turning to greet Darrell and his inevitable barrage of questions, she smiled to herself. She wasn't about to complicate her life further by getting involved with tricky Jason or the eminently nice Mark. Getting romantic with the punters always led to a whole heap of trouble.

'New skip's here,' Darrell said. 'But we'll need another. It's already half full. And I needs you to make a decision on lights for the restaurant. Make it quick and we can order them snappy like and get 'em in. Oh, and put the kettle on, love. I'm gasping.'

All thoughts of romantic runaway lovers, the enigmatic Jason, and Mark with his concerned hazel eyes and floppy dark red hair fled. Falling back to earth with a bump, she followed Darrell's burly overalled figure into the pub.

CHAPTER 8

Limoncello – a classic Italian liqueur, sharp bitter top notes based on a
sweet syrup

The interviews were not going well. So far Livvy had seen three young lads, none of whom could string a sentence together or add up; and Brittany, who was slightly more promising. Livvy recognised the brittle posh girl façade; she'd been to school with the type. Rich parents, no attention. In fact, Brittany could have been her ten years ago. Having failed her cabin crew training, Brittany moaned her mother had threatened to throw her out unless she got some kind of job. The only problem she was desperate to go travelling as soon as she had funds so Livvy wasn't sure how long she'd be around.

She'd have to ditch the impractical fake nails, Livvy thought, but, from a poor choice, she seemed the best on offer. Livvy had told her she'd think about it and, once Brittany had gone, had looked gloomily through the other applicants. No one suitable for cellarman or chef. The phone rang, startling her. It was Jason.

Bearing in mind what Mark had said about him, even so, when she'd replaced the receiver, her spirits were in a much better state. He had the number of a chef she could use. He came highly recommended and was available straight away. It seemed too good to be true, but she was desperate.

Sitting in the pub kitchen two hours later Livvy began the interview. She hesitated and re-checked the online form the man had completed. 'Fabio, is it? Could you summarise your experience please?'

As the man talked, without a hint of the Italian accent his name suggested, Livvy studied him. Early thirties, ridiculously good-looking with luxurious dark hair and limpid brown eyes. It would be a shame to hide him in the kitchen.

'Catering college of course,' he was saying. 'Samphyre in Exeter, Rolandaz in London, spent time in the States cooking for celebs.' He named two of the biggest film studios.

He was certainly well-qualified. Overly so. She was suspicious. 'You said you're originally from the west country. What brings you back? And would you really be happy cooking in a small pub? Will we be able to offer you the challenge you so obviously need?'

Fabio's eyes gleamed. 'I could make it so much more. That would be the challenge. Building from nothing to something. To a destination eating experience!'

Livvy suppressed a smile. She liked the arrogance. 'Putting aside the insult that The Runaways is nothing, would cooking here be enough for you? You're obviously very ambitious. How would I know you'd stay?'

'Livvy, I'm back here as my mama is ill. I want to spend some time with her.' For a second tears shone in the dark eyes. 'While I can. Cooking for you would be a gift. If you trusted me to do what I want in the kitchen, then I'll promise you I'll stay as long as it suits us both. And, by the way, my real name's Fred but Fabio goes down better with the clientele.' He gave a shrug. 'Mama is Italian but I'm from Honiton. Devon boy, me.'

Livvy stared at him. He seemed, the name thing aside, to be genuine. But she didn't want to rush into anything and make the wrong decision, no matter the urgency. 'Fabio, would you be prepared to cook for me as part of your interview?'

'Of course! It would be my pleasure. But mostly yours. And the menu – is that up to me?'

'Entirely up to you. Just let me have the bill for the ingredients so I can reimburse you.'

He smacked a forefinger and thumb to his lips in a gesture so overtly Italian, it made Livvy want to hire him then and there. 'Then I shall prepare a tasting menu, the likes of which you have never had. Will it just be for you?'

The thought of eating this promised banquet all alone had Livvy's mood plummeting. 'No,' she said, as something occurred to her. 'There'll be two of us.' After Mark's kindness over the auction, she owed him a favour.

'Then it will be a meal *per due*,' Fabio said with a flourish and grinned. Then he added, 'Leave it with me, my lovely,' rapidly resorting to Devon.

Having possibly appointed a chef, it became apparent the need for other staff was paramount. It was a risk to take them on when she hadn't got the business up and running but so was opening on a shoestring. Better to start off how she meant to continue. Fabio would need a sous chef and she and Brittany would need help behind the bar and, at this her feminist principles rebelled, someone strong to look after the cellar was vital. Barrels of beer weighed a ton.

Her saviour came, once again, in the unlikely form of Pete. With the kitchen operating, she'd kept the skittles alley open. She could offer limited beer and cider, and burgers. It went down well with the players but was surprisingly hard work. After the Wednesday match, a local derby bitterly contested between teams from The Runaways and The Toad and Flamingo, the locals' pub on the other side of town, he stayed back to help clear up.

To her surprise, Mark popped by and offered his help too. 'Was driving home and saw the lights on,' he said. 'Thought you might need a hand.'

Livvy sighed out her gratitude. 'Thank you, Mark.' There was something about his presence she found reassuring.

'The lass is doing too much,' Pete grunted from the far end of the alley where he was carefully, and at a glacial speed, stacking chairs. 'Take that empty barrel out, will you?'

Mark grinned, saluted him and rolled his sleeves up. Tipping the barrel over on its side, he rolled it out to the car park. Returning he said, amazed, 'How much do that lot drink? There's five barrels out there.'

'I'm not complaining. Keeps my income ticking over when I don't have anything else coming in.' Livvy began to collect the empty pint glasses and then gave up; she'd leave it until the morning. 'And thank you for taking the barrel out. I'm looking for staff but apart from one girl called Brittany who I'll think I'll take on, and a possible chef, I haven't found anyone else suitable.'

'Wish I could help. But I can't think of anyone looking for work. Lullbury is like most seaside places; the young move away, the retired rarely want to commit to regular paid work again. You'll have more joy in the summer when the students come in looking for seasonal work.'

'Except I can't wait that long. I want to launch when the refurb is done and open with a fireworks party.' She gave an exhausted grin. 'Open with a bang if you like. And there are going to be times when I can't be here. I need someone reliable, someone trustworthy to take my place.'

Pete shuffled towards them. 'You need a good cellarman. Do the grunt work. Someone good behind the bar an' all.'

'Nothing wrong with your hearing, Pete,' Mark said.

'I'll ignore that,' the old man muttered. 'There's Young Karl. Just been made redundant, he has.'

'Oh come on, Pete,' Mark answered before Livvy could get a word in. 'Young Karl is sixty-three. He's not going to want to hump barrels around.'

'And still going to the gym. Don't tar everyone with the same brush, they'm not all pen pushers like you. Young Karl'd take out three of them barrels to the one you just rolled out.'

'Touché,' Livvy put in. 'Thanks, Pete. I'll certainly consider Karl for the job if you think he'd be interested. How can I get hold of him?'

'Give me here that beer mat. I'll jot down his mobile,' Pete said, a little surprisingly. Peering down at the piece of cardboard, he scribbled down a number. 'He'd be glad of the work, 'specially with Christmas coming up. Expensive time is Christmas.'

'It is,' Livvy said faintly, feeling steam-rollered.

'I'll say my good nights then.' Pete whistled to Skip, who got stiffly to his feet and trotted after his master and out through the door.

'Thank you for all your help, Pete,' Livvy called after him. In reply, he put a hand up.

'Pete, do you want a lift home?' Mark asked, receiving a curt no in answer. He watched him go. 'It's a cold night. I hope he'll be okay. It wouldn't have been any trouble to drive him back; he doesn't live that far from me. Think he likes the stroll back up the hill though.'

Livvy tucked the beer mat into the back pocket of her jeans. 'I'm in danger of staffing the place completely by personal contacts. Saves on the cost of an ad, I suppose.'

'It's the way it works in small towns. Everyone knows one another and everyone knows one another's business.' Mark gave a tight grin. 'Can get claustrophobic at this time of the year without the tourists to dilute the mix a little. If it gets too much for me, I disappear up to London. A few days in the Smoke usually reminds me why I moved to Dorset.'

'I'm sure it does.' Livvy looked at Mark thoughtfully, pondering why he had become the brunt of local gossip. Getting back on topic, she said, 'Maybe I'll give Karl the benefit of the doubt.' Shrugging, she added, 'I mean, what have I to lose? Thank you for your help, Mark. Again!'

'You okay to lock up?'

'Absolutely fine. You go home. Perhaps you'll catch Pete up on your way.'

As she heard the Mercedes's familiar growly engine start up, she wondered where Mark had been coming from. *None of your business, Livvy my girl,* she reprimanded herself. The headlights swept the car park and left her in the dark.

A gull keened mournfully overhead and far below her, the sea shushed and murmured. After the busyness of the skittles match it seemed very lonely. The car park yawned, empty, into the darkness and to the beer garden beyond.

On the other side of the pub was attached a three-storey Georgian town house but the car park faced onto the blank back wall of an office block. Its metal escape stairs rattled in a sudden blast of wind. Wishing she hadn't been so hasty as to insist Mark go, she turned to lock the door of the skittles alley and then stiffened.

Sensing rather than knowing, she felt someone was watching her. A prickle of fear traced down her spine. Keys shoved between her fingers, she braced herself and then turned back to face the car park. 'Hello? Anyone there?' The security lights flared on, temporarily blinding her. There might have been a shadow, maybe a figure flitting the far end, towards the road, but it had gone before she'd really registered.

Unnerved, she ran to the pub's side door, unlocked it and ran in before the security lights cut out again. Her hands shook as she locked the door and double checked it was secure. Her heart pounded into her throat. Ridiculous to be so spooked but she was convinced someone had been out there, watching. Probably bored teenagers. Leaning her forehead against the door and deliberately calming her breathing, she made a note to get the security lights fixed.

CHAPTER 9

Cognac – eau de vie! A classic post prandial digestif

*L*ivvy called Young Karl and interviewed him the following day. He was a compact, stocky man with tattoos and muscles. The very sight of him reassured her he'd be useful to have around, not only for the heavy lifting, but should there be any trouble from customers. She was skilled in deflating tension and dealing with drunks but there was the odd occasion when even she admitted a man with muscles was the only answer. Karl's outward appearance belied his quiet, intelligent personality and, as Pete had suggested, he was glad of the offer of a job, having been made redundant from his warehouse manager's role.

What was even better, Karl had worked his dues in pubs when younger so he knew the job, although confessed he might need retraining. Livvy was relieved. He was perfect. After last night's spook, it would be good to have someone reliable and fatherly around to help lock up.

Once he'd gone, she popped into the function room, now stripped of wall coverings and flooring and asked Darrell if he'd take a look at the outside lighting, bribing him with chocolate digestives and a giant mug of strong tea.

'Will do, my lovely,' was his cheerful response. 'Reckon they can be a bit temperamental, like. Sea air don't help. Damp gets in everywhere.'

Thanking him and blessing the tradie gods who had sent him her way, she left the entire packet of chocolate digestives with him.

Despite the discouraging interviews of the other day, she then had a run of more successful ones and soon filled the other staff vacancies. Stewie, a part-time catering student, tall and skinny with a thatch of bright red hair, grabbed the opportunity to be sous chef, and she took on Eli Wiscombe as part-time bar help for Brittany. She was a little uneasy about Eli, despite his good references from his other job at the animal sanctuary on the outskirts of Lullbury. However, he'd been upfront about the spot of trouble he'd got in a few years ago and she'd appreciated his honesty.

Good-looking, with a broad face and his dark hair gelled into a quiff, he came across as overconfident. But then, he was eighteen. It came with the territory.

All were employed on a trial basis. They'd have to prove themselves, as would she as a good boss. She eased her shoulders, shaking out her hair. It had been a satisfying day's work. Now there was one more phone call she needed to make.

If Mark was surprised at being invited to dinner the following evening, he didn't show it, he simply accepted with a pleasure that was obvious.

The Three Ds had nearly finished the bar. The stone flags had yet to be cleaned up and the lighting and wood burner weren't installed but there was room for a table for two. With light coming from the bar area and a couple of fat candles on a table salvaged from the skip and covered with a snowy tablecloth, and a standalone heater taking the edge off the chill, it just about passed muster.

'After all,' Livvy muttered to herself as she fished out cutlery from a yet unpacked box and laid the table, 'it's not as if it's a date. It's actually an interview, or dinner with a friend. I haven't got time for dates.'

Fabio poked his head out from the door to the kitchen and heard. 'If your dining companion is the guy I've just seen getting out of a taxi, maybe you should rethink that philosophy, babes.'

Livvy laughed and tweaked the position of the napkin and the water glasses. 'I really haven't time for dating, Fred.' She turned. 'Or should I call you Fabio?'

'Just call me Fab-u-lous darling,' he answered camply. 'That'll do. *Amuse bouche* at eight. Get him sat down by then.' He gave a little wave and disappeared.

Mark duly admired the work in progress that was the bar and sat, as instructed, at the little table. It was wobbly and Livvy hoped the wedge of *The Lullbury Bay Echo* she'd shoved hastily under one leg would last the evening. She flicked his napkin open and spread it on his lap. 'What can I get you to drink, sir?' she asked, on a laugh. 'I've a good Sicilian white open, or a local Pinot Noir. Or would you rather a gin and tonic as a pre-prandial cocktail?'

'Perfect.' He grinned. 'I'm glad I decided not to drive.'

Livvy squeezed past Darrell's toolbox and went behind the bar. She decided to join Mark in his choice of drink and poured two glasses of locally produced gin. Adding ice and lemon, she put one in front of him, and she slid onto the chair opposite.

Mark picked up his glass and chinked it with hers. 'Cheers,' he said. He nodded to their surroundings. 'Might catch on, you know. Shabby chic.' He pulled a face. 'Or should I call it builder's chic? Looking good so far, though.'

Livvy sighed. 'It seems to be taking forever. I mean I know it isn't, but I'm not blessed with patience. I'm dying to get the place up and running. There's been a delay on the stove; that should have been installed by now and the Three Ds weren't even here today, they were finishing another job over in Weymouth.' Livvy had hated being alone, without their jaunty, noisy presence. She was a determined cynic when it came to ghosts. She'd lived and worked in places with a haunted reputation and thought it was all a load of nonsense. Even so, the pub was a rambling, rabbit warren of a place to be in on your own.

'That's builders for you. The Three Ds?'

'It's what I call them.' Livvy blushed. 'To my shame I can never remember which is which, although I'm pretty sure, by now, that Darrell is the dad.'

Mark gave a low rumbling laugh that Livvy liked very much. 'They're good blokes though. They'll finish on time. Or thereabouts.' Picking up his water glass, he studied her over the rim. 'Thank you for inviting me, by the way.'

Livvy felt her face heat again. 'It's to thank you for the day at the auction. And for popping by the other night to help clear up. Besides, I didn't fancy eating on my own. I'd value your opinion of the food too, of course,' she added, worried she sounded needy.

'Looking forward to it,' Mark replied warmly. 'And, if you take this Fabio on, there's every chance I'll be eating here regularly. It's no fun cooking for one.'

'Amen to that. It's why I'm a beans on toast fan.'

'Well, if I may say so, the diet suits you.' There was a pause. 'And what have you decided to do about the name? Are you sticking with The Runaways, or changing it?'

'Haven't decided. It was a coaching inn at one point. I've been doing some research while it's been shut. The London to Exeter coaches stopped here, apparently. It was probably called the Coach and Horses or something like that.'

'And that's not what you had in mind?'

'Not entirely sure. I'd like something classy, something unpretentious.'

'There's a new pub opened up over in Bridport called The Bell and Colander. And there's our very own Toad and Flamingo on the other side of Lullbury.'

Livvy pursed her lips. 'That's one thing I've definitely decided I don't want. A made-up name like The Fig and Florin, or Parrot and Pug.'

'You're no fun. What about The Key and Loch? The Ferret and Parsnip? The Brain and Artichoke?'

'The Flag and Quiche?' she countered. 'The Fox and Fart?'

Fabio interrupted their laughter. He stood importantly by the table, a silver salver resting on his arm. 'Your *amuse bouche*, sir, madam.' With a flourish, he removed the lid and deftly served two plates of tiny, exquisite-looking food – scallops in a sauce.

After they'd eaten it, Mark sat back in his chair and said, 'That was delicious. The lemony sauce was amazing.'

Livvy perused the handwritten menu Fabio had supplied. 'Leek velouté with lemon gel,' she read.

'Gorgeous. If the rest of the meal is half as good, I think you should get in that kitchen and snap up that chef. And if you don't, I will!'

The rest of the meal was good. It was better than good. It was excellent. After a six-course tasting menu including a winter salad of caramelised walnuts and pickled beetroot, pollack with an oyster sauce, tender strips of dukkha spiced steak, a creamy cauliflower risotto, marmalade and blood orange pudding and a rhubarb parfait, Livvy and Mark sat picking at a cheese board.

'It's no good,' he moaned. 'I can't do justice to this Ticklemore and it's too delicious to eat just for the sake of it.'

'Time for coffee?'

'I could possibly, just possibly, squeeze down an espresso.'

Livvy left him at the table and went to find Fabio. He was wiping down the food prep tables. 'Fabio, that was the best meal I've ever eaten.'

He shrugged, completely without humility. 'Naturally.' Straightening, he tossed the cleaning cloth into the sink. 'So, the job's mine?'

'Of course the job's yours! Come and join us for coffee and cognac.'

'I wouldn't be intruding? You and Mark seem to be getting on well tonight.'

'You wouldn't be intruding at all. We're just friends. I told you earlier, the last thing on my mind is a boyfriend. I haven't the time, for one thing.'

'Just wanted to add my congratulations,' Mark said, making Livvy jump. She hadn't heard him come in. 'That was a magnificent meal, Fabio. I hope Livvy's given you the job?'

'Looks like it.' Fabio grinned. 'You two go back in, I'll get a pot of coffee on.'

When he joined them, bringing home-made petit fours, Livvy had set out three brandy glasses and a bottle. 'Delamain Pleiade,' she said, opening it. 'Aged for sixty years. I've kept it to one side for a special occasion.' Adding a measure to each glass, she raised her own and added, 'Which this most certainly is. Welcome aboard, Fabio! Welcome to The Runaways.'

They clinked glasses and sat in silence for some time, savouring the spirit as it warmed its way down.

'You still going to call it The Runaways?' Fabio asked, unbuttoning his chef's white tunic.

Livvy swirled cognac around her glass, staring at the mellow tones as they shifted and caught the light from the candles. It had been a bottle her father had given her and not one for sale behind the bar. He'd know exactly what to name the place. Something that would sum up what it was all about. Good food, seasonal and mostly locally sourced, great company, decent beer and wine. Branding had been something the Smith-Lygott organisation had excelled at.

Over the last few weeks, she'd often considered giving him a ring and asking his advice. But she wanted her pub to be just that – her pub. Not part of her father's empire. Some stubborn part of her wanted to prove to him that she could do this herself, go it alone. 'I don't know. I don't like the name, but I don't, as yet, have an alternative.' She put the glass down carefully. 'Do you happen to know what it used to be called, Fabio? I might reinstate the original.'

'I do, as a matter of fact.'

Something in his tone worried her. 'Oh God, don't tell me it was The Hang'd Man or something like that?' she asked, horrified.

'Nah, babes. Nothing so gruesome. It was The George.'

'The George,' Livvy repeated. She thought it over. A not unusual pub name, especially for one of this age. Ordinary but classy. 'It might just do,' she said out loud.

'And what about the restaurant?' Mark put in.

'Something simple,' Livvy answered, while thinking it through. 'Eat at The George?'

'The George,' Fabio added. 'Eat and drink and a warm welcome awaits.'

'Or The George. Drink. Eat. A warm welcome. That's it!' Livvy cried.

'Perfect,' the men chorused.

'Perfect,' Livvy echoed. 'I think this calls for another drink, don't you?' She poured them all another measure. 'Thank you, Fabio,' she said as she toasted him. 'And thank you, Mark. To a successful partnership, and friendship.'

For a second Mark's eyes flickered, then he raised his glass. 'To friendship,' he murmured.

CHAPTER 10

Dry white wine – crisp and no nonsense, with aromatic and tangy secondary notes. Hidden depths. Quaffable.

The following day, after talking Brittany through how she saw the pub working and introducing her to the contactless payment system, and till, Livvy suggested they have a quick look around what their competitors in town were doing. 'Lunch, or maybe several lunches, are on me,' she offered with a grin. She thought it would give her the ideal opportunity to get to know her new employee.

With Brittany bribed with a free lunch, they drove down the steep Harbour Hill to Lullbury Bay. Livvy caught sight of a beautiful Victorian cottage charmingly called Christmas Tree Cottage. It already had a huge tree erected outside, fully decorated and with an enormous white star on top. She parked the van behind a row of yachts, dry moored for the winter, their halyards clinking in the stiff breeze coming off the sea.

'This is the pub where the RNLI crew drink,' Brittany drawled an explanation as she led Livvy to The Old Harbour Pub.

Livvy eyed the enormous Father Christmas figure lashed to the door frame. It appeared to be knitted and wobbled slightly in the wind whipping across the harbour. *Odd thing to greet your customers with.* Following Brittany to the bar she ordered drinks from the gruff man serving and sat down.

'Is it a locals' place?' she asked, looking around at the intricate rope knots and framed pictures of the lifeboat hanging on the walls, all bedecked with red tinsel. A Christmas tree stood in a corner near the wood burner, chaotically decorated in baubles and tinsel. 'Santa Baby' played jauntily in the background. She could just about glimpse a pool table in the adjoining room. It smelled of the sea in here, damp and salty and was, apart from themselves, completely empty.

'Suppose.' Brittany flicked back a long lock of blonde hair and took a sip of her white wine. 'But it's popular with the grocks in the summer. Grockles. That's local lingo for the tourists,' she explained at Livvy's blank look. 'Super place to sit out in the sun and watch the weekenders get their 4x4s stuck as they try to tow their boats out of the mud at low tide. Great laugh.' She grinned. 'It was always the place to get a pint of cider when you were underage. Claude, that's the landlord, turns a blind eye.'

'Risky. You could lose your licence.'

'Don't think old Claude is bothered. He's been here donkeys. He's pretty ancient. Heading into retirement any time.'

Livvy observed the man behind the bar who she assumed was Claude. White-haired, with a shaggy beard and an impressive handlebar moustache he looked quite a character. The place had all the feel of somewhere ticking over until its owner decided he'd had enough. 'Do they serve food?'

Brittany shook her head. 'Not really. Or not what *I'd* consider food. Claude puts on sausage rolls and bacon baps and stuff but no more than that. He's good at doing food whenever there's a fundraiser on, though. Like the New Year's Day Dip, or the Blessing of the Boats Ceremony. On New Year's Day everyone gets decked up in fancy dress and goes for a swim in the sea. It's to raise money for the lifeboat fund.'

'Sounds mad. Think I'd rather just bung them a cheque.'

Brittany laughed. 'Yah. Probably is. It's actually surprisingly good fun though. And everyone packs into here afterwards for a bacon roll and coffee. Trust me, you need it after swimming in the sea in January.'

'I suppose wild water swimming is all the rage but that takes it to another level.'

'Gosh yes, but I think it predates cold-water swimming. The tradition's literally been going for yonks in Lullbury.' Brittany pointed her glass at her. 'You should give it a try. Clears the head awfully well from the night before.'

'Maybe.' Livvy wasn't convinced. She pulled a face. 'Not sure I've ever had a hangover bad enough to warrant swimming in sub-zero temperatures.'

Brittany giggled.

'Tell me about the Blessing of the Boats Ceremony.'

'Ar, that's a good'un, that is.' Claude appeared at their table. 'Hello young Brittany. Haven't seen you in here for a while.'

'Hi, Claude. Yah, I've been away.'

'Have you now. Where then? And anywhere compare with Lullbury Bay? Hard place to beat, is this town.'

'Oh, Australia, Thailand, Dubai, you know.' Brittany flashed a beseeching look at Livvy.

Livvy let the lie pass. A girl didn't like the whole town knowing her failures.

'I don't know, my lovely. Never stepped foot out of Dorset, my girl. And who's your friend here?'

'I'm Livvy.' Livvy extended a hand. 'I've just taken over The Runaways, I mean The George as it's now called.'

'And very nice to meet you.' He smoothed the points of his moustache. 'Come in here to check out the competition?'

Claude obviously wasn't as daft as he looked. Livvy smiled. 'No harm in seeing what else is on offer in town. I've heard very good things about your bacon rolls.'

He grunted. 'Just the thing on a cold day.'

'And I hear you cater for the Blessing of the Boats too?'

He scratched his head. 'Not sure I'd go as fancy as saying it's *catering*, like, but it's my contribution to the day. It's when the town gets together to give thanks for the boats that fish for us, give us our fun and sometimes saves us from the sea. Vicar comes down, we has a sing-song and a prayer and then all pile in out of the wind.'

Livvy was struck by the sincerity in his voice. 'It sounds marvellous. I'll make sure to attend. When does it happen?'

'Not 'til May. Joke is, we waits until the weather's better.'

'And it's absolutely freezing!' Brittany butted in.

'Tis that. But got to do it if you'm a seaside place. That sea out there is a pleasure and our supermarket but it's a treacherous place if you don't respect it.'

'I've a lot to learn about living in a seaside town,' Livvy said.

'You'm come to the right place.' Claude gave a wheezy grin, yellowing teeth just about visible beneath his whiskers. 'Nowhere friendlier. We'll have you part of the community in no time. Pop next door to the lifeboat station while you're down here and get a collection tin. Stick it on your bar. Brings in a few pennies.'

'I will. And I couldn't help notice your magnificent Father Christmas outside.'

'Ar, we likes our Christmas, do us Lullbury folk.'

'So I've heard. Is that something to do with the RNLI too?'

'No, my lovely. That's The Ninja Knitters.'

'The who?'

Brittany spluttered with laughter. 'The knit and natter group. They yarn bomb the town. Knitted hearts in the park for Valentine's, giant yellow chicks for Easter. They literally go all out for Christmas. One year we had a full-sized nativity scene outside the church and knitted holly and ivy all along the promenade railings. My sainted ma is a sometime member when she can be bothered. They meet in The Sea Spray and knit and, well, natter.'

Another form of community. Lullbury Bay seems good at it. 'Sounds great,' Livvy said. 'I'm hopeless at that kind of thing but I'd love a Father Christmas for the pub.'

'You would?' Brittany looked appalled.

Livvy grinned at her. 'If you can't do tacky at Christmas, when can you?'

'I know, darling, but there's a limit.'

'You won't get no Father Christmas in time for this year,' Claude said. 'You has to put in a request months afore. Takes a deal of time. You might land a knitted holly wreath, I suppose.'

Livvy registered Brittany's horrified look and smiled. 'I'll think about it. Thanks, Claude. And thanks for your hospitality.'

'Off to The Ship now then, I reckon?'

'No getting past you, Claude.' Livvy tipped back her drink and rose. 'I need to check out the rest of the competition. Are you coming, Brittany? I'll stand you lunch, I hear the pies are good in The Ship.'

Brittany got to her feet. 'Would rather a burger in the Toad, darling,' she said, brooking no opposition.

As a compromise they ate burgers in the Toad and Flamingo, a pub which looked to be family-orientated, and popped into The Ship for coffee. Livvy loved how it was hidden away along an alleyway off the main street. She also enjoyed the feel of history shifting off the half-timbered walls. She drank her coffee while Brittany flirted with two likely lads at the bar. If she could train her up properly and instil any kind of work ethic, Brittany would be an asset. When she forgot to maintain the cool, posh girl façade, there was a charm. Combined with a no-nonsense brusqueness, it would serve her well behind a bar.

Looking around at The Ship's interior Livvy thought this might be her closest rival. A simple menu which showed they had confidence in their food; a convivial atmosphere; an enormous inglenook fireplace belting out welcome heat; what looked to be a thriving darts team judging from the cups displayed in a cabinet; and it clearly appealed to locals and tourists alike. As she was making a note of what beers they had on tap, two burly blokes dragged in a Christmas tree.

Lenny, who she'd discovered was the landlord, resplendent in a Deep Purple T-shirt and faded Levis, supervised exactly where the tree went. Fitting snugly into the alcove next to the open fire, it would look wonderful when dressed and twinkling with lights. She put one on the list of things to order for her own place.

As they left, one of the lads at the bar called over. 'Oi, Brit. Give us a snog.' He grinned and gestured to the bunch of mistletoe hanging above their heads.

'You should be so lucky, darling,' Brittany shot back. 'Whatever makes you think you can afford me?'

Livvy grinned and followed her out. She was right. With a guiding hand, Brittany would be a real asset to The George.

As they walked down Lullbury Bay's steep main street to where she'd parked the van, a white sports car shot past. It was driven by a very chic blonde. And Mark was in the passenger seat.

CHAPTER 11

*Bourbon – barrel aged American whisky primarily made from maize
corn. Can be harsh on the palate*

*L*ivvy had two more days until The George's soft opening
and there was one more place in Lullbury Bay she
wanted to check out. In her experience, it paid to get to
know your competitors. It was also an advantage to build up
links with other traders. She needed to know what they offered
so she could develop The George's unique selling point. Little
sense in offering what all the others were.

The Old Harbour had the obvious advantage of position. Who
wouldn't want to sit under a glowing sunset right by the sea? The
Toad and Flamingo did exceptional home-cooked food and,
judging from the play equipment in its beer garden, aimed itself
at families. The Ship had its history to offer and was slap bang in
the middle of town, once you'd found it.

She needed to offer something in The George that the others

couldn't. She wasn't confident a dilapidated skittles alley, however popular, would quite cut it.

The one place she had yet to try was The Old School Kitchen. Not a pub but a restaurant. If she was to make good food The George's main attraction, she needed to pitch it differently to the town's main restaurant.

It was almost embarrassing to ring Mark again. He laughed uproariously at her invitation but added he'd pick her up that evening. Having made an online booking, Livvy was impressed with the restaurant's website and added it to her list of ever-growing things to do. Her phone buzzed. Thinking it was Mark, she saw, to her delight, it was her best friend from boarding school.

'Yolly! Hi. How's life in the diplomatic corps?'

'Hard work, doll. I keep running out of cocktail dresses.'

'How awful,' Livvy replied, not hiding her sarcasm. 'How's Cosmo?' Yolanda had married a diplomat who had been posted to the British Embassy in Washington.

'Oh he's loving it. You know Cosmo. Even if things are rather tricky with the Special Relationship at the moment.'

'You don't sound so keen. Is everything all right?'

'I'm fine, Liv. I'm sorry I haven't been in touch. The move over here has been mad and I've the most awful morning sickness.'

There was a pause and then Livvy clocked what Yolanda was saying. 'Oh my God! You're pregnant?'

'I am. It's why I keep running out of frocks. I'm growing like billyo. Doesn't help Cosmo is six foot three, I suppose. Trust me when I say, get sprogged up by a normal sized guy. Not looking forward to the hatching, I can tell you.'

Livvy laughed and then a snatch of envy caught at her, taking her by surprise. She'd thought she and Gavin would have children at some point. Tricky to run a business and have a family but not impossible. A wave of loneliness overwhelmed her, accompanied by self-pity. She brushed it away and said, more forcefully than she meant to, 'Congratulations, Yolly, my love. I'm so pleased for you and Cosmo. When's it due?'

'Not until March. Took me by surprise to be honest. Thought it was all the stress about moving out here but turns out I'm up the duff. And there's more. It's twins. Another reason why I'm so bally enormous.'

'Oh, Yolly, that's amazing. Trust you, you never do things by halves.'

Yolanda giggled. 'Of course. I mean, if you're going to do something, you may as well do it properly. Rather hoping Cosmo will be happy to stop at two and then I'll be done in one fell swoop. Just as well we have staff over here.'

'Get you.'

'I know. I'm rather enjoying it. It's all rather marvellous fun. Apart from the fact I can't keep anything down and I can't even have a sniff of a drink.'

They chatted for a while about the pregnancy and life in Washington and then Yolanda said, 'Now, what about you? Have you got over the beastly Gavin and are you surrounded by heavenly men?'

It was Livvy who giggled this time. 'There are quite a few men around but I'm not sure I'd class any of them as heavenly.' She went on to describe The Three Ds, Jason, Young Karl and Old Pete, and the skittles team. 'I swear they've got an average age of a hundred and three.'

'None of them sound at all promising,' Yolanda reproved. 'I can't have my bestie marooned in deepest, darkest Dorset and be man-less.'

'I'm not looking for anyone, Yolly. Too much else to do and after what Gavin did, I'd find it hard to trust anyone again.'

'But that's no way to live. You've got to get out there again. Not all men are like Gruesome Gavin. Aren't you lonely, darling?'

'I am a bit. When I have the time. Mostly I'm too exhausted to dwell on the fact I'm on my own. I suppose there's Fabio.'

Over the airwaves Livvy could hear Yolanda's ears pricking up. 'Who?'

'My new chef. Looks like Jack Savoretti and cooks like a dream.'

'Oh my. Now *he* sounds promising. I'd give my virginity to a man who looks that good and who could cook me lobster thermidor. Or rather I would, had I not lost the Big V years ago and can't currently eat anything.'

'And he's my employee. It would all be far too messy. It's been hard enough finding staff as it is. And there's lovely Mark. He's been so kind.'

'Lovely Mark?' Yolanda's voice rose excitedly then she paused. 'Ah. Kind? Friend material?'

'Yes, I think so. Hope so. I saw him out with a very glam blonde the other day so he's probably with someone anyway. The funny thing is, we seem to end up eating out rather a lot. In fact, we're eating together tonight.' She explained why and then went on to outline her plans for The George.

'It all sounds rather wonderful. I'm so pleased for you. Looks like your dreams may come true and so they should, especially after what that bastard Gavin did.'

'Gavin? Gavin who?'

'That's the spirit. Speak soon, lovey, and have fun with Lovely Mark.'

Livvy clicked off her phone thoughtfully. The spasm of envy had passed but it had left a residual ache of uncertainty. She gazed around her bedroom hearing the sea batter the cliffs below. Just what was she trying to achieve here? Was she going to be successful? Lack of confidence swamped her. And then, spotting the time she yelped and ran for the shower.

'You know,' Mark said, leaning towards her over the table, an impish expression on his face, 'If we continue eating out together like this, people will begin to talk.'

Livvy lifted her face from the menu. She had been right. Food was serious business in The Old School Kitchen. She and Fabio were going to have to raise their game to offer any kind of competition. 'I'm sorry, what did you say?' She returned his smile. He was looking good in a white shirt and chinos. The lights caught his glossy dark hair turning it chestnut.

He flicked a heavy lock off his forehead. 'It doesn't matter. It's good to see you again, Livvy.'

'Thank you for being my running mate. My fellow gastrophile.' She pulled a face. 'Is that even the right word? I've been so busy my head's exploding and I've lost the power of speech.'

'Gastrophile will do fine. And, a night at home with a Marks and Spencer ready meal, or dinner here? Tough decision. I've been meaning to eat here since it opened but never got round to it. Got to say, it's got a great feel.'

'It has, hasn't it?' Livvy's expert eyes took in the simple décor. Someone had had a clear vision. Bare brick walls, a mixture of long sharing tables and tables for two, white linen, real napkins – a nice touch – and candles and fresh flowers. On the walls were enlarged black and white photographs of when the building had been a school, and nestled in corners were tall leafy plants which softened the look. Apart from the stunning white wreaths made with tightly clustered gypsophila and twinkling white lights, there was nothing Christmassy on show, though carols played quietly in the background. It was classy, understated, with the emphasis on what was important – the food. It was exactly the sort of vibe she hoped for in the restaurant.

A waiter came to take their order. Livvy asked some probing questions which were skilfully fielded. Not only that, expert advice on what wine to choose was offered. It was going to be hard work training up Brittany to a similar professionalism.

Aware of Mark giving her a speculative look and that she'd been ignoring him, she said, 'This all looks pretty perfect, doesn't it?' She sipped her water. Even that was stylish, served in good quality plain glasses from a jug brimming with lemon and ice. 'It's just all so… exactly what I want for The George.'

'And your place will be perfect too.'

She pulled a rueful face. 'I'm getting cold feet.' Gesturing around she added, 'This all looks so good. Classy but unpretentious. It's hard to pull off. And look, there's only one long sharing table empty and that's on a midweek night in early November.'

'Give yourself a chance. You haven't even opened The George yet. You've been working too hard. You're too close to it. When you actually open, I'm sure everything will fall into place. And you've got one outstanding asset.'

'Fabio? Yes, he's great.'

'I meant you.'

Livvy blushed. 'Thank you. You're very good at this.'

'Eating out? I'm excellent at it. Have some wine, it's positively moreish.'

'No.' Livvy giggled, feeling instantly more relaxed. 'I meant this thing you do.'

He frowned.

'Listening then saying exactly the right thing. Bolstering confidence.'

He paused, took a sip of wine and then answered. 'I've been told I'm a good friend.' He laughed shortly. 'Lots of women see me that way.' Spreading his hands he added, 'Don't get me wrong, I'm not complaining. At university most, if not all, of my closest friends were women. I seem to get on better with women than men. Perhaps it's because I've a sister I'm very close to. Listening is part of my job too. I analyse company accounts, give advice on profit and loss, how to move forward. There's a surprising amount of counselling involved.' He twirled his wine glass around by its stem, not meeting Livvy's eyes. His mouth worked. 'It would make a change, sometimes, to be seen as the sexy alpha guy though.'

Livvy didn't have time to answer, nor had she one ready. She didn't think Mark needed to be the sexy alpha guy. He'd do just as he was. 'Oh look,' she said in relief, 'here are our starters. The prawns with aioli for you? And yes, mine's the goat's cheese and beetroot.'

For the rest of the evening they managed to keep the conversation light. Livvy stopped sulking about how perfect The Old School Kitchen was and concentrated on learning from what they were doing and Mark kept up a charming commentary about nothing in particular. It succeeded in keeping Livvy entertained and her mind occupied.

Once they'd reached the coffee stage, a man circled the room. Tallish, with dark hair and smiling eyes, he worked his way round the tables, stopping to chat to diners.

'Hello, I'm Rick, the owner,' he said as he reached them. 'I hope you've enjoyed your meal this evening.'

Livvy held out her hand. 'Livvy Smith. It's been perfect. My plaice was excellent.'

Rick's eyes brimmed with humour as he shook it. 'Livvy! So nice to meet you. You've taken on The Runaways, haven't you? Congratulations.'

'Thank you. Now renamed The George.'

'Good choice of name. Much more appropriate.'

Livvy smiled. 'I think so. We've our soft opening this week. Please come if you can.'

'I'd be delighted.'

'I love your white Christmas wreaths. Can you tell me where I could get some?'

'Absolutely. My fiancée makes them. Daisy Wiscombe. She runs Va Va Bloom. It's a few doors up from here. You can get your Christmas greenery from her too.' He looked around at the restaurant, now gradually emptying. 'I haven't gone to town on Christmas yet, I always wait until at least Bonfire Night is over, but I'll have one of her trees in here. She orders them in from a local Christmas tree farm and can deliver.'

'Brilliant. I'll do that. And I agree with not starting Christmas too early.' Livvy hesitated. 'This is Mark, my friend.' The two men said hello. 'Forgive me but we noticed how good your meat is. Mark said his beef was incredibly tender. Do you source locally?'

'When I can. I was in the supply business before I opened up here. I had lots of local contacts in place already. My philosophy is to source locally and keep food seasonal. Where I can. It's not always possible, of course.'

'My philosophy too.'

'I can email over a list of suppliers if you like. And have you thought about joining the local trade association? It's well worth it.'

'That would be amazingly kind. Thank you.'

Rick shrugged. 'It can be tough when you're starting out. I had lots of input from Caroline over at The Station House – do try their cocktails by the way – so I'm happy to pass it on. And get *The South West News and Views* onside. I'll email the link. It's a what's-on blog. Fairly influential. A review on there is worth gold. Oh,' he said, as an afterthought, 'I don't suppose you're looking for a cleaner? Ours has a sister looking for work. Candice.'

Livvy was overcome. 'I do need a cleaner. I've been putting off advertising for one as I've had builders in and I didn't want a cleaner to be scared off. The George has been in rather a mess. I'd love to meet Candice. Thank you and thank you for all the information. It's so good of you.'

'No worries. One of the things we do really well here in Lull-bury Bay is community. We all help each other. I'm glad you enjoyed the meal. Hopefully we'll see you both again.'

As Mark and Livvy walked through the alley to the shoppers' car park behind the restaurant, Livvy wondered how The George would even begin to compete with The Old School Kitchen. It had been pretty perfect.

Mark unlocked the Mercedes. 'Great evening. Wonderful food but it occurs to me that the one asset The George has that The Old School Kitchen lacks is plenty of parking. An enormous free, easily accessible car park. Counts for a lot, especially in high summer when Lullbury Bay will be rammed and folk will be fighting for a space.' He smiled at her over the roof of the car. 'Get in. I'll take you home.'

Livvy slid onto the passenger seat. She felt a huge rush of affection for Mark. He always knew exactly the right thing to say. And, what's more, she agreed. The Old School Kitchen, while perfect in its own way, perhaps didn't have absolutely *everything* sorted. Much as she'd liked Rick and was grateful to him for his help, she couldn't help but preen just a little.

CHAPTER 12

*Hot milk – sweetened with sugar or preferably honey. Ideal for those
who have trouble sleeping*

 ivvy had been so busy and was so exhausted by the time
she hit the sheets, she was usually fast asleep in minutes.
Tonight, though, worry about reopening the pub was
keeping her awake. Tugging the duvet up around her shoulders,
she shivered further down into the bed, promising herself an
electric blanket as soon as she had time to hit the shops. The
weather had turned cold, and she was discovering the damp in
the sea air never seemed to quite leave the building.

The plan was for a soft relaunch before the fireworks party
and grand opening at the weekend, by which time The Three Ds
had promised faithfully the restaurant refurb would be complete.
She and Fabio had planned a three-course themed menu culmi-
nating in fizz and fireworks around the bonfire. It was a sneaky
way to get rid of any burnable stuff they'd stripped out of the pub
and Darrell's sons had built an impressive bonfire at the far end

of the beer garden. Once lit it would look magnificent against the sea backdrop. She'd splashed out on a professional pyrotechnics company who assured her it would be a good show. Bookings weren't too bad for the restaurant, and she hoped for walk-ins too. It would be a busy night. But first, she had to get through the soft opening when any snags or issues with the team would get ironed out. Hopefully.

Worry and the cold kept sleep at bay and it was the early hours before she'd eventually dozed off. And then, for some reason, she sat up with a start, not knowing what had woken her, and lay there, her heart beating madly. Had she heard something? Shoving her head under the covers completely, she lay listening to her own thumping heartbeat and straining to decipher a sound beyond it. What was that? Mice? She needed a cat who was a good hunter in that case. Or was the scrabbling something else?

She visualised herself going through the locking up process. Main door locked and bolted. Kitchen door ditto. All windows shut tight. Trap door to the cellar secured. She was suddenly very aware that she was alone in a large, rattlingly old building. Sometimes the disadvantages of going it alone were too much. For a second, she wished there was a sturdy male body next to her in bed. Her thoughts drifted to Gavin and she almost smiled. He'd been a bigger wuss than she.

The image of Mark's solid, reassuring presence rose up in her imagination. Her lip curled in amusement; he'd be capable of tackling most things. The window casement clattered making her jump. The advantage of having this as her bedroom was the magnificent view. The downside was the wind coming right off the sea hit this side of the building with force. It was a wild night; the remnant of an Atlantic storm had battered the southwest coast for the last couple of days. Livvy relaxed infinitesimally. Just the wind then. A squall threw itself at the window, spattering the glass with rain so hard it sounded like pebbles from the beach far below.

Livvy's shoulders sank back to their more normal position. It had just been the weather which had woken her. Then she heard it. The side door of the pub, the one leading to the kitchen, far below her, rattled violently as if someone was desperate to get in. Livvy froze. Had she locked it? Screwing her eyes shut she again went through her movements of the evening before. Yes, she definitely remembered locking it and putting on the alarm. Shoving herself up the bed, she switched on the light. Wind battered the window and howled around the corner of the building. It was the wind then. Only the wind. Plus exhaustion, stress and her over-active imagination.

Tripping downstairs to open up for deliveries next morning, she tried to shrug off the sounds of the night before. A noisy wind can catch at the imagination when alone at four in the morning and whirl into being things that just aren't possible. Old buildings had their fair share of hauntings and pubs were notorious for ghosts, but Livvy didn't believe in the spirit world and refused to entertain the idea that The George was haunted. Of course, that left the possibility it was an intruder. Livvy couldn't decide which was worse. No, it had been the wind and her over-hyped nerves about the opening, that was all. Swinging back the kitchen door with vigour, she greeted the vegetable delivery man with a smile of such forced gaiety stitched onto her face that he recoiled.

'Wishing you all the best for today,' he said, looking startled. 'I'll be along later with the missus.' He waved and shot off to his van.

'See you.' Livvy humped the boxes of veg into the kitchen and shut the door firmly on the frigid breeze that whipped up off the sea.

Fabio and Stewie would be along in an hour to begin prep.

Fabio had suggested, until the restaurant was up and running properly, it would be wise to stick to a basic pub menu. Good burgers, a steak and ale pie made with meltingly tender beef, a roasted Mediterranean vegetable lasagne and a rich and creamy fish pie. They'd also offer thrice-cooked chips and a range of baguettes for lunchtimes. It all sounded good to Livvy. Then doubt assailed. For a second lack of sleep overwhelmed her. She pushed a hand through her hair and stared at the boxes of potatoes, onions and assorted peppers piled up in front of her. Could she really pull this off? Resolutely heading for the kettle, she switched it on. There was little that a good cup of coffee couldn't cure.

A knock came at the kitchen door again. Another delivery but this time it was flowers. Two bunches. Reading the card that came with the international delivery made Livvy's heart swell:

Knock 'em dead, doll. Hugest of best wishes for this week's grand opening. Will be over to check out The George asap. Luv Yolly, Cosmo and the Bumps xxx.

She couldn't think who the others could be from. Sending flowers wasn't the sort of thing her parents did even when they approved of something, so it was with some curiosity that she read the second card:

Sending good luck wishes from Daisy and Rick, and all at The Old School Kitchen. Welcome to Lullbury Bay!

She'd arranged them in vases, was on her second coffee and beginning to feel the buzz of the caffeine when Fabio arrived, his nose pink with cold. Unwinding an extra-long scarf from around his neck, he muttered, 'One for me and make it quick.'

Fabio was definitely not a morning person. She assumed it was from years of working late nights in restaurants. Also assuming she'd get nothing out of him bar monosyllables until he'd had his caffeine hit, she poured him a mug, added a dash of cream, just as he liked it and went through to the bar to check the last-minute details.

She stood in the middle of the pub and admired the simple refurb. The chairs and tables bought at the auction looked perfect, the stone flags had cleaned up to a mellow grey and cream and the white-washed walls made everything look fresh and light. The wood burner was laid and ready to be lit and the bar gleamed with glossy optics and bottles, thanks to Candice who was proving a treasure. It was simple and understated and just as she'd wanted. She'd kept the old station clock and it ticked reassuringly into the quiet. Apart from that, the walls were blank; she hoped to find some local art to display.

She was envisioning seascapes and abstract prints when Fabio came up behind her and surprised her by pulling her backwards into him in a fierce hug. Resting his chin on her shoulder, he said, 'It'll be fine, babes, you'll see.'

'Thanks, Fab.' Livvy felt tears prickle. The man could be difficult, but he was free with his affection and praise and sometimes you just needed a hug.

'I'll be in the kitchen if you want me. Chillax, *bambina*. It'll be a riot. Today's special is heritage turkey and stuffing baguettes with home-made cranberry. Shove it up on the chalkboard, there's a love.'

Livvy shook herself into action and meandered around, tweaking the bar towels and drip trays, tucking a chair in, adjusting the bottles on the shelves. She resisted rearranging the mass of white lights she'd put above the bar. They gave off the merest hint of Christmas. Her competitors were already in full Christmas mode, so she'd hung delicate glass decorations from the new wall sconces too. Again, only a pointer to the upcoming season. She didn't want to go full-on Christmas until the tree she'd ordered had arrived. She wasn't doing anything useful or necessary, but it helped. Just before eleven, she poured snacks into the pretty glass bowls she'd bought cheaply at the antiques market in Bridport, took in an enormous breath and unlocked the front door. Stepping outside for a moment, she admired the sign proclaiming the pub's new, or rather original, name. Darrell had found it under a pile of decrepit garden furniture in one of the outhouses. It had come up a treat with a deep clean. And the wooden furniture would burn like kindling on the bonfire.

The George was open for business. Again. And this time it really felt like her place.

Inevitably it was Pete and Skip who were first to arrive. She settled both in a corner by the now merrily flaming wood burner and handed the old man a pint of cider and a newspaper from the rack by the door. 'First one is on the house today. And here's a dog biscuit for Skip.' Not brave enough to hand the treat straight to the cantankerous dog, she put it on the newly scrubbed pine table. 'I hope you like the changes I've made and they're not too drastic.'

Pete harrumphed into his glass. He took a swig and gave Skip the biscuit. 'Looks alright.' Nodding to the wood burner, he added, 'Like the stove. Cosy for the old bones.'

Livvy grinned. It was as much praise as could be hoped from him. 'Glad you approve,' she said softly.

Young Karl arrived and got into position behind the bar, keeping himself busy by polishing already clean glasses.

Brittany turned up at midday for the food service, looking as if she'd only just rolled out of bed. Livvy hoped the girl was awake enough to wait tables; she'd had a good training session with her so was reasonably confident. Once you got past Brittany's sulky, slightly superior air, the girl had a sharp brain. Livvy just hoped she would stick around for a while before going travelling. The team, Livvy included, wore a simple uniform of a black T-shirt and long stone-coloured aprons embossed with the pub's logo. A grumbling Brittany was made to tie up her hair.

For thirty anxious minutes, it was just Brittany, Karl, Livvy, Pete and Skip the collie. Livvy could sense Fabio and Stewie idling impatiently in the kitchen. She stood behind the bar watching the door and praying for customers. She'd put notices on the local Facebook page and had taken out a paid ad in the online version of the local paper. She hoped that was enough.

And then the door opened. Mark first, closely followed by Jason and a sprinkling of walkers who had been tackling the South West Coast Path. Rick arrived, accompanied by a vivacious dark-haired woman wearing a Va Va Bloom T-shirt who Livvy assumed was Daisy. Keeping an eye out for Brittany who was being tutored by Karl, she made her way over.

'Thank you so much for coming. It really means a lot.'

'We came to wish you all the luck in the world.' Daisy gave her a hug. 'Nice to have a new place in town.'

Livvy hugged her back. 'And thank you for the flowers. They're gorgeous!'

Daisy grinned. 'Got to be some advantages to being a florist. Just let me know if you'd like a regular order for the restaurant.'

'I will.' Livvy laughed. As well as being kind, Daisy was obviously an astute businesswoman. She nodded. 'I loved the flowers you did for The Old School Kitchen, so I'll pop by to discuss something similar.'

'Happy to oblige. Oh, and the tree will be with you early December.' Livvy had spoken to Daisy yesterday about ordering a Christmas tree and she'd been efficient and friendly. 'And I'll get the wreaths delivered as soon as I've made them. They're popular so I'm out of them at the moment but Rick said you weren't majoring in Christmas until after your party at the weekend. I'll get them to you with the tree. Promise.'

'Brilliant.'

Daisy leaned nearer. 'And, take it from me, although you'll want to put all the hours God sends into working, remember to take some time out. I've learned that the hard way. Come for a drink one night. Maybe we can do cocktails at The Station House?'

There was something about Daisy that reminded Livvy of Yolanda. Maybe she could be a friend? 'You're on!' Turning to Rick, she thanked him for the information he'd emailed. 'I've had a good look through it and I'll discuss the suppliers with my chef. And I can't thank you enough for Candice, she's a one-woman miracle worker. Now, what can we at The George tempt you with? There's mulled wine on, seeing as the weather has gone decidedly wintry and I can definitely recommend Fabio's burgers. Not sure how he does it but they melt in the mouth.'

Daisy giggled. Flicking a cheeky look at Rick, she said, 'Two burgers then. I'm rather partial to them.'

Letting what was obviously an in-joke go over her head, Livvy showed the couple to a table opposite Pete where Daisy managed, wonder of wonders, to charm Skip. Livvy's admiration for the woman grew and she vowed to ask for dog taming tips.

Less than an hour later, the bar was full, and Fabio and Stewie were churning out delicious food from the kitchen with efficiency. Karl was proving reliable behind the bar and Brittany was putting on a charming front. Even Pete ordered a turkey baguette and chips which he shared with Skip.

Livvy, in a rare quiet moment, stood back and surveyed the scene. Brittany brought out two steak pies for Mark and Jason, the group of walkers were ploughing their way through lasagne and chips, the wood burner flickered comfortingly in the newly opened up chimney and there was a contented hum of chatter from satisfied customers.

As the first real day of business, it would do.

CHAPTER 13

Sassi Vino Bianco – expensive tasting. A cheeky little number

As the pub began to empty Livvy felt herself starting to relax, although her eyes were gritty with stress and fatigue. Jason paid his bill, mouthed the words, 'It was excellent,' put up a hand and left. He passed a woman walking in and they stopped and greeted one another. She was tiny, blonde, very attractive and looked familiar. Livvy suppressed a grin at the way most people seemed to know one another in Lullbury Bay. It was very unlike where she'd worked last.

The woman came up to the bar and smiled. 'Well, darling, I've just heard great things about the food from Jason, but I suppose I'm too late for any today?' She reached a hand over. 'I'm Simona Stratton, your neighbour for your sins. I've been away, otherwise I would have popped in before.'

Livvy shook Simona's hand in response. 'If I sweet talk Fabio, he might rustle you up a baguette. Welcome to The George. Can I get you anything to drink?'

'Oh, sweetie, a large dry white please. I'm absolutely parched. Ye gads, please excuse me for a mo, I've just spotted the love of my life.' She tripped across to the end of the bar, reached up and enfolded Mark in a bear hug. Livvy watched and then it clicked. Simona was the woman driving the flashy white sports car she'd seen him in the other day.

There was a large Georgian house adjoining the pub; Livvy had always admired its symmetry. It was the sort of house she'd like to own when she grew up. So this was who lived in it? Pouring Simona's glass of Pinot, she tried to not to watch as the woman had a very animated conversation with Mark. She wondered if there was something going on between the two. Simona's hands were all over him, stroking his arm, hugging it to her, gazing up at him as if she could eat him up.

Leaving the wine on the bar, Livvy went to check with Fabio about whether he could do one more food order and came back to see Simona and Mark still deep in conversation. Collecting the wine glass, she took it over and presented it to Simona with a flourish saying, 'One white wine. It's a good Italian Pinot so should hit the spot. Fabio has one hot smoked salmon and cream cheese baguette left if you'd like it. Or a turkey and cranberry roll. I twisted his arm, and he said he could do a few chips too.'

'Oh angel!' Simona rolled her eyes in pleasure. 'That sounds heavenly.' She turned to Mark and pouted. 'But you can't join me? Are you sure you have to go?'

Mark extricated himself. 'I've already eaten and some of us have to work for a living, Si,' he said, softening the words with a smile. Turning to Livvy, he surprised her by kissing her on the cheek. 'So glad the reopening has gone well so far. Congratulations. If I can, I'll pop back for a swift pint later. Tell Fabio the food was as delicious as it was the other night.' Then he went before she could answer.

Simona rounded on Livvy. 'Ooh now, *that's* intriguing! The other night, eh? What have I missed out on by being stuck in

Tuscany?' She put her hand through Livvy's arm. 'I simply insist you join me for lunch and tell me all about it.'

Livvy glanced around the bar. There were hardly any customers left. Karl and Brittany were perfectly capable of taking it from here and she hadn't eaten since... actually she hadn't eaten anything. The two cups of coffee drunk first thing that morning had been all that had passed her lips. 'I'd like that. Let me just pop into the kitchen and see what else Fabio has left and I'll be right back.'

Ten minutes later, apart from Pete snoozing in the corner, the pub was empty. Karl, Brittany and Stewie would eat lunch with Fabio in the kitchen and then leave, before returning at seven when the whole thing would start up all over again.

Livvy poured two glasses of wine and took them over to Simona, who was sitting at the same table where Daisy and Rick had sat. 'Food won't be a minute.' She put the glasses down. 'I took the liberty of pouring you another and thought I'd join you.'

'Oh yummy.' Simona clapped her hands together. 'What fun to have the place doing decent wine and nosh again. I've missed it. So handy being right next door. Not far to totter home.' She finished the dregs of her first glass and sipped at the second. 'So,' she tapped the table with French manicured nails, 'sit yourself down and tell me how a gorgeous honey-blonde creature like yourself has ended up in Lullbury Bay running a public house of all things.'

Livvy collapsed onto the chair. 'Ooh, feels so good to sit down. It's been hectic.' She took a slug of wine and then said, 'I'll give you the short history, shall I?' She stuttered through an explanation, leaving out the Gavin part.

Simona's eyes widened when she mentioned her parents' hotel chain. 'Ooh, I've stayed at The Olde Gates in Broadway. That's part of your parents' group, isn't it? It was the most delicious place. If The George becomes half as good, I'm going to rather enjoy having it on my doorstep.' Her mouth dropped open as Fabio came through the swing door from the kitchen, carrying their lunch. 'Talking of delicious… Now, my darling, *who* is this?'

Amused, Livvy introduced them and grinned at how Simona kept hold of Fabio's fingers just a little too long, breathing, 'You're dreamy,' up at him.

Simona showered salt on her chips, watching Fabio disappear into the kitchen and giggling. 'Now, he's far too gorg to hide away. What a dreamboat. If he can cook as well as he looks, I may well have to move in.'

Livvy's tummy rumbled. Picking up her turkey and cranberry roll and not able to wait, she bit into it with relish. 'I had exactly the same thought. And, oh yes, he can cook,' she added, spearing a chip.

Simona picked up a chip too. 'British fries,' she said, going slightly cross-eyed with greed. 'How I've missed you.' She bit it in half and ate it, leaving the remainder on the plate. 'Oh my, oh my. I've never had anything so wonderful in my mouth.' She sniggered. 'And I'm not about to let you in on just what I've had in my mouth. I really don't know you well enough yet.'

Livvy snorted a laugh. She was beginning to like Simona.

The woman gave Livvy a steely look from narrowed eyes. 'So, if I spill the beans all about myself, my darling, will you reciprocate and tell me why you were having dinner with the divine Mark? Don't you just adore him? That dark red hair is to die for.' She broke off a fragment of bread and popped it in her mouth, chewing delicately.

'It wasn't really dinner,' Livvy protested. 'Well, it was but not in the sense you mean. I asked him to join me in trying Fabio's tasting menu, as part of Fab's interview.' She pulled a face. 'I didn't relish eating on my own. And he helped me reccie the competition when we ate at The Old School Kitchen.' She paused and took a sip of wine. 'That *was* dinner, I suppose.'

'Oh yes. Marvellous place.'

'It was a thank-you for taking me to the auction where I was able to bid on the furniture for this place.'

'The auction house in Bridport?'

Livvy nodded.

'You two *have* been spending some time together,' Simona said slyly.

'Not in the way you mean. We're just friends.' Again, Livvy wondered about the relationship between Mark and Simona. 'He's been very kind.'

'Kindest man I know.' Simona opened up her baguette and slipped out a sliver of smoked salmon. 'Delish,' she declared. 'Absolutely delish.'

'So, what about you?' Livvy asked, not sure if the delish was aimed at the food, or at Mark. She dipped one of Fabio's fabulous chips into his home-made ketchup. 'Are you on your own in that gorgeous big house?'

'Me?' Simona made a face. 'I'm a widow, darling. Rich as Croesus but all alone in the world.'

'Oh I'm sorry,' Livvy said, aghast. 'That was so crass of me.'

For a second, the fun-loving mask slipped from Simona's face. She reached over and patted Livvy's hand. 'Don't be absurd, darling. How could you possibly know?' She pushed away her plate of food, hardly touched, and picked up her wine glass. Sipping thoughtfully, she added, 'I married Terence when I was twenty-four. He was thirty years older and, despite what all the gossip mongers said, it was a love match. I loved him with all my heart.' She stared into her glass and swirled the remaining wine around. 'We had twenty blissful years together but then he died. I have plenty of money, a rather nice car, a house in Italy and a pied-à-terre in London, and my lovely Georgian pile next door but I'd swap it all in a heartbeat if I could bring back my lovely Terence, even for a second.' She frowned fiercely and Livvy saw she was trying not to cry.

'I'm so sorry.'

'Well, there you are.' Simona shrugged herself back into flip-pant mode. 'And if you ever dare to feel the teeniest bit sorry for me again, I might have to never talk to you.' Once more, she patted Livvy's hand. 'And that would be an awful shame as I would rather like us to become friends. It would be so cosy to have a girly neighbour.'

Livvy thought of the cavernous spaces below her in the pub when she was in bed and how lonely it made her feel. She wasn't sure how much she had in common with Simona but it would be good to have a friend next door. 'Then there's only one thing to say,' she said solemnly.

'My, why so dour?' Simona giggled. 'What's that, kitten?'

'Fabio does a mean sticky marmalade pudding.'

'Oh, sweetie,' Simona cried, fluttering her eyelashes and putting her hand to her heart. 'Who could resist?'

'Clotted cream?'

'Oh, clotted cream,' Simona breathed in ecstasy. 'Can I share your pud, though? The only way I can maintain this svelte figure of mine is not to eat. It's utter torture, darling. I shall require the merest *soupcon*.'

'I think that can be arranged. I'll see what I can do,' Livvy answered, liking the woman's honesty, and went into the kitchen.

CHAPTER 14

Hot mulled cider – perfect for bonfire parties and barbeques. Add Calvados, cloves and allspice for an extra kick.

The day of the bonfire party dawned bright and clear, with watery turquoise skies. Even the wind which seemed to have taken up a permanent job of battering at The George's sea-facing walls had eased. The storm had blown itself out and washed the sky clean.

Livvy breathed a sigh of relief that it wasn't raining and hummed happily to herself as she bustled about the kitchen, ticking off the list of things she'd had to do. Local media alerted, stocks replenished, menu agreed, jobs allocated, timings organised. Staffing would be tight; one reason to only serve food in the restaurant, but she had faith in her team and Mark and Pete had kindly offered to help out where they could. She'd asked them to be bonfire wardens.

As well as the launch proper, the party was her thank you to all those who had helped her get this far. She was so grateful. Fabio and Karl were already proving themselves staunch allies even in the short space they'd worked together.

And now, she was standing in an empty restaurant which, in under an hour's time would hopefully be full of contented diners. The Three Ds had done a fantastic job in here and she couldn't believe they'd finished in time. The laminate flooring that she'd been so snobbish about but which Darrell insisted would look great for a restaurant floor, would prove hard-wearing and easy to clean. The walls, stripped back to their rough plaster, had been painted the same stark, clean white as in the bar and new wall sconces had replaced the eighties monstrosities that were there before. More mismatched tables and chairs were dotted about and dressed with white linen, gleaming cutlery and sparkling glassware. It looked just as she hoped; unpretentious and welcoming, if perhaps a little bare. Something on the walls was most definitely needed. Livvy felt a wriggle of excitement. Her vision was coming together.

No bar food tonight: they were pushing people into here. If anyone wanted to eat more casually, they could buy sausages, burgers and toffee apples at the kitchen door to eat by the bonfire. Her anticipation mounted; she was really looking forward to this.

'Well, kitten,' yelled Simona into her ear, three hours later. They were standing in front of a blazing bonfire, their faces hot and reddening, the cold circulating draughtily behind. 'I rather think you can consider yourself very much put on the map. I'm hearing the most wonderful compliments about Fabio's food. Do you think he can come out to play any time soon?'

As she spoke, words muffled by her enormous fur-trimmed

hood, Fabio arrived to stand next to them. He leaned into Livvy. 'Stewie's in charge of the bonfire snacks. Apart from that, The. Kitchen. Is. Closed.'

'Thank you, Fabio. You've been… fabulous.'

'Of course.' He shrugged. Then he grinned and threw an arm around her shoulders. 'We make a good team, *bambina.* Congratulations!'

'And it *has* been a real team effort, Fabio. Really couldn't have done it without you.' She was curious to see a strange emotion flicker across his face but was unable to say more as the first of the fireworks erupted. Several rockets shot high into the sky, trailing glistening streams of multi-coloured light across the sky, reflecting in the indigo sea. Everyone cheered. She looked around at the happy faces, gleaming in the flames from the bonfire. The beer garden was packed. Surely tonight's success boded well? A glow of contentment warmed her and she hugged Fabio's arm in sheer happiness.

Afterwards, Fabio, Karl and Livvy stumbled back into the bar, everyone else having finally departed.

'Quick drink before you go home, chaps?'

They shook their heads.

'I have to drive home.' Fabio came to her and kissed her on the forehead. 'Great night. Toodle-pips *bella.*'

'Night, Fab. And thanks, once again, for everything.'

'And I have to get back to the missus,' Karl said. 'Been a good night, Livvy. Folk'll be talking about this for a while. Got the Christmas season off to a smashing start. Heard someone say the fireworks were as good as they've seen anywhere, including Lyme Regis. And that's saying something. Night, Fabio,' he added, as the chef exited out of the front door. 'Livvy, can I have a quick word before I go?'

'Of course.' Livvy lifted the bar hatch and, slipping behind the bar, began to load the washer with the first lot of glasses.

'I came back here to use the lav,' Karl began. 'For some reason I checked if the door to the bar was locked and it wasn't. Fabio was supposed to have locked up when he'd finished in the restaurant so there would be no access to here. Stewie was running burgers and whatnot from the kitchen and doing plastic glass sales from the kitchen door. Limited range like beer and cider.'

'Yes, that's what we agreed. He seemed to be coping.'

'He was. Wasn't too busy. Think folk were too busy watching the fireworks to think about eating.'

'So, what's the problem?' Livvy abandoned what she was doing and faced him, panic gripping her stomach. She knew she should have got in extra agency staff. They'd been stretched too thinly. 'There's nothing missing, is there?'

'Not that I can see. But a bloke was having a good old nosey around in here. In the bar. Jason Lemmon, think it was. Tall geezer, thin, hair no particular colour, mousy like.'

'Wearing a black coat, oh and a mustard-coloured scarf?' Livvy asked, frowning.

'That's the badger. I asked him if I could help. Said he was on the way to the gents so I showed him where it was.'

'I don't think we need worry about Jason taking anything, although it is strange… He knows the place; he'd know where the loos were.'

'Just thought I'd tell you. He looked right shifty.'

'Thanks, Karl. I appreciate you checking. I'll have a word with Fabio about being more conscientious about locking up. Hopefully no harm done. Now you get off home to your wife. It's been a long night.'

'Will do. Night, my lovely.'

'Night, Karl.' Livvy saw him to the door and then made her rounds checking all windows and doors were locked. She keyed in the alarm and went wearily upstairs. *Funny about Jason. Prob-*

ably just having a look around, seeing what I've done to the place. Yawning, she barely had time to undress and brush her teeth before she collapsed into bed.

CHAPTER 15

*Cappuccino – espresso based, prepared with steamed milk, milk foam,
cocoa powder. The perfect morning pick-me-up.*

On Monday, the only day The George shut, Livvy braved the piercingly cold and very Christmassy weather to visit the art school. She decided to walk, wanting to get some fresh air. Daisy's words nagged at her. It made sense to take time for herself. Work-life balance was important, but she had no earthly idea how she'd achieve it.

She marched briskly down the hill into town, swinging her arms to keep warm. Above her was a sky of peerless blue and the sea sparkled shades of sapphire and green, topped with foamy crested waves. Lullbury Bay, on a day like this, was a good place to live.

She found the art school eventually. It was tucked away behind a housing estate and next to some tennis courts. Crossing over the unpromising-looking car park she went inside to be greeted by white corridors hung with photographs and paintings and followed the hubbub of noise and a sign saying, 'Artisans' Show This Way' to an enormous, light flooded studio. Standing at the doorway she paused for a second to take it all in. The white walls were hung with huge seascapes and some abstracts; a gigantic Christmas tree dominated one corner decked in tasteful white and silver; and arranged around the room were trestle tables crammed with crafts for sale. Snatches of 'Santa Claus is Coming to Town' could be heard when there was the occasional lull in chatter.

'Hey, Livvy!' It was Daisy calling her from the corner opposite the tree. She was dwarfed by a collection of wicker baskets brimming with winter greenery, next to a table heaped with wreaths of all sizes and colours.

Going over she said, 'Hi, Daisy. Thanks for the invite. When you rang and mentioned a Christmas craft fayre, I didn't anticipate anything like this.'

'It's brilliant, isn't it? One of my favourite things to do in the run-up to Christmas. This is slightly different to the usual ones. They're usually full-on Christmas with mulled wine, carols and mince pies. Dave, who runs the place, is booked up with stuff in December so he decided to try a more streamlined version out. Make sure you have a good look round. There's some really excellent stuff for sale and all made by the artists who work here.' She plucked a length of holly from one of the baskets, the bright red berries gleaming against the glossy leaves. 'And don't forget all your Christmas greenery. It's traditional to bring some evergreen in at this time of year!'

Livvy laughed. Daisy never seemed to miss a selling opportunity. 'I won't. I'll come back for some holly and mistletoe.'

'Ooh, who are you planning on kissing this Christmas?'

A stocky middle-aged man in dungarees and a red beret approached. It saved Livvy the embarrassment of having to answer. Who *did* she want to kiss this Christmas? With Jason,

Fabio and Mark around she had quite the choice. *Not to mention the Three Ds and Old Pete,* she giggled to herself.

Mr Red Beret handed Daisy a mug of steaming hot chocolate. 'There you go, my lovely. No marshmallows but best I could do.'

Daisy took it, cupping her hands around the mug emblazoned with, 'Father Christmas does it Up the Chimney'. 'Thanks, Dave. Have you met Livvy? She's taken on The George.'

He clasped Livvy's hand and pumped it vigorously. 'Nice to meet you, my friend. Dave Wiscombe. Bloke in charge for my sins. I was at your bonfire and fireworks on Saturday. Had an ace time. Good to see the place open again. And our Eli is going to work for you, I understand? He's my nephew. Good lad but easily led. Firm hand and he'll do okay for you.'

'Thanks.' Livvy smiled. 'I'll bear that in mind. I've got Karl Comberford working for me too.'

Dave brightened at the name. 'He'll help you sort him out. Good bloke, is Karl. Now, my lovely, make sure you look at Jago Pengethley's stuff. His glass light catchers make great presents. And check out the pottery and jewellery. All made on the premises. We've got eleven artists and crafts people working here now. Lots of excellent Christmas present ideas.'

'Thank you, I will.' She looked at the painting on the wall behind them. It was simple but effective, broad creamy stripes of sand against deepening shades of blue. A thought occurred. 'Dave, would you consider letting me display some of your paintings in my pub?'

A cunning look crept into his eyes. 'What, for sale you mean?'

Livvy nodded. 'I'd like to showcase some local talent. My walls are very bare and paintings like the one there would be the perfect backdrop.' She pointed out the landscape.

Dave turned to look. 'That's by Vivienne Little. She's very talented. Does a lot of seascapes. Dunno though, not sure I'd want to risk some of 'em in a pub. Can get a bit lairy, like, in a bar sometimes. Wouldn't want them wrecked.'

'Neither would I,' Livvy said, horrified. She hadn't considered that. 'Maybe just in the restaurant then? It'll be seated meals, waiter service in there. And I run a strict house. Anyone getting drunk gets thrown out.'

'Tell you what, I'll have a chat with Viv, see what she says. She'd get more eyes on them than they get down here, that's a fact.'

'Thank you. And do pop in for a pint one night.'

He tugged his beret in a salute. 'Will do.'

Livvy said her goodbyes and wandered the craft fayre, going from table to table. She bought three glass robin tree decorations and a beautiful light-catcher scene of a yacht bobbing on a turquoise sea, all from a piratical-looking man with curly dark hair and an earring. Taking his card, she saw it was Jago Pengethley. Having had a brief chat with him and admiring the large glass panels he also made; she wondered if she could squeeze one in the pub somewhere. From the next table along, she bought a pair of amber drop earrings which she knew her mother would love. She'd add the glass light catcher to them to make up her mother's Christmas present. Her father was more difficult to buy for.

She'd been happily browsing some beautifully carved wooden bowls when she turned too quickly and bumped into a tall gazelle-like woman behind her. 'Oh, I'm so sorry. I didn't see you there. I do apologise.'

'Not a problem. I wasn't looking where I was going. Too many lovely things to distract me. I'm going shop happy.' The woman frowned, gazing at Livvy more closely. 'Didn't I see you at the bonfire party on Saturday? Are you new to Lullbury Bay. Forgive me, out of the holiday season, everyone generally knows everyone else.'

'I'm Livvy Smith. I own The George.'

'Of course you do. I'd heard it had been taken over. Welcome to Lullbury Bay. The bonfire party was fantastic, by the way, I had such a lovely time.' The woman extended a hand. 'I'm Bee. I run the bookshop and community café. Look, I don't know about you but I'm getting buyer fatigue. Do you fancy a coffee and some cake? They've turned the staff room here into a pop-up café.'

'Perfect.' Livvy groaned. 'There are so many nice things here if I'm not careful I'll max out my credit card.'

Bee exclaimed in mock horror. 'And it's far too soon before Christmas to do that. Come on. Let's find cake.'

They squeezed through the tiny gaps between the tables in the makeshift café. It was busy. Bee waved and said hello to lots of people as they settled at a table; she seemed to know everyone. Although cramped, the café hummed with the comfortingly sweet smells of vanilla and sugar, and good roasted coffee. A curvy woman with bright pink hair served them and Bee introduced her as Tracy who usually ran The Sea Spray Café on the seafront. 'You have to try Tracy's cooked breakfast,' Bee added. 'Best in Dorset.'

'Ah!' Livvy said. 'I've heard it's the place to go for hot chocolate too. I met Alan, no I've got that wrong, Austin, is it? We shared a friendship bench and he recommended the hot chocolate at The Sea Spray.'

'Austin's one of my best customers.' Tracy rested a hand on a comfortably ample hip. 'Come down one day, maid, and I'll treat you. Only doing tea, coffee and cake here mind but we do have some mincemeat shortbread which is melt in the mouth and don't half go down well.'

'Sold,' Livvy said. When Tracy had gone, she turned to Bee. 'Austin also said you'd won a community award. For the friendship benches. Have to admit I didn't have a clue what they were when he began talking to me but I can see it works really well. It's a fantastic idea. Congratulations.'

Bee nodded. 'Simple idea but effective. Even in a town like this one where everyone knows one another, or is related,' she grinned, 'usually to the Wiscombe family, there are still the lonely, the ones who don't find it easy to strike up a chat. Or the ones who aren't into joining clubs or societies.'

Livvy thought of Pete. 'Would it work in a pub, do you think?'

Bee frowned. 'Always thought pubs were where conversations happened spontaneously anyway.'

'You have a point, although I'm not sure people find it as easy post lockdown. Some have lost the knack of talking.'

'I agree. Ah, here comes our coffee and shortbread. Thanks, Tracy.'

'You're welcome. I put you a slice of coffee and walnut each too. Enjoy!'

Livvy nibbled the mincemeat shortbread. She moaned. 'So good.'

Bee laughed. 'Don't know how she does it, but Tracy's got a knack with food.'

'Between Fabio, that's my chef at the pub,' Livvy explained, 'and The Sea Spray, I'm going to be the size of a house.'

'The sea air doesn't help. Makes me permanently starving.'

'Tell me about your community café, Bee. I've been impressed by what I've seen of Lullbury's community spirit so far.'

'It's a wonderful place to live,' Bee said warmly. 'I wouldn't live anywhere else. As you probably know it's tough keeping a bookshop going. I had this space attached to the shop so thought I'd open it up as a community space. I do very limited food, nothing like The Sea Spray, of course, and offer hot drinks and groups can use it as a meeting place. Once or twice a week I hold tea and chat sessions where you can come along and meet a few people, and there's a Death Café–'

'A what?' Livvy spluttered her coffee out.

'It's where people meet to have guided discussions on death,' Bee explained gently. 'Whether it's your death you're facing, or you're grieving for someone, or about to lose someone. It helps to meet up with other people and the leader offers practical help too. We have quite an elderly demographic in Lullbury Bay so it's popular.' She smiled. 'But a lot of people react like you when I first mention it.'

'I'm dreadfully sorry. It sounds marvellous now you've explained it. It just sounds a little–'

'Brutal?' Bee supplied. 'Avril Pengethley, Jago's mum, runs it. One thing she tries to do is be honest about the process, the problems and the practicalities. She calls them The Three Ps. She also runs an advice service in the café but that's for any kind of problem. Legal problems with housing, probate, that sort of thing.'

'How wonderful. Must be an invaluable service.'

'It is.'

'I'd really like to offer something community based. Something similar to what you're doing but don't think either would be quite right and you've got them covered anyway.' Livvy ruminated, ideas running through her head. 'Maybe a board games afternoon? You know, Scrabble and Monopoly. With tea and biscuits? Do you think that would work?'

Bee nodded enthusiastically. 'Excellent idea. I can see that sort of thing going down really well. And a pub is a different environment to a café. You might get more men attending and it's often men who don't develop their support networks enough. Go for it. Get some flyers printed and I'll put them up in the café.'

'Thanks, Bee. I'd like to have a noticeboard in the main corridor of the pub when I get the chance to put one up. I could point people your way then, too.'

'Think you're getting the hang of the Lullbury community spirit.' Bee laughed. 'Now, let's get down to the serious business of eating cake!'

CHAPTER 16

Sloe gin – a British liqueur made with sloe fruits picked after the first frosts of winter. Popular amongst ladies in the nineteenth century. Sweetness can be adjusted.

Livvy rushed back. She had a hot date with a chimney sweep. She half jogged up the steep hill back to the pub and arrived hot-faced and breathless just in time to see a smart black and silver van pull up in the car park. Despite all best efforts, and after much early promise, the wood burner was smoking and not giving out the expected heat. It had proved impossible to book a sweep before the stove was fitted.

The sweep's name was Jonquil and she was as gloomy as her name was sunny. A tiny, wiry middle-aged woman, she stood in front of the newly installed wood burner and tutted with violence. 'Just as well I'm here. You can't go using this old chimmley when it ain't been swept for I don't know how long. You'll have the whole place burning down round your ears.'

'Well, I'm very glad you got to me in time then,' Livvy

"

answered, trying to keep her temper. She'd rung at least three times before the woman had got back to her. 'As I said to you on the phone, ideally it would have been better to sweep it before having the wood burner fitted and lit. I'll leave you to it, shall I?'

'Cuppa wouldn't go amiss,' Jonquil said, unfolding a huge white sheet and laying it down. 'Two sugars, drop o' milk.'

'Coming right up.' Livvy banged the kitchen door open, ignoring the woman's mutters of, 'Bloomin' townies.'

Having taken Jonquil tea with some added biscuits in the saucer, Livvy returned to the kitchen, the ash and soot from the chimney was making her cough. Poor Candice would be dusting it off surfaces for days. Her phone buzzed. It was her father.

'How's it going, Liv? How was the grand opening?'

'Went really well, Dad. Got great reviews for the food and everyone loved the bonfire and fireworks.'

'Well, they'll lap up anything free. Make sure you charge entrance next year.'

Livvy's heart shrivelled a little. Was it too much to hope he'd say a simple congratulations?

'You need to get online reviews,' her father continued. 'Tripadvisor is the thing folk read before they make decisions about where to eat. Times are hard. They don't want to spend their hard-earned cash unless they're sure of what they'll get. It's tough in hospitality. We got shafted during Covid and the industry's never recovered.'

'Yes, Dad.' Livvy had heard this complaint for years. 'I'm trying to build a community pub though.'

'Are you?' Brian Smith-Lygott sniffed in derision. 'Doesn't sound much like your original vision. Thought you were going foodie gastropub?'

'I was. Still am. But I'd like to develop the idea of the pub being a hub of the community too.'

'Look, darling, you of all people should know if you're not

clear about your vision, it gets diluted, and you don't succeed. It's not how we brought you up.'

'I know.' In her head Livvy had a hundred arguments to put forward. She wanted to do something different with The George. Her parents didn't agree and couldn't see why she'd broken away from their business model, so she remained quiet. It was useless to argue.

'We're coming down to see what your George is all about. Just before we go on that cruise. We'll have an early Christmas together.'

Would have been nice to be asked. 'Great. I hope we'll do you proud.'

'Well, we'll see. Speak soon.'

The phone went dead. Livvy stared at it, exasperation and panic warring. Getting a room ready for her parents was yet another job to add to the list. She blew out a frustrated breath. Nothing would come up to her mother's stratospherically high standards.

After nursing a mug of tea debating whether she'd be better giving up her bedroom and camping out in one of the others, she ventured back into the bar with another mug for the not so jovial Jonquil.

Jonquil appeared to be glad to see her, or it might have been the tea. 'Aw, smashin'. Thirsty work doing this.' She took the mug and drank.

Livvy retreated to the bar and perched on a stool. 'How's it going?'

'Just as well you called me in when you did. Reckon that last lot what owned the place never let the chimmley see a brush. I've got a ton of stuff down.'

'To be fair, the chimmley, I mean, chimney, was blocked off and there was an electric fire in place.' Livvy sipped her tea, the soot getting to the back of her throat. Her admiration for what Jonquil did rose.

Jonquil gave a visible shudder. 'Can't be doing with blocking off a perfectly usable chimmley.'

'I agree. I much prefer a wood burner.'

'Can't beat 'em. You got Darrell and his boys to do the work?'

'Yes, although they had to call in a specialist to fit the stove itself.'

Jonquil finished her tea, leaving sooty fingerprints on the mug. 'Good team, they are.' She jerked her head to the stove. 'Did a good job with this 'un. It's a right bobby-dazzler.' She put the mug down on the now grey groundsheet and, picking up a long-handled brush, shoved it up the chimney. 'Nearly there. Took a while, this did, and take my advice, it'll need another go next spring. Can only get so much out in one go.'

'I'll book you in again before you leave then.' Livvy had slipped off the stool to return to the kitchen when she was halted by Jonquil making a guttural sound.

'What we got here then? Brush is wedged.' She shoved harder and something fell out, landing on top of the sheet covering the stove. 'Well, looky here.'

'What is it?'

'I finds all sorts stuck up chimmleys. My old Dad was a farmer an' he used to stick a bull's heart up to keep his cattle from getting sick.'

Livvy was still processing this bizarre statement as she went nearer. Jonquil was an eccentric in a town full of them and she didn't know how to take her. Hardly wanting to look, she peered down at the blackened and twisted object. Then she recognised it. 'Oh my God!' She flinched back violently.

'Yeah. It was a cat, alright.' Jonquil's eyes gleamed. She was the most animated Livvy had seen her.

Looking more closely, Livvy could see quite clearly the outline of the cat's features, even its ears pointing above its domed head. It wasn't a skeleton, more a preserved, albeit flattened, carcass.

'Mummified,' Jonquil put in. 'By the looks of things. Dried up by the heat from the fire.'

'Did it get stuck? Poor thing.' Livvy felt bile rise. She remembered the scrabbling sounds from the other night. 'Was it after a mouse?'

'Nah. Someone put it up there. To keep the witches away. Old building this. Folk used to think a chimmley was a passageway between this world and t'other. They used to stick all sorts up a chimmley to keep evil away. I've come across shoes, witches' bottles, flanks o' bacon stuck with pins to catch the witch on her way down.' Jonquil cackled. 'Never fails to surprise me, what I find.'

Livvy backed away. 'But to put a cat up there. That's horrible.'

'Must have been some pretty strong magic they was afeared of. Don't you worry, my lovely, the cat is likely to have been dead long afore they shoved it up there. Poor critter.' Jonquil shook her head. 'Thems were cruel times back then, though.'

'It's still horrible. I don't believe in all that stuff. It's ridiculous.' To her embarrassment Livvy found her voice was shaking.

'I'll see what else is up there, shall I?'

Livvy was torn. If there was anything as horrific as the cat she didn't want to know. On the other hand, she'd rather Jonquil got everything out.

Jonquil pulled the brush down, along with a shower of soot. The smell was choking. 'I'll just give him one last go. Might have found me a nook or cranny.' She pushed the brush back up, stopped when it was halfway and appeared to be listening. 'Just a wink to the right,' she whispered and then shoved hard and pulled back.

This time the object was smaller and, to Livvy's relief, less obviously macabre. Jonquil picked it up and brushed centuries old soot and ash off. 'Reckon this one's a book,' the woman said, feeling it. 'Wrapped in old, waxed cloth, by the looks of it. I'll unwrap it, you take it.'

Livvy hovered, hardly able to breathe. She was very aware of the cat's body still lying on top of the stove and braced herself should it be anything as horrific. It wasn't. Jonquil peeled back the cloth to reveal, as predicted, a book. It was black and leather-covered. Livvy took it between finger and thumb. It wasn't very big, probably about the same size as an A5 notebook. She took it to the bar where the light was better. Hardly daring to touch it, she opened the front cover. It revealed a dedication in beautifully written script:

"To my love, my secret love, my one and only."

'Poetry, by the looks,' Jonquil said. 'Fancy.'

Livvy started. She hadn't heard her come up behind. 'I think it's a notebook.' She turned another page. 'Poems and, look, some sketches.' They stared at a pen and ink sketch of a young woman. She had hair dressed in ringlets on either side of her face and had on a dress with a scooped neckline and extravagantly puffed sleeves. 'She was beautiful,' Livvy breathed.

'She was. I'll take this poor puss out your way, shall I?' Jonquil said, bringing Livvy back to earth. 'Might take the poor beggar up the museum. Got a lot of folkie type stuff in there. You should take a looky. Someone might tell you about that there book.'

'Thank you, Jonquil. I'll do that.' Livvy focused. 'And thank you for taking the—' she couldn't bring herself to say the word body. 'I appreciate it.'

'No worries.' Jonquil tenderly wrapped the corpse in a sooty groundsheet. 'Poor pussycat. I hopes you had a good life afore you met your end.' She glanced up at the blackboard with the specials chalked up and became much more matter of fact. 'Might bring the old fella by. We likes us a good steak and chips.'

'Please do.' Livvy was warming to her. 'Please come and eat. First drinks on the house.'

'Aw well, in that case, it's a no-brainer.' Jonquil grinned. 'And

I'd like to know about this old book an' all. I'll just clear up and that's me finished then, I reckon.'

Livvy took the hint. 'I'll pay you by BACS, shall I? And book you in for the next time.'

When Jonquil had gone, thankfully taking the mummified cat with her, Livvy returned to the kitchen. Placing the notebook carefully on a shelf, she switched on her laptop. Intending to email Yolanda, she found herself putting in a search for cats in chimneys. What Jonquil had said about scaring witches must be a load of old nonsense… It appeared not. Several sites came up with numerous examples of items found in chimneys and the theory behind it. It was horrible. Feeling sick, Livvy shut down the computer and reached for her phone. Determined to put it all to the back of her mind, she sent a chatty text to Yolanda instead.

CHAPTER 17

Lager – matured in cold storage, distinguished by the use of bottom-fermenting yeast. Simple and unsubtle flavour.

With Brittany shaping up, and Stewie working with Fabio in the kitchen, a little of the pressure lifted from Livvy. She didn't feel she had to be on the premises at all times. Karl quickly proved himself to be utterly reliable and trustworthy and she was happy to leave him in charge as bar manager so she could take the occasional night off.

Fabio declared Stewie a triumph in the kitchen, and they were already planning new menus for the run-up to Christmas.

It was only Eli over whom she had doubts. There was nothing concrete; it was just something about him. Taking Karl into her confidence, she got his assurance he'd keep a close eye on the boy. The one advantage of employing Eli was he attracted his enormous extended family along on Sunday evenings. Assorted uncles and cousins boosted wet sales considerably on an evening when it was generally quiet and there was no food on offer. Most of the family, like Dave Wiscombe and Eli's older sister Lucie, and cousin Daisy she welcomed, but there were a few members who could get a little unruly.

On the first Sunday in December Livvy returned from the local DIY store with a van load of Christmas decorations. She'd also invested in strings of outside lights although was still working out exactly how she was going to put them up. Karl met her in the car park and helped carry the boxes through into the kitchen.

Fabio put his hands on his hips. 'And where do you plan to put this lot, *bambina?*' He reached into the nearest box. Pulling out a garland of tinsel, he grimaced. 'Horrid stuff.'

'At least it's fairly tasteful,' Livvy rebutted. 'I've gone all white and silver. Nothing garish.' After the incident with Jonquil and the chimney, she'd wanted to do the utmost to banish anything dark and gloomy. She was determined to fill the pub with white light and Christmas cheer.

'Nothing wrong with tinsel,' Karl added loyally. 'Me and the missus likes a bit of it up at Christmas. Although we usually go for red and green.' He picked up an enormous sparkly silver tinsel star. 'And this is the badger, all righty.'

'Quite,' Fabio said, glacially. 'If you don't mind, I'll be off. Stewie will clear up after the Sunday lunch service. There's only one couple left eating. And then I suppose you'll be invaded by the Eli hordes again.'

'At least they drink,' Livvy said cheerfully. Sometimes Fabio's snobbishness got a bit much. 'Otherwise there wouldn't be much point opening on a Sunday evening. They're the only customers we get in then and I'm very grateful.'

'Whatevs.' He shrugged himself into his jacket, winding his long scarf around his neck. 'Toodle-pips. See you on Tuesday.'

'Bye, Fab,' Livvy said. Karl winked at her as if to say, 'Take no notice.'

Stewie came in, carrying an armful of empty plates. 'Diners said to pass on their compliments to the chef.' He looked around. 'Oh he's gone.' Putting the plates next to the sink, he said, 'Ooh ace, Christmas decs. Want a hand putting them up?'

Livvy beamed in gratitude. She was becoming very fond of him. He was a hard worker and willing to turn his hand to anything. 'Oh, Stewie, that would be great but I think you've got your hands full in here.'

Stewie shrugged. 'Won't take long.'

'I'd really appreciate your help in that case, but I don't want to keep you.'

'Where's the tree coming from?' Karl asked.

'It's being delivered,' Livvy checked her watch, 'ooh, in about an hour. I ordered it from Va Va Bloom.'

'Luvverly,' Karl said, rubbing his hands together. 'Can't beat the smell of a real tree. I'll give you a hand bringing it in.'

For a moment Livvy was overwhelmed. She'd taken a chance employing Karl and Stewie and both men, in their different ways, were proving invaluable. Karl, glad to be in employment at the end of his working life, was old-fashioned and courteous and couldn't do enough for her. Stewie, nineteen and just as enthusiastic, made no effort to hide his gratitude at being able to learn from a master chef.

She knew she'd lose Stewie to his own kitchen at some point but that was the nature of employment in this business. Stupid tears prickled. She was making friends in Lullbury Bay and no longer felt quite so alone. 'Thanks, guys,' she managed, through a lump in her throat. She wagged a finger at them. 'Don't forget to eat.' It was one thing she stipulated. It was important to look after her staff well; training opportunities must be available, and they must eat.

'Don't you worry,' Karl said with glee. 'I'll make time for Fab's roasties. Don't know what he does to roast potatoes, but I've never tasted anything like those bad boys.'

'He uses goose fat and couscous,' Stewie replied. 'Makes them extra crunchy.'

'Does he now? Well I never.'

'Put any spare bowls of roasties on the bar, please, Stewie,' Livvy instructed. 'People seem to like them as bar snacks on Sunday evening. But make sure you eat too.' She picked up a box of outside lights, staring at it, hoping it would inspire her with an idea of how to put them up. The George was a tall building. Did she have a ladder long enough? Did she even have a ladder? All sorts of random stuff was secreted in the outbuildings. She hadn't had time to sort through any of it yet.

'Mind you, some of Eli's lot would eat anything that's free,' Karl observed. 'They're wasted on them. They just want their lager. And their tequila shots.'

'They'd be wasted anyway,' Livvy replied. 'Delicious though they are, we can't eat them all. I'll have a word with Fab about quantities. He's over catering. Now, chaps, any ideas how I'm going to put these up?' Livvy brandished the box of lights. 'I'm really not sure I've a ladder long enough to get these up where I want them.'

'You don't want a ladder, my lovely.' Karl's eyes gleamed. 'Our Ernie will have just the thing. Leave it with me.'

Evening service resumed and, with Eli manning the bar, Livvy was free to decorate the tree. Stewie insisted he stay on to help. They were interrupted by a loud rumbling outside. The pub's walls shook, lights flashed in through the windows and a deafening horn sounded. Startled, Livvy peered out through the window, relieved to have an excuse to go outside to investigate. Tree dressing had been accompanied by raucous carol singing from various members of Eli's family. They'd gone through most of the *Come and Praise* bangers.

Earlier, Livvy had watched in concern as there seemed some kind of argument between Eli and an older relative, possibly his Uncle Gerry. Eli had appeared to calm things, and all was cheerful enough now, well-oiled by several rounds of her finest lager. The quality of singing had deteriorated in direct correlation to the amount of alcohol consumed, however, and she was glad of the break.

Going outside, with Stewie at her heels, it was to find Karl standing in the evening gloom with another man. Behind them was a monstrously large green and yellow tractor. It loomed, slightly threateningly, in the seaside drizzle.

'This is my little brother Ernie,' Karl said. 'He drives the fastest John Deere in the west.' The man nodded and grinned. Wearing navy overalls, he had a battered tweed cap pulled down over his face and was chewing a match.

Livvy looked at them blankly.

'Maybe you need to be a certain age to get the joke,' he added, 'you're too young. Ernie said you can borrow the tractor to put the lights up.'

'I can? How?'

'You get in the cherry picker here and he'll hoist you up.' He turned and cheerfully slapped it with his palm.

Livvy's mouth dropped open. She looked at the tractor and then up at the roof of The George towering above her. Then she eyed the cherry picker. It was no more than a large bucket attached to the front. 'Get in there?' she squeaked. 'It doesn't look as if it'll hold me. I'm not doing that.'

'Go on, Liv. I'll get in with you.' Stewie was obviously up for the adventure. 'I'll hang on to you while you fix the lights. It'll be a right laugh.'

'You'll be fine,' Karl reassured her. 'Ernie's won all sorts of ploughing competitions. He's a dab hand at the wheel of his tractor.'

'He may well have won ploughing competitions,' Livvy

protested, glancing at the man doubtfully, who still hadn't said a word. 'But hoisting me up in his cherry picker thingy is a different matter.'

'Don't you like heights, my lovely?'

'It's not that, Karl. I'm just not convinced it's safe.'

Karl shook the cherry picker making it rattle. 'It's okay, Ernie's got it on lock. Haven't you, Ern?'

The silent Ernie nodded enthusiastically. His only comment was the match lifting skywards.

Karl jiggled the bucket again to underline his point. 'See, it's not going nowhere. Won't swing around. Safe as houses. Reckon it'll be a whole load easier than perching on the top of a ladder.'

He had a point. Livvy wished she'd thought through the Christmas lights plan beforehand. What was the alternative though? A dark, undecorated pub? It hardly gave off seasonal vibes and she wanted her first Christmas to be perfect. Thinking of all the other decorations already up in Lullbury she said, 'Well, if you're sure.' She gazed up in trepidation at the soaring walls of the pub and at the steep incline of the roof. She blew out a defeated breath. 'I can't see how else I'm going to do it.'

'Sweet,' Stewie cried. 'I'll go and get the boxes of lights. After all, it's not Christmas without lights.'

'What you got to attach the lights to the guttering, then?' Karl asked, rubbing his hands against the chilly air, his breath misting out.

'Some of these plastic ties.' Livvy pulled one out of the pocket of her fleece. 'Do you think they'll be strong enough?' she asked, showing him. 'It gets pretty windy up here.'

'That's the badger. If I was you, I'd only put 'em on the car park side where it's more sheltered. The wind'll whip them off in no time on the seaward facing walls. I'd go up and do it myself.' Karl huffed a bit. 'But Jen wouldn't hear of it.' Jen was his wife. From what Livvy had heard, she wouldn't argue with her either.

Stewie returned, carrying the pack of ties and the pile of

lights. Livvy was beginning to wish she hadn't bought quite so many.

Ernie swung himself into the tractor cab and the engine shuddered and rumbled into life. Livvy was overcome with a fit of nervous giggles and had to have help from Karl to clamber into the cherry picker bucket, with Stewie getting in behind. Two seconds too late, the smell rose up in a great swell of acrid animal waste.

'Oi, Ern,' Karl yelled. 'What was the last thing you used this bucket for, mate?'

A voice rose over the tractor noise.

'What did he say?' Livvy asked, brushing something greeny-brown and pungent off her jeans.

'I'm really sorry, Livvy.' Karl wrinkled up his nose. 'He was shunting round some muck on the farm and a whole load fell into the bucket. He didn't have time to clean it out.'

'Muck?' Livvy wailed. 'You mean—'

'Gross.' Stewie hooted. 'Oh, Liv, we've got cow manure all over us.'

Livvy was about to tell Karl she'd changed her mind when the bucket began to rise, taking them with it. 'Oh fuck,' she swore uncharacteristically and hung on for grim death, to the teenager. She began to giggle again. Never, in her wildest dreams, did she think owning a seaside pub would involve standing in a shit-smeared cherry picker being raised eleventy-million feet.

The cherry picker wobbled to a halt. Stewie waved at Ernie to move them closer until they were near enough to the guttering for Livvy to begin to attach the lights. Livvy had to force herself to let go of Stewie and had a bad moment when she looked down at the expectant faces below but then got herself under control. *You're up here now, Livvy, girl. And besides, who else have you got to do it? It's your pub!*

Stewie unravelled the lights and passed the plastic ties over as needed. They worked methodically until shouting down to Ernie to shunt them along to the next section. Once her legs had stopped shaking and she'd got used to the height, Livvy even began to enjoy herself. The view, over the rooftops of the town was fabulous. She could see the line of lights leading downhill on the main street, the white lights along the promenade and even the lit up RNLI station on the harbour. The harbour wall curled round and the sea shifted and gleamed against the dark sky in the bay beyond. It wasn't something many would be privileged to see.

An inquisitive seagull swooped low, cackling. It brought her back to the task in hand and Stewie waiting patiently to pass over another rope of lights. 'Sorry, Stewie. I got distracted.' She chuckled. 'It's not bad up here once you get used to it. And just as well Darrell fixed the security lights, eh? Otherwise we wouldn't have been able to see a thing.' Then she noticed how he was shivering with the cold, his nose and ears pink. 'Best get on, though. Pass me the next set of lights.'

Three-quarters of an hour later, she was lifted out of the cherry picker by Gerry, Eli's drunken uncle. He and his cronies, having caught wind of the excitement, had gathered to watch the fun.

'Ooh, girl, you don't half stink.' Gerry belched and handed her to another man, standing in the gloom of the cold December evening. Much as Livvy had ended up enjoying it, she was very glad to have her feet firmly back on terra firma.

'It may be ungallant in the extreme to agree with Gerry but I'm afraid you do.' It was Mark. He steadied her as she wobbled violently. 'What you need is a stiff drink. For one thing, you're absolutely frozen.' Throwing an arm around her shoulders, he began to guide her back inside.

'Just as well I run a pub, then,' Livvy managed through chattering teeth.

'Indeed,' he replied cheerfully.

The Wiscombe crowd followed them to the bar. Mark settled

Livvy on a stool and ordered a whisky, and coffee. The carol singing began in earnest again. This time, 'Little Donkey' thundered out.

'Fabio or myself would have been happy to help, you know. You only had to ask,' he murmured on a smile.

'I had my intrepid helper at my side.' As Stewie passed, Livvy caught him by the arm. 'Get yourself a hot drink.'

'Thanks, I'm frozen.' He grinned and nodded. 'Never thought I'd be doing that on a Sunday shift.' Blushing crimson, he added, 'I love working here, Livvy. Never know what to expect next.'

She smiled at him. 'Make some hot chocolate and sit by the radiator and then get yourself home. You should have finished hours ago.'

Aware of Mark's eyes on her and the fact she hadn't answered, she turned back to him and said, 'Can you see Fab in a tractor bucket up fifteen feet?' Grinning she sipped her whisky. 'And Eli had his hands full in here. I seized the moment. I know I said I didn't want to go full-on Christmas too soon but even I've got to admit the lights have gone up late. Most of the rest of the town is decorated already.' She felt the fire of the whisky steal through her. 'And actually, it was great fun.' She shivered. 'Once I got used to it. And learned to duck the seagulls.' She leaned over the bar and ordered drinks for Karl and the silent Ernie. 'On the house,' she told Eli.

'Good. If that's how you feel about it, just as well I took some pictures.' Mark withdrew his phone from his jeans pocket. He flashed a grin.

'Oh, I'd love to see those!' He handed over the phone and Livvy scrolled through them, laughing. 'That's a brilliant one,' she said and shared the shot of her clambering out of the cherry picker. It wasn't flattering but Livvy had never taken herself all that seriously. The picture of her being hoisted around the waist by a red-faced Gerry was hilarious. Hair tumbling any old how, sticking out an all angles and filthy jeans, she wore a triumphant grin. Who needed Gavin?

'What about sending them to the local rag? It's the sort of story *The Lullbury Bay Echo* would lap up. Great publicity too. That's if you don't mind your dignity being injured.'

Livvy laughed again. She plucked at her filthy jeans. 'No dignity left. None whatsoever.' She winced at the particularly raucous chorus of 'The Twelve Days of Christmas' coming from behind her.

Mark peered round her to check on them. 'It's all right, they're being loud but Eli's coping.'

'Thanks,' she said, gratefully. 'He came across as being confident at the interview, too much so but I think that was nerves talking. He's not half as cocky as he seems and he's a bit young to deal with that sort of crowd even if most of them are his relatives.'

Mark checked again. 'Actually, I think the only Wiscombe is Eli's Uncle Gerry.' He pulled a face. 'You might want to keep an eye on that one. He got banned from The Old Harbour last winter. The Wiscombe family are well-regarded in Lullbury but he's the exception.'

'Consider me warned. Did you enjoy the fireworks? I didn't see much of you.'

'Me and Pete were being conscientious about our bonfire duties. Have to take that role seriously.' He smiled, the warm twinkle in his hazel eyes belying his stern tone. 'It was a great night. I didn't see much of you either but presumed you were busy. I saw you with Simona and Fabio,' he added lightly. 'Watching the fireworks.'

'Oh yes. He'd just finished in the kitchen and came to gloat about all his satisfied customers.' Livvy remembered Fabio's casual arm around her shoulders and felt an urge to explain. But why should she feel the need to explain a friendly gesture? She gazed at Mark, her cheeks heating. Probably the whisky, or the heat from the wood burner in contrast to the chill outside. She thanked Eli for the coffee he brought her, grateful for the interruption. 'I'm thinking of setting up a board games afternoon,' she said, deliberately changing the subject. 'With tea and cake maybe, plus anything anyone wants from the bar.'

'Sounds a good idea,' Mark said neutrally. 'Do you think Pete will join in?'

Livvy laughed. 'He may just about tolerate the interruption, but it's Skip I'm more worried about. Daisy Wiscombe has a knack with him but he's my only customer so far who I haven't won over.'

'I can only suggest copious amounts of dog treats. Seriously though, the board games idea sounds wonderful and even Old Pete enjoys a game of dominoes.'

'I'll order some in, or I might have look in the charity shop in town. Might strike lucky.'

'Haven't you any games from when you were a kid?'

'No. Didn't really have that kind of childhood,' Livvy answered, not elaborating. Her upbringing didn't feature cosy family games around the fire. Her parents were too busy working. 'I'd like to set up a noticeboard as well, you know, with advertised events. I'm leaning into making the pub a community hub.'

'And one with great food. Interesting concept.'

'Isn't it just?'

'And what about the skittles alley?'

Livvy sighed. 'Now that's something I haven't decided on. It's practically falling down. Would need so much investment to repair, I'm not sure I can afford to lay out capital for what might be little return.'

'It's a community asset though.'

'I know. I'll have to do some head scratching over the accounts. Can't do it up unless I have the money to invest.'

'O Little Town of Bethlehem' thundered to its conclusion at the other end of the bar.

Mark's mouth twisted. 'At least that's one community service you're doing.'

'What's that?'

'Keeping that lot here so their better halves can have a peaceful evening to themselves!'

CHAPTER 18

Jagerbomb – a shot of Jägermeister dropped into an energy drink. Some take it as a hangover cure. A mistake.

*L*ivvy came awake with a start. Too much whisky and the promise of a rare day off had had her in bed as soon as she'd closed up last night. It had been tricky prising Gerry's lot away from the bar, but they'd gone home eventually.

She had twinges of concern as she saw them off the premises, still singing loudly. She had a duty of care not to let her customers drink too much and also to her neighbours; she'd lose her licence if there were complaints about rowdiness at closing time. She was touched that Mark had hung on until she'd bolted the main door. Having had his fair share of whisky, he made the wise decision to walk home and collect his car later. As she'd made her way upstairs, she wondered where he lived. Somewhere not too far away presumably.

Turning over in bed, she glanced at the alarm clock and

groaned. It was ten to five. Pulling the duvet back over her head, she tried to get back to sleep and failed. A raging thirst, coupled with the need to wee kept sleep at bay. Giving up, she threw off the bedding, switched on the lamp and padded into the bathroom.

Downstairs in the kitchen, she flicked on the kettle to make tea. It was still pitch black outside and wouldn't get light for at least another three hours. It felt like the middle of the night and, with the darkness of the hour, all the fun and bonhomie of the previous evening leached away.

She'd thought she was feeling her way into the community, making friends. Now she felt very on her own in a huge building. The sharp tang of pine wafted through from the Christmas tree in the bar bringing comfort. She'd hung fairy lights in the kitchen to bring some seasonal cheer to Stewie and Fabio, well mainly for Stewie. Reaching up she switched them on enjoying their soft glow. It was, at last, finally beginning to feel a little more like Christmas.

The kettle bubbled to a noisy boil, clicked off and left a silence in the kitchen that was profound. Livvy's stomach dropped as the familiar doubts assailed her. Why did everything always seem three times as bad at this time in the morning? Or was it just her hangover? Intrusive thoughts chased themselves around her pounding head. Would she ever make a success of the place? Food orders were picking up, but she'd never make a substantial profit until she got the reputation of the restaurant properly established.

She couldn't rely on Fabio being around permanently; despite his protestations, her little pub wouldn't be enough for his ambitions long term. And timing was an issue. She needed to make money to see her through the quiet period. January through to Valentine's Day would be deathly quiet. She didn't make much from the scattering of regular drinkers who came in, even if their numbers were bolstered by Gerry's Sunday night gang, so her true profitability depended on food sales.

Unease slid over her. There was something about the Sunday night gang she didn't trust and she hadn't liked the disagreement between Eli and his uncle. As promised, Karl had kept a close eye on Eli and had reported nothing untoward so far. She wasn't sure she entirely trusted Eli either. She knew from experience it was all too easy to have a finger in the till. Still, she couldn't dismiss someone on a gut feeling and she didn't want to discourage Gerry and his friends just because she didn't like them very much. She was a publican; she couldn't hope to like all her customers. She just needed to make sure they didn't drink themselves insensible or cause trouble.

The silence in the kitchen thickened and Livvy got up to put teabags into the pot. Fabio would have shuddered, had he known. He always made tea properly, with leaves. As she reached up for a mug off the shelf, she dislodged the little book she and Jonquil had discovered in the chimney.

Pouring some tea, she settled at the work prep bench and gingerly opened the notebook. Again, she admired the sketch of the young woman. She was very beautiful. The artist had hinted at dark hair and eyes and a well-shaped mouth that curved up at the sides in an expression of perpetual amusement. She must have been very young when the portrait was drawn as she still had the bloom of childhood on her rounded cheeks. Livvy wondered who she was and leafed through the book to find a clue. As well as some other sketches, most not as accomplished, there was some poetry. Livvy scanned the first. She had no idea if it was any good, but it was clearly a love poem:

> *A smile bestows her face*
> *With a womanly hue so pure.*
> *An unawak'd beauty with shy good grace*

Life's wondrous treasures yet to endure.
And yet! Such joy!
Her gaze alights upon this soul
The bright orbs heateth my form.
Love claims its mystic fee
And captures mine heart within me.

One or two words had been scribbled out and replaced. It had obviously been a work in progress and Livvy found it touching. At the bottom of the page, was a date. It was written in pencil and faded with age, almost indecipherable: December eighteen something. Was that the year the couple had met? The early nineteenth century, a time when The George would have been at its height as a coaching inn.

With mounting excitement, Livvy realised she had in her hands the evidence of a romance. A memory flickered. Hadn't Mark said the pub had been named after some runaway lovers? Had this little book belonged to one of them? As she turned the back pages, something slipped out. It was a coil of hair. So dark as to be almost black but still with its reddish lights in place.

Then she heard it. A thump. Dropping the book with a start, she froze. Another thump but this time a slighter sound. The noises were coming from the car park. The security lights flared to life. She jumped a foot as the kitchen door rattled. Fear licked icily down her spine.

And then a surge of white-hot fury raged through her. How dare someone muck about in her car park? Teenagers again. She remembered how she'd felt watched as she locked up after the skittles match. Anger blazed within her. She could ignore them and go back to bed but she knew she wouldn't sleep. No, she needed to do something about this. There was no one else here and it was her pub, so it was up to her to sort it.

Flinging open the kitchen door she yelled, 'Whoever you are

and whatever you think you're up to, you need to get the fuck away now or I'm calling the police!'

The car park appeared empty. The newly repaired lights were merciless and shone into every corner. She turned to return to the kitchen. It was cold out here and she was dressed only in her dressing gown and slippers. As she did so, she could swear she heard the scuffle of feet running away. The little bastards!

CHAPTER 19

Hot chocolate – gained in popularity recently, especially at Christmas. Ideal when in need of comfort and warmth.

*L*ivvy needed to get away from the pub for a while. Despite trying to shrug it off, the incident in the early hours had shaken her. Plus, she'd been eating, sleeping, living the pub ever since she'd taken over and it was beginning to feel all a bit too much.

As soon as it was properly light, she drove into Exeter. The air was satisfyingly crisp and seasonal as she climbed into the van and she tuned into Bay Radio which blasted out some cheesy Christmas hits. She sang along to 'Step into Christmas' as she turned down the hill to drive through town to hit the main road west.

She needed to hunt down a Christmas present for her father and hadn't found any inspiration on the internet. What she craved was a good browse through a department store. After tracking down a parking spot big enough to take the van, all the time wishing she'd taken the park and ride, she found herself in the civilised atmosphere of John Lewis. Enjoying the Christmassy muzak and the tastefully decorated white Christmas trees dotted about she discovered some cashmere scarves in the menswear department. She wondered if she should get Mark something. It was tricky; she'd only known him a few short weeks, but he already felt like a good friend.

'Christmas shopping?'

She turned with a jolt. It was Jason Lemmon. 'Oh hello.' There was something about him which unnerved her. Maybe it was because everything about him was pale. There was no warmth to the man. Prematurely greyed hair, icily pale blue eyes, the whitest of skin.

He lifted a carrier bag. 'Me too.' Grimacing, he added, 'I like to get it all done well before the day. Have you much to buy?'

'Not really.' Livvy shook her head. 'Think I've got presents for my mother. The difficult one is my dad. I never know what to get him.'

'Men are tricky to buy for, I agree.' Jason gave a charming smile. 'I'm afraid I've given up with my parents, they insist they don't need anything, so I take them for a decent meal somewhere instead. Gives us time to catch up a little, too.'

'What a good idea.' Livvy warmed to him. 'Much better than spending loads on something unsuitable.'

'I entirely agree.' Jason blinked his pale eyes slowly. 'And, of course, I get to enjoy the treat too. I'm considering bringing them to The Runaways, or should I say, The George, this year.'

'And we'd be delighted to host you all.'

'So, what does your father like to do? Has he any hobbies? I might be able to suggest something.'

Livvy shook her head again. 'He was always too busy running the hotel chain to have any hobbies. Now he's semi-retired, although not as retired as Mum would like him to be, they've developed a new career.' When Jason raised an elegant brow in query, she added, 'They like to cruise. Preferably somewhere hot and sunny.'

'In that case, I may have the perfect solution to your present buying quandary.' He took her arm gently and propelled her to a corner of the store.

After Jason's help with her shopping, it seemed churlish to refuse his offer of coffee so she allowed him to lead the way to nearby Gandy Street. A narrow, medieval thoroughfare, full of trendy shops, bars and cafés, it thronged with Christmas shoppers. White lights were strung across the lane; the short December day was growing gloomy, a sea fret beginning to gather. The lights cheered everything. Livvy made a vow to buy yet more for the pub. It was a dark time of year.

They settled in the first coffee shop they came across. The café was heaving with Christmas shoppers, but Jason hovered over a table where two women were idling over their empty cups and something about his presence made them move.

Livvy eased into her seat wedged against the wall and looked around while they waited for the waiter to take their order. On each table was a hideous red and green lamp in the shape of a Christmas troll. Red and purple foil garlands hung in heavy swags all around the walls, festooned with flashing multi-coloured fairy lights and dangling gold lanterns. Covering each large window looking out onto the street were light curtains shimmering lime green and pink. Two corners were dominated by enormous fake trees smothered in vivid pink and white fluffy decorations and with yet more flashing fairy lights. It was Christmas but with added punk. If you entered without a migraine, you'd have a fairly good chance of leaving with one.

'They really love Christmas in here.' She grinned, thinking of her restrained, colour coordinated decorations back home in The George. Jason gave a superior smile in return and snapped his fingers at the waiter. Livvy ordered a hot chocolate. There was something about the contrast between the suave Jason and this joyously chaotic café that made her crave a rebelliously childish comfort. 'Gandy Street is somewhere I'd like to explore more.'

'It's a charming little place. Well worth investigating. I've heard it's the street JK Rowling based Diagon Alley upon.' He added, 'She attended the university here, I understand.'

'Well, in that case, I'll definitely have a good look around. I was a huge Harry Potter fan as a kid.' Her hot chocolate arrived, and she began to pick off the star shaped marshmallows. Eating one, she sighed. 'I feel as if I've hardly stepped foot out of the pub recently.'

'Mm. The perils of running a business. But you have staff? How is that working out?'

'Oh, Jason!' Livvy put a hand to her mouth. 'I'm so terribly sorry. I've completely neglected to thank you for suggesting Fabio. He's been amazing.'

Jason batted her apology away. He preened slightly. 'I was only too happy to put his name forward. There's absolutely no need for thanks. And, after all, I get to sample his food so it's a win-win situation all round.' He lifted his coffee cup. 'Here's to a very fruitful partnership between you two.'

There was a slight edge to his voice that Livvy couldn't interpret. Ignoring it, she replied, 'Thank you. I think the restaurant is really going to showcase his talents.'

'Do I detect a hesitation?'

'I'm not sure Fabio will want to commit to the restaurant long term. Much as I have ambition for it to become a destination eating place, I suspect it won't be big enough for him. He's worked in such prestigious venues.'

'True. He won't stay around forever.'

'He's back because his mother is ill, I understand.'

'His mother is dying,' Jason said succinctly.

Livvy lapsed into silence, sipping her hot chocolate, thinking. It was troubling to have her fears about how long Fabio might stay confirmed. 'I had no idea it was that bad,' she said eventually.

'Poor Fabio.' *No wonder he's moody and taciturn.* 'And there's no guarantee, without Fabio, that The George will be as successful.' Last night's doubts were still playing on her mind.

'Also true. There's never a guarantee of success in business, no matter how hard one works. But I'm sure that won't be the case with The George,' Jason pointed out equably. 'Take my advice, make sure there isn't anywhere else in town that's doing quite what you're offering. I think that's key. Develop your unique selling point.' He smiled graciously and leaned back. 'Although I'm sure I'm not telling you anything you don't know.'

'No, you're not,' Livvy thought, wondering why he was so invested in someone else's business. However, it was also a relief to talk to someone who obviously understood the issues. 'But that's easy to say, more difficult to do. I think, at the moment, I'm offering a combination of the community feel of The Ship and the food of The Old School Kitchen. I'm not sure that will be enough long term.'

'As long as the restaurant menu is a tad more sophisticated than the current bar one. The bar food was excellent, but I think you'd be wise to offer something really exceptional in your restaurant.'

Livvy smarted. The bar food *was* exceptional. It was just a pared down version of the restaurant menu. 'It will be if Fabio has anything to do with it.'

'Then I really don't think you can lose.'

'That's good to know.'

'I'm confident.' Jason paused. 'As long as you can keep Fabio, of course.' He drained his flat white.

'That's the crux of the matter. Chefs like him are few and far between.'

'Then you'll have to cross that bridge when you come to it. Just one thing. What have you planned for the skittle alley?'

'Nothing at the moment. Leaving it be.' Livvy pulled a rueful face. 'And it's the one thing The George can offer which no other pub in the town can.'

'Then I'll just leave this thought with you. An old-fashioned skittle alley may not fit in with the image you hope to achieve.' He smiled but it didn't quite reach his eyes.

Livvy stared down at her mug and swirled the cream into the chocolate. Irritably, she tucked her hair behind her ear. Jason was voicing what she'd been concerned about. Plus, the skittle alley, due to its age and run-down condition, was costing her a fortune to heat. Her father was right, she needed to be clearer about what she was trying to do with The George. Was it too hopeless to marry a gastropub with a community hub? Could it be both or was she diluting the concept and risking excelling at neither? 'I may have to close it,' she admitted. 'I'm not sure how Pete and his gang would feel about that, though.'

'Really, Livvy. Is Old Pete and his even more aged dog your target demographic?'

Livvy looked up quickly. She wasn't sure she liked how he was talking about Pete. 'Lots of things to think about,' she said, breezily. 'Lots of decisions to make.' She gave a tight smile, unwilling to continue the discussion. What she did, or did not do with The George was up to her. And it was what she did that would dictate whether it would fail or succeed. The responsibility was crushing but it was hers alone.

Jason took the hint. 'Indeed.' He lined up his coffee cup handle with the teaspoon in the saucer in a fastidious manner. 'I hear you've found something rather interesting in your chimney.'

Livvy was taken aback at the change of subject. She wasn't sure she wanted to discuss that with him either. She remained silent but this time Jason didn't take the hint.

'I bumped into Jonquil. She sweeps the chimneys in some of the properties I develop. She mentioned a mummified cat? How very intriguing.'

'I suppose you know all about these things?'

'Only the bare minimum. I'm more of a scientist.'

Livvy could believe it.

'These witches' charms and so forth. Very common in Dorset. Nothing more than superstition, of course.' He gave a slight shudder. 'Primitive stuff, and nonsense. Can't have been pleasant for you, though.'

Livvy gave a quick shrug. She refused to be drawn on the subject of the mummified cat. It still freaked her out to think about it. 'I'd heard a story about a couple of star-crossed lovers connected to the pub. I don't suppose you know anything about them?'

'Star-crossed lovers, eh?' Jason's eyes glinted. 'Well, that's a bit more like it.' He pursed his lips. 'I've only heard something vague about the tale. Why not pop into the museum? I believe Barbara is well versed in local history.'

'I will. Thank you.' Livvy began to gather her things. 'And thank you for the hot chocolate and showing me the delights of Gandy Street.' She stood up. 'And now, if you'll excuse me, I've more Christmas shopping to do.' It was a flimsy excuse and, moreover, a lie but she had a sudden need to get away. And get away from him.

When she offered a ten-pound note to pay, he batted it away. 'You can treat us next time.' He caught her hand as she passed by him. 'I hope there will be a next time, Livvy.' His thumb caressed her knuckles in a way which made Livvy's skin crawl. 'I'd really like there to be.'

Livvy gave him a stiff grin. 'Bye, Jason,' she said through gritted teeth, and navigated the confusion of tables, chairs and shopping bags on her way out of the café. *I'd rather sup with the devil.* She was grateful for him pointing out the silk cummerbund and matching bow tie for her father's present but refused to extend their friendship beyond that.

CHAPTER 20

Sherry – a fortified wine made from white grapes. Popular in the nineteenth century and gaining in popularity now. Some consider it quite the neglected wine treasure.

The following day was quiet in the pub. Old Pete and Skip came in and a few were booked in for lunch but that was about it. Livvy dug out some Christmas CDs and played one softly in the background. The wood burner, thanks to Jonquil, was burning cheerfully and the bar looked tastefully decorated but far too subdued after the café in Gandy Street. While she had no desire for its headache-inducing excesses, a few more decorations and lights wouldn't go amiss.

The tree was beautiful and smelled fragrantly of pine but the silver star on top wasn't enough of a statement. To her delight one or two customers had given her Christmas cards so she'd strung up ribbon in amongst the white lights over the bar and hung them there. She hummed along with Michael Bublé, agreeing that it was 'Beginning to Look a Lot Like Christmas'. But it needed more. After all, it wasn't a season for restraint.

Livvy knew she could leave Fabio, Stewie and Karl in charge so headed out to the shops. The town was definitely getting its Christmas groove on. Mini trees, wreathed with lights, poked out over the shop windows, a huge tree had been erected in the square and lights were strung between the buildings over the main street. It looked festive now, during the day, but would be spectacular when darkness fell. She hadn't made it to the Christmas lights ceremony, as she was working in the pub, but a number of customers had popped in on their way home glowing with excitement and reporting how beautiful the lights were this year.

'No more gold hot pants,' Craig from the auction house had said. He'd delivered an antique pine bench he thought she might like. He was right; it would look perfect in the bar. His comment had confused her until he explained. 'Last year's lights looked absolutely perfect until lit.' He chuckled, his laughter rumbling from deep within his enormous frame. 'Then everyone saw they formed the rather unfortunate and unmistakable pattern of underpants when lit.' He laughed again. 'Real Kylie gold hot pants, they were. Such a hoot. The mayor was apoplectic when he clocked them. Story's passed into Lullbury Bay legend.' He wiped the tears of mirth from his eyes. 'Such a shame there's no repeat,' he'd said. 'I rather miss them.'

Now, Livvy noticed, as her van struggled up the steep hill which was the main shopping street, to the soundtrack of 'Jingle Bell Rock', that many of the shops had their windows decorated for Christmas. New this year, was the Best Decorated Shop. It would be announced at the Late Night Shopping Event and she promised herself she'd make it.

On the way back from the DIY store and the Cash and Carry, with a load of crisps, nuts and soft drinks, and another couple of boxes of lights and decorations, she avoided the busy main street, diverted and drove past the town's museum. It, too, had entered into the Christmas spirit and, in the car park outside, had a tall tree elegantly decorated with shiny red baubles, topped with a gold star. She drove past thoughtfully and then, on an impulse, pulled into the next road and turned around. She ignored the horn which blared out behind her, she assumed from an irate motorist who had been taken by surprise at her sudden manoeuvre. Retracing her route, she drove into the museum's car park. As she parked up, a sleek grey Mercedes slid in behind her and parked alongside. It was Mark.

'Hi there. Didn't you hear me hoot?' He locked his car and came over to her.

Livvy leaned against her van. She crossed her arms. 'So, it was you being a road-hog?' she reproved, playfully.

'Only when stunningly attractive pub owners suddenly turn left in front of me without signalling.' He flashed a grin.

'I take the compliment and thank you.' Livvy looked down. 'Especially as I'm dressed in my scruffy dungarees. Sorry to cause you confusion. I was on the way back to the pub when I decided, to hell with it, Karl and Fabio can cope without me.' She pulled a mischievous face. 'I'm playing hooky.'

'Sounds intriguing. Can I join in?'

'Please do, I don't think it'll be all that exciting.' She jerked her head towards the museum. 'Thought I'd find out more of the pub's history. I've been instructed to seek out Barbara.'

'Then count me in.' Mark looked up at the building. 'I don't know how many times I've driven past this place and I haven't been in yet.'

'It's an impressive looking place, isn't it? Especially against today's blue sky. Looks as if it was once a big house. Georgian maybe, possibly the same vintage as the pub. I love the tree.' Livvy took his arm. 'Come on then, let's get you and the museum acquainted. Don't want to hang about out here, it's freezing!'

They walked into the foyer. At one time it must have been the grand entrance of the house and still showcased impressive black and white floor tiles. A magnificent staircase led upstairs, dividing into two at a half landing in front of a tall window. A Christmas tree stood beneath and looked perfectly in place. Wound around the banisters was a mass of red tinsel and 'When a Child is Born' played softly in the background.

Waiting at the desk and while Mark perused the leaflets on display, Livvy took in the sight of another two beautifully decorated trees. She admired the giant silver stars on top and recognised them as the same as the one she'd just bought. Red tinsel had also been hung all round a noticeboard and she made a note to do the same to the one Karl had just fixed to the pub's corridor wall. She wandered about in the hope of spotting someone, but the place was deserted. Returning to the desk, she spied an old-fashioned brass bell and twanged it. After a few minutes, a middle-aged woman bustled out from a door hidden underneath the sweeping staircase. Raucous laughter, and Slade followed her out.

'Oh my,' she said, snatching off a paper party hat. 'Have you been waiting long? We're officially open but never get many visitors at this time of the year so we're having our Christmas party.' Her small brown eyes darted left and right. 'Only don't tell anyone, will you? We'd get in trouble if the directors knew we were doing it when open.'

Livvy smiled warmly at the woman. 'We've only this minute walked in so you haven't kept us waiting at all. And I wouldn't dream of saying a word. I'm sorry if I'm interrupting your party and I don't know if you can help but it's been suggested I need Barbara.'

'I'm Barbara. What can I do for you?'

When Livvy explained, Barbara's eyes lit up. 'Ooh, I've been meaning to try the food at The George. Jonquil said the menu looked great. She popped in with the cat you found. We still haven't put it on display, but it'll find a place. Great find!'

'We found a mummified cat when the chimney was swept,' Livvy explained to Mark.

He pulled a face. 'As you do. Intriguing.'

'Oh it is, it is,' Barbara exclaimed. 'We're going to add it to our folklore section. We have quite a collection of items designed to keep witches at bay.'

Mark looked even more baffled.

'Things shoved up chimneys to ward off evil spirits and witches,' Livvy added.

'Ah, that explains everything,' he said, clearly not under-standing a word.

Livvy gave him a quick look. 'This isn't your thing, is it?' She could see he was trying to keep a straight face.

'It's so not my thing.'

'Well,' Barbara put in, rather stiffly, 'even if it's not your thing, as you put it, young man, it's still part and parcel of our local history.' Having dealt with Mark, she turned back to Livvy. 'What did you hope to find out?'

'If you've anything about the history of The George, that would be wonderful.'

'Come this way,' Barbara said, looking animated. 'We've defi-nitely something that will interest you.'

She led them up the main stairs and into a large room on the second floor. High ceilinged, it was painted a classic but chilly pale green. Elaborate gilt framed portraits hung from the picture rail, an impressive marble fireplace yawned cold and unlit and display cabinets stood rigidly to order. Apart from the three of them, it was empty of people. 'As I said, we don't get many visi-tors at this time of year. I suppose everyone is too busy Christmas shopping.' There was a faint note of disapproval in Barbara's voice. 'It seems to begin earlier and earlier and get more commercial every year.'

'I agree,' Livvy said. 'I've only just decorated the pub and I'm weeks behind the rest of the town.'

'Well, I suppose you have to make the effort when you're running a public house. I have to say, Livvy, it's good to meet *someone* who's taking an interest in our local history.' Barbara gave Mark a reproving look. 'This room is dedicated to Georgian and Victorian Lullbury.' She swept a proud arm to indicate. 'The seventeen hundreds is when the coach began running from Exeter to London. There used to be an inn at what is now a nursing home on the main Exeter road. The coach – The Arrow it was called – had been running along the main route for a while but the construction in 1820 of Lullbury's only road into the centre of town made it possible for passengers to travel right into the middle. That's when The George came into its own. The horses would need changing, stabling was necessary, and passengers would need refreshment and possibly accommodation too. As you'll see when you look at the displays, it wasn't a popular route because of its steepness.' She gave a dry laugh. 'The modern bus drivers still don't like the climb up and down that hill.'

'Neither does my van,' Livvy put in. 'I drove up it earlier this morning. I came back the other way, to avoid the hill and the congestion. It's why I ended up popping in here.'

'Yes well, that's as maybe,' Barbara said briskly, the engine capability of Livvy's work van obviously of no interest. 'Your pub, or coaching inn as it was then, 'developed a lot of trade and it's when it was rebuilt. The original structure is probably medieval but the outside shell is what was built in the early nineteenth century and that's what you can see today.' She stopped to take a breath. 'Goodness, sorry for the history lecture. I do tend to go on once I get started.' She gestured to the display cabinets. 'You can read it all for yourself, so I'll leave you in peace. If you've got any other questions, pop by the desk on your way out or take a look at the museum's website. And now I must dash. I'll be missing Pass the Parcel.' She disappeared and they heard her clatter down the stairs, presumably to return to the staff party.

'Mummified cats?' Mark said, incredulously, into the swirled-up air Barbara had left.

'Only the one. We found a book of poetry and sketches in the chimney too. That's why I'm here really. Looking for clues who the book might belong to.'

'And maybe why that was shoved up the chimney?'

'Exactly.' Livvy scanned the room. Spotting a large portrait of a young woman, she went over to it. 'Oh.' The sound came out as a long-drawn-out syllable. 'She's so beautiful.' The dark hair, the enormous eyes and the beautiful rosebud mouth was very familiar.

Mark joined her. 'Adela Dickson,' he read. 'She *was* beautiful, wasn't she?' Bending down to peer closer at the tiny writing on the information board, he read, 'Adela Dickson was the daughter of William and Augusta Dickson whose house this was.' He looked up. 'Oh, so she lived here. This was her house.' He whistled. 'Some house.'

'What else does it say?' Livvy stamped down her impatience as Mark got out his glasses before reading the rest.

'Adela never married. It is believed she suffered an early romantic tragedy. She went on to live a full and adventurous life, undertaking a Grand Tour as well as investing in many charitable and benevolent enterprises. She was thought to be an acquaintance of Ada Lovelace. Ada Lovelace. Wow.' He straightened. 'Now, this is much more my thing.'

'Who's Ada Lovelace?'

'Byron's daughter. Some say she invented computer programming.'

'Computers?' Livvy forgot about reining in her impatience and went closer to Mark to read the information herself. She tried to ignore how good he smelled. 'When are we talking about exactly?'

'Says here she was born in 1808.'

'Who? Ada Lovelace or our Adela?'

'Adela. Born 1808. Died 1883. A wealthy woman by all accounts. She would have been a rough contemporary of Ada Lovelace's. Ada was an astonishing woman.'

'Computer programs in the nineteenth century? Really?' Livvy scanned the portrait again. 'Wonder if Adela was as clever? She was certainly beautiful. Why didn't she marry? I'd imagine it was the expected thing back then.'

Mark nodded. 'Ada Lovelace did. And had children. She was only in her thirties when she died. Who knows what she would have achieved had she lived longer.' He pushed his specs up his nose in an endearing gesture. 'Maybe Adela thought an independent life was the better option.'

Livvy thought of Gavin. 'She might have had a point,' she said, drily. Examining the portrait more closely, she added, as realisation dawned, 'You know, she looks exactly like the woman whose sketch is in the book I found in the chimney. I can show you, if you like, it's back at the pub.' She frowned, trying to get her head around it all. 'But, if it is Adela Dickson in the notebook, why would a sketch of her be in a book found stuffed up the chimney in The George?'

'No idea,' Mark said, cheerfully. 'But I think Barbara's converted me. I'm finding this all very intriguing. I'd love to have a look at the drawing.'

'There's some poetry in the book too.'

'Any good?'

Livvy grinned. 'I'd say he was a better artist than writer.'

Mark grinned back. 'Ah.'

'To be fair, I'm no expert in early nineteenth century literature.' Livvy beamed at him. 'It was worth coming into the museum for this alone.' She moved on to a display case. 'Oh, Mark! Here's a drawing of The George. I'd love to get hold of a copy. Look, you can see the arch over the entrance to the car park. It's attached to what is now that office block. Must have been where the old horse-drawn coaches entered. Funny that it's still the way into the car park. And look, it says here it had stabling for fifty horses. Wow.' She giggled. 'The stables must be those decrepit outhouses I've inherited. At some point, in the far distant future, I plan to convert them into holiday accommodation. Oh, this bit is all about a carriage crash. It says just as the coach was coming down the hill into town it overturned.' She reared back in horror. 'A passenger died. How awful. No wonder the route wasn't popular. Too dangerous. Not sure I want The George to be associated with such a tragedy. Maybe I'll rethink that local history display.'

Mark slung a comforting arm around her shoulders. 'There must be loads of memories of The George that people can share. Perhaps ones not so old and sad. Birthday parties, people getting together. Maybe ask people for happy photos to put up.'

'That's a much better idea. I can't believe my pub was the scene of such drama.' She shuddered. 'It's horrible.'

Mark tightened his arm. 'And a long time ago,' he said kindly. 'Do you want to look at anything else, or shall we get out of here? Come on,' he added, teasing, 'let's take a leap back into the twenty-first century. Or do you want to stare at a few mummified cats?'

Livvy elbowed him in the ribs and shook her head. 'No thanks.' At that precise moment her stomach gurgled. 'Sorry,' she blushed. 'Didn't have any breakfast.'

'Think I should remedy that. Come on, I know just the place.'

CHAPTER 21

Acqua frizzante – crisp, refreshing and the perfect sparkling
accompaniment to food

They left the van parked up at the museum and Mark drove her to an Italian restaurant in the next town. 'They do fantastic pizzas here,' he explained, as they sat down.

When their food arrived, Livvy had to agree. 'Would be super to do something like this at the pub. Maybe in the summer when the beer garden's done.'

Mark took the last slice and held it up, trying to catch the dangling cheese. 'You reckon? Would need a proper pizza oven and an authentic dough recipe. Nice idea though.' He took an enormous bite and pleasure spread across his face. 'That was so good,' he said, when he'd finished. He picked up a wodge of paper serviettes and wiped his fingers. 'Nothing like pizza for a quick lunch.'

'How do you find these places?' Livvy gestured around at the restaurant which was barely more than a café and which was tucked away up an alley off the main street. It, too, had entered into the Christmas mood. Dean Martin crooned 'Let it Snow' over the sound system, the restaurant glowed softly with walls covered in curtains of white lights and a fat Father Christmas figure stood on the bar gyrating along. 'If I hadn't been able to smell garlic, I wouldn't have known there was anything here.' She touched the carafe holding a spluttering red candle and around which had been wound ivy and mistletoe. Despite its humble setting the place was deeply romantic.

'Word of mouth, I suppose. Italian food has to be my favourite, and this place is rumoured to bring pizza wannabe chefs from Naples here to learn their craft. Been owned by the same family for generations. I love places like this. There's always room for big swanky showy-off restaurants, but you can't beat these little places. Italy does them well.'

'Have you travelled much in Italy?'

Mark nodded, halfway through drinking some *acqua frizzante*. 'My favourite place on earth,' he said, as he put the glass down. 'It's one place I could see myself living.'

'Whereabouts would you go?'

'Too many wonderful places to choose from. Umbria maybe?' He grimaced. 'Bit hackneyed though. I love Sicily and the Cinque Terre, and the east coast is spectacular as well. And I'm sneakily fond of Sorrento, despite the tourists.'

'Sounds like you *have* travelled a lot in Italy.' Livvy smiled but the thought of Mark settling in another country was upsetting. She'd miss him if he went away from Lullbury. *Only as a friend,* she added, hastily, in her head. *We are just friends, right?*

'Sounds as if you've travelled a lot too'

'I have, and when I was a kid, with my parents, before I went to boarding school. Although they were mostly working, so it was me and the nanny.' Livvy thought back to the succession of nannies and au pairs she'd had looking after her as a child. Some kind, some fun. One or two neither. It had been a lonely existence. Gilded but lonely. 'So, on paper at least, I am extremely well-travelled, but I can't say I've got to grips with anywhere. Not as you obviously have.'

'Perhaps we should do a research trip to the land of the pizza.' Mark grinned broadly.

'Perhaps we should,' Livvy answered, knowing she could never get enough time away from the pub to make it happen. The thought of travelling to one of the world's most romantic places with Mark filled her with joy. *But we're just friends*, she reminded herself again.

Mark raised his water glass, and she did the same. 'To Italy,' he cried as they made the toast. 'To lots of lovely research.'

The waiter, attracted by the noise, came over. 'You've enjoyed?' he asked.

Mark rattled off an answer in Italian which had the waiter looking impressed. 'Some *gelato* to finish?'

'Regrettably, I'm full. Would you like some ice cream, Livvy?'

'Maybe another time when I've eaten less delicious pizza. An espresso would be marvellous though.'

'Of course,' the waiter said. *'Molto bene.* And come back another time. We always have pizza for lovers.'

Livvy blushed scarlet and hid her face in her water glass.

Mark roared at her discomfort. When the waiter had left to get their coffee, he said, 'Don't think he's got the concept of men and women being friends. There always has to be the *inamorata.*' He paused, gazing at her reflectively. 'Don't worry, Livvy I'm not about to make a move on you. We're just pals, aren't we?'

Livvy nodded. It was what she wanted, wasn't it? She didn't have room in her life for a boyfriend. But even as his words sank in, that this was how he saw her – as a friend – a little bit of her shrivelled. Part of her, in another life, at another time, would like

Mark as a lover. She found her voice. 'Of course we are,' she answered, stoutly. 'The best kind.'

There was an awkward silence broken only by the waiter returning and serving them coffee with a flourish.

Mark stirred in a lozenge of brown sugar. 'I hope you don't mind me saying but you look tired. Are you sure you're leaving enough to the others? You've a good team behind you now. They should be able to shoulder more responsibility.'

'They are. I'm really lucky to have them and I am leaving more to them, I promise. Like today. It's been so good to get out and leave the pub for a while, even if we did end up researching its history. I promise I'm not going to become one of those people who are only about their business, although it's hard not to be when you're just starting up.' She sipped her espresso wondering if the caffeine hit was worth the risk of a sleepless night. 'It's just that I haven't been sleeping well.'

'Oh no, that's rotten. Why?' Mark's sympathy was immediate and sincere.

'Just disturbed nights. Kids playing about in the car park in the early hours. Banging the kitchen door, waking me up.'

'Idiots. Can't they find something more productive to do?' He frowned. 'Must be frightening when you're all on your own.'

'It can be, even though I'm pretty sure it's just bored teenagers but it does make me aware I'm alone in a very big building.'

'You've got a security system?'

Livvy nodded. 'And now, thanks to the genius Darrell, a superb set of security lights.'

'Ring me, if you need to. Or Simona. She's only next door and she's actually, contrary to appearances, pretty good in a crisis.'

'Thanks. I appreciate it but I'm made of strong stuff.' She shrugged. 'It might just be mice.'

'Big mice!'

'Yeah.' Livvy managed a laugh. 'I was thinking of getting a cat.'

'A dog might be a better idea. Even if it's not a guard dog as such, the barking will put people off.'

'You may have a point. I've never yet met a cat who was an efficient mouser anyway.'

'Have you been in touch with Tom up at his animal sanctuary? It's on the hill leading out of town in the other direction to the pub. He often has dogs he rehomes.'

'I haven't. I didn't know he rehomed animals.'

'Might be worth a visit. If nothing else a dog is excellent company.'

'Thanks, Mark. I'll do that. And, what's a pub without a pub dog?'

He grinned. 'As long as it gets on with Skip.'

'Only Daisy gets on with Skip,' Livvy said gloomily. 'I'm not even sure Pete is all that fond of him.' Changing the subject, she added, 'You know you mentioned a young couple who met at the pub, and it didn't end well?'

Mark's brow creased. 'Did I?'

'It was the first night you came in when I'd only just taken over. You asked if I was planning on changing the name and said the chain had named it The Runaways after a couple who used to meet there back in the nineteenth century and it ended tragically.'

'Oh yes. It's an old story. Speaking of Pete, ask him about it. He used to sit at the bar and tell tales for the price of a pint of cider. That's when his hip allowed him to sit on the bar stool. His arthritis is too bad now. All I know about them is they used the inn to meet one another when they got off the stagecoach from London.'

'Just as Barbara in the museum said. The George was a coaching inn.'

'Like lots of other pubs in England. You'd have to ask a historian about it. Not my area of expertise.'

'You seem to know a lot about Ada Lovelace.'

'Ah yes. My father-in-law, or should I say ex-father-in-law, has an obsession with her. He was in the defence industry back in the day and found out that the computer programming language he was using at the time was called Ada after Ada Lovelace.' Mark grinned. 'Now he spends his retirement trying to convince the world to recognise her for the genius she undoubtedly was. He bends my ear about her every time I go to see the in-laws.'

Livvy remained silent. It was charming that Mark was still on such good terms with his ex-in-laws. Civilised.

'But you were talking about the runaway couple.' Mark picked up an almond biscotti and crunched it.

'It was the portrait in the museum that did it.' Livvy warmed to her theme. 'The more I think about it, the more I'm sure she's the same woman as in the book of sketches and poetry I found stuffed up the chimney. If she's Adela Dickson, who suffered a romantic tragedy early in life and then never married, what if she was one half of the runaway lovers who met at The George?'

'It's a bit of a reach, Livvy.'

'Yes, it is, isn't it?' She deflated.

'But I can see it means a lot to you. What are you going to do next?'

'Research Adela, I suppose.' She smiled ruefully. 'In all the spare time I don't have. I don't know why but I'm really drawn to this story of thwarted romance. I love the idea that The George was the meeting point for all these people, these lovers. Just think how many assignations have happened under the roof of my pub.'

Mark laughed. 'And still are.'

'And still are.'

He glanced at his watch. 'Suppose we'd better go. It's gone four.'

'Has it?' Livvy was startled. 'Time's flown.' She peered outside. 'Gosh yes, it's gone dark. I need to get back, unload the van and get geared up for opening time. Perhaps,' she added cheerfully,

'I'd best concentrate on getting my new business up and running and forget all about nineteenth century lovers.'

'Maybe.' Mark called for the bill, then turned to her, looking serious. 'Going back to these annoying teenagers, ring me if they're a problem again. Any time, day or night.'

'Thanks, Mark. That means a lot. It's good to know I have a friend to rely on.'

A strange expression flickered across his face. 'Always. Now, come on, let's get you back to pick up your van.'

Darkness misted around them as they drove back to the museum car park. Lullbury Bay's main shopping street was awash with Christmas colour and hope. The mini trees above the shop windows were now lit and the lights strung across the street twinkled with a myriad of red and green stars. Definitely no Kylie hot pants in evidence. The huge tree in the square was also lit and filled the chilly, damp sea air with a warming glow.

As Mark changed down to turn into the car park where the van sat, Livvy said, 'I'm determined to make the Late Night Shopping Event. I missed the lighting up ceremony and I really regret it.'

'That's a shame. The lighting up is great fun. Think I actually prefer Late Night Shopping, though. There's usually a lantern parade, the carnival floats come out, loads of stalls. Last year there was a German Market but not sure that's happening again. Might be bands on in the square instead with lots of street food.'

'Carnival floats?'

'Carnival is big here in the southwest. Until you've seen some of those floats, you won't believe your eyes. Loud, bright, anarchic. Great fun.'

Mark eased the Mercedes smoothly into a parking space. Livvy began opening the passenger door to get out but changed her mind. To hell with being friends. She reached over and quickly kissed him on the cheek. 'Thanks, Mark. Thanks for everything. Let's go to the Late Night Shopping. Together.'

If he was taken aback, he had the good manners not to show it. Flicking a heavy lock of glossy red-brown hair back, he grinned. 'It's a date. See you, Livvy.'

'See you, Mark.'

CHAPTER 22

Craft made west country cider – subtle apple bouquet, sharp on the palate, effervescent

Livvy floated through the rest of the evening, a silly grin on her face. She really did enjoy being with Mark and was determined to take it at face value. Yes, she was up to her eyeballs running a business, but it didn't mean she couldn't have a personal life. Daisy had warned her about making sure she kept a work-life balance and that's what she was going to do.

Humming along to 'Rockin' Around the Christmas Tree' on the sound system, she approached the customer waiting at the bar. 'Hi, Lucie, what can I get you?' she said to Eli's sister. She was in her mid-twenties at a guess, with hair dyed a fierce red.

'Hi, Livvy. I thought I'd drop in and see how he's getting on.' She waved at Eli who was at the other end of the bar serving Jason.

Livvy said warmly, 'Eli's doing well, as you can see.' They

watched as he and Karl joked around at the glass washer. 'What can I get you to drink?'

'Cider please, a local one if poss. And a packet of salt and vinegar.' Lucie leaned over the bar looking anxious. 'And do you think I could have a word?'

'Of course you can. Find a table and I'll bring your drink over.' Livvy watched Lucie speculatively as she found a table well away from anyone else. It was the table nearest the Christmas tree and most people avoided it claiming the sharp pine needles pricked. Lucie sat down, the lights playing over her bright hair. She still looked uneasy. Had she come to complain about Eli's working conditions? If so, there was no possible basis. Eli was paid more than the minimum wage, all his food was included and, where possible, shifts were negotiable. Staff were looked after at The George. She poured half a cider, found the crisps and took them over to the table, along with a white wine for herself. 'On the house,' she said and sat down.

'Ooh, thank you. It's lovely in here.' Lucie looked around appreciatively. 'Eli said you'd done a good job, but you know what blokes are like, they don't do the interior decorating deets. I couldn't take in much the last time as it was rammed and I only came in here once when it was The Runaways. Had the atmosphere of a morgue. I love what you've done. It's so much nicer.'

'Well, I'm aiming for an atmosphere slightly more welcoming than a morgue.'

'Soz.' Lucie grinned. 'I have a habit of speaking then thinking.'

'Then I hope we'll see you in here some more, maybe to eat? Our food's really good, even though I say so myself.'

'I'd love that.' Lucie sipped her cider. 'Eli waxes lyrical about your food. He pisses Mum off something rotten as he says she can't cook anything like Fabio can.'

'Oh dear. I'm sorry about that. It sounds as if Eli is happy working for me and certainly Karl says he's a quick learner, even if he gets a bit flustered when we're busy. Oh, and we have to nag him to put his phone away but that's teenagers for you.' Livvy took a measured sip of her wine, feeling it glide coolly down her throat. It had been busy tonight, and this was the first chance she'd had to sit down. 'Forgive me, what have you come to complain about?'

'Complain?' Lucie looked shocked. 'I haven't come to complain. If anything, I'd like to thank you for giving Eli a chance. He's been a bit,' she paused, choosing her words carefully, '*wild* in the past. You and Tom Catesby up at the animal sanctuary are the only people who have shown any trust in him.'

Livvy nodded. 'Tom gave Eli a good reference. Eli was quite upfront about what he'd done as a kid when we interviewed him.'

'Oh. Good.'

'It was joy-riding and vandalism, wasn't it? A while ago now, though.'

Lucie nodded. 'Mum was mortified about the whole thing. I mean, Eli's growing up now, holding down two jobs, got a girl-friend – or did have, they've split up – but our family has a name in Lullbury Bay. We're well known. It was awful for her.'

'I can imagine. But, if Eli is sorting himself out – which I hope he is – why have you felt the need to check on him?'

'Is Gerry coming in here to drink?'

'Gerry? That's your uncle, isn't it?'

'Technically a great uncle. He's from the side of the family Mum and Dad don't have anything to do with.' Lucie bit her lip. 'They're not nice people. They don't live in Lullbury Bay but come here to drink. They've already been banned from the other pubs in town.'

'Thank you for the warning, then. I'll make sure I keep an eye on Gerry and his gang.' Livvy paused. 'But why are you worried about Eli? You are, aren't you?'

'We are. Eli's a basically good lad but he's easily led. I don't trust Gerry as far as I could throw him, and I worry he'll be a bad influence on Eli.'

'In what way?'

Lucie blew out a breath. 'I don't know. Anything.' She flapped her hands. 'Everything. As I said, Gerry doesn't have anything to do with our branch of the family and vice versa so they haven't crossed paths until now but when Eli came home after his shift the other night and told Mum his Uncle Gerry had been in, well, we feared the worst.'

'What can I do to help?'

'I don't know really. Keep an eye on what's happening, make sure Gerry isn't up to anything. We know he deals, is into petty crime. As I said, he's not a nice bloke.'

Livvy took Lucie's hand. 'I promise I'll keep a watch out and I'll get Karl to do the same. Karl and Eli work together all the time and I'd trust Karl with my life. He'll look out for Eli.'

'Hey, sis, what you doing up here?' Eli approached their table. 'This all looks very cosy. What's going on?' He looked suspicious.

'Just in time,' Lucie said brightly. 'Another round of drinks here, please. We're discussing a Christmas Quiz. In aid of–' she began to flounder.

'The RNLI,' Livvy supplied with a flourish. 'What else.'

'Yeah. What else.' Eli snorted. 'That's all I ever hear from Luce and Jamie. RNLI.'

'You'd better hope you never get into difficulties at sea, then, little bro,' Lucie said, crisply.

'Whatevs.' Eli shrugged. 'Same again?'

'Best make mine an orange juice,' Lucie added. 'I've got the car.'

'Good. I'll bag a lift.'

Lucie raised an eyebrow. 'Only if your manners improve.'

Eli sighed, rolled his eyes heavenwards. 'Please can I have a lift home?' he parroted.

'You can.' After he'd gone, Lucie turned to Livvy. 'And you say you never have any problems with him?'

Livvy giggled. 'Always says please and thank you to me but then I'm his boss.' She grinned, leaning back into her chair. 'Well, it looks as if The George is holding a quiz night.'

Lucie looked at her sheepishly. 'I'll get my Jamie on board to help. That's my husband. He'll have a vested interest; he crews for the lifeboat here. And I'll get Jago and Honor along. Jago's crew too. Honor's the deputy at the primary school so she'll be up to her armpits in end of term stuff but tell her it's Christmas and she'll be here. She's obsessed with anything Christmas. She's married to Jago.'

'Lucky Honor. I met Jago at the craft fayre. I bought a light catcher off him.'

'God yeah, he's gorg, isn't he? All that dark curly hair. Very easy on the eye. Uncle Dave and Daisy and Rick will come too.'

'Actually, it's not getting people along to the quiz I'm worried about. It's writing the damn thing.'

'I'll do that. Happy to be quiz master too. It's the least I can do seeing as I landed you in it.' Lucie grinned. 'I love a chance to boss people about. Don't stand for any nonsense, me.'

'So I saw.'

'You mean, with Eli? Older sister's prerogative. Got to be some perks to being the firstborn.'

'I wouldn't know. Only child here.' Livvy smiled, liking Lucie more and more. She looked around but there was no sign of Eli with their drinks. Seeing Mark come in she waved. 'We may as well go up to the bar to get our drinks as your brother has disappeared. I was hoping he could tell me more about Tom's animal sanctuary. I'm hoping to get a pub dog.' She stood up.

At the word dog, both Pete and Skip woke up. Pete wiped his mouth and grunted and Skip let out a low growl.

'You getting a dog, Livvy?' Pete said.

Nothing wrong with your hearing when you choose to listen to things you shouldn't, Pete. 'Maybe.'

'Better make sure my Skip likes it.'

'Absolutely.' Livvy cast a humorous look towards Lucie. 'I wouldn't dream of introducing any animal Skip doesn't approve of. Another pint, Pete?'

'Ar. Don't mind if I do.'

The women went to the bar. Livvy slipped behind it, pulled Pete's cider and poured Lucie an orange juice. 'Ah, Eli, there you are. Could you take this to Pete please?'

'Only if I get paid danger money.'

'Skip's not that grumpy.'

Eli picked up the pint glass. 'Wasn't talking about the dog.'

Livvy suppressed a grin. 'Hi, Mark. Usual?'

'Yes please. Lunch made me thirsty.' He shot her a conspiratorial grin.

'What do you think about a quiz? A Christmas themed one.'

'Excellent idea. Love a quiz.'

Eli rejoined them. 'Pete says you're thinking of getting a pub dog?'

'One thing I've learned about this town,' Livvy said, on an exasperated sigh. 'You can't breathe without everyone knowing how you do it.' She handed over Mark's beer.

He saluted her with it and then sipped. 'It's both the curse and blessing of living in a small town.'

'Tell me about it,' Eli said, feelingly.

Livvy experienced a flicker of compassion towards him. It must be rough to mess up when young, in a town where everyone knew what you'd done and had long memories about it. 'Do you think Tom at the animal sanctuary might have a suitable dog?' she asked him.

He leaned against the bar, thinking. 'Not at the moment. Tom's not keen on rehoming animals so close to Christmas, even if he had any dogs. He's got lots of guinea pigs,' he added, brightening.

'Not sure a guinea pig, no matter how cute, will be the company I'm looking for. I've thought about getting a cat but that was when I thought we had mice.'

'Haven't seen any mice. Or rats. I can tell what they are by their droppings.'

'I haven't seen any either. No mice or rats at The George. Thank goodness. Health and Safety would have our guts for garters if we had them. For such an old building, it's surprisingly clear of pests. Haven't seen even so much as a silverfish.'

'So, you're looking for companionship?' Lucie asked. 'I always think a pub dog is a nice thing to have about the place. The Old Harbour used to have a smelly old retriever, but he's long gone.'

'It would be comforting to have something around when I've closed up,' Livvy answered.

Lucie nodded. 'I can imagine. Big old place to be in when you're on your own.'

'Livvy, I'd offer my services but I'm going to be tied up with stuff in the run up to Christmas,' Mark said, causing Lucie to give him an impish look.

More grist for Lullbury' s gossip mill, Livvy thought but giggled all the same. 'What sort of service did you have in mind?'

Lucie leaned her elbows on the bar next to her brother. 'Yes, Mark. What did you have in mind?' She quirked a suggestive brow.

Mark shifted, thrusting an embarrassed hand through his hair. 'I was going to offer to stay over. Having another living, breathing human in the place might reassure you.'

Eli, patently bored now the conversation had veered from animals, wandered off to collect glasses. Lucie gave Mark, and then Livvy a blank look. 'Why do you need reassuring, Livvy?'

'It's nothing really. I've had a few kids messing about in the car park at night. I thought a dog might warn them off. It's either that or I get the police involved but I can't see them taking me seriously. They haven't actually done anything.'

'Ah. I can see how a guinea pig might not do the job then. And good luck with the police. By the time they've come all the way from Bridport the little scrotes will have long gone. If we still had a manned police station in town maybe the kids round here wouldn't be tempted to cause trouble.'

Livvy knew Lucie was thinking of Eli. She turned to Mark. 'Thanks for the offer. It's very kind of you but I completely understand if you're too busy. Actually, my parents have promised, or should I say threatened, to come to stay soon so I'll only be on my own for the next couple of weeks. I'll probably be working so hard once my head hits the pillow, I'll be asleep. Or at least that's how I'm planning it. And if these kids persist, I'll set Mum on them. That'll scare them. She's worse than any guard dog.'

They laughed.

'Got it!' Mark rapped the bar so hard, the couple at the table nearest them stopped chewing halfway through their turkey and cranberry burgers and stared.

'What?' Livvy smiled at his enthusiasm.

'Pete,' he called over. 'Is your mate still looking to get rid of his gun dog?'

Pete shifted to his feet, stood for a second to feel his balance, and came over, Skip obedient at his heels. 'Ar. He is. Too old to do a full day's shoot now and he's trained up a new dog. He don't know what to do with the old girl. Why you asking?'

'She'd be perfect for Livvy, here in the pub, don't you think?'

Pete sucked his teeth. 'Might do an' all, I s'pose.'

'What's she like?' Livvy asked, trying not to get drawn into the idea.

'Little bitch springer called Angel. Coming up to eleven, bit arthritic,' Pete said.

'What happens to Angel if she isn't rehomed?'

'I can answer that,' Lucie supplied. 'Some beaters aren't very sentimental about their animals.'

'I get it,' Livvy said bitterly. 'Having worked for him all her life, now she's no use that's it.' It was no good. She already wanted to rescue little Angel.

'Not that simple, girl.' Pete huffed. 'Norm rehomes his. He's just waiting for the right place to take her. He's got a kennel full of gun dogs. One in. One out, like. But he can't afford to keep a dog that don't earn her keep.'

'I can see that but I'm not sure I can take on a dog.' Livvy was desperately backtracking, but she knew a stitch-up when she saw it. 'Not with all my other commitments. I mean, is she even house-trained?'

'Oh ar.' Pete reached a hand down to check Skip was there and caressed his ears. 'He trains his dogs. She'll be more used to kennels, like, but he'll have her house-trained. Apart from a walk a day, I don't think Angel will be too much trouble. Reckon she'll make a beeline for the rug in front of the fire and sleep there most of the day.'

'If it helps, I'd take her out,' Mark offered. 'I could do with some exercise. The George's good food is beginning to have an impact on my waistline.' He patted his completely flat stomach. 'She'd be company for you,' he persisted. 'Particularly at night. And every pub has to have a pub dog.' He grinned, disarmingly.

'I've always said if I get to come back, that's what I'd like to be reincarnated as, as a pub dog!' Lucie said, on a giggle. 'Angel sounds like the perfect solution, Livvy.'

'We've already got a pub dog. Sort of.' Livvy glanced doubtfully at Skip currently looking as if butter wouldn't melt.

'It would be nice to be greeted by something other than a snarl and breath so rank it could fell a tree,' Mark said.

'Oi! Watch your words,' Pete defended. 'When you're as old as Skip here, you'll be bad-tempered too.' He scratched Skip's head, making the dog grin, tongue lolling.

Livvy reeled back as she caught the full blast of Skip's breath. 'Skip's not so bad. Pork scratchings are the answer.'

'See, you're a natural with dogs,' Lucie said. 'Why not go and meet Angel and see what you think.'

'This is all so unfair. You know exactly what will happen if I actually meet her. What colour is she?' she added, intrigued despite her misgivings.

'Black and white,' Pete said. 'Sweet-natured little bitch. Soft as anything, like.'

'Stop it!' Livvy put her hands over her ears. 'This is emotional blackmail.'

'True,' Mark agreed. 'But if you had her, you'd be doing me a favour too. I've got too many commitments at the moment to take on a dog, much as I'd like to. If you let me, I could share ownership with Angel. Do the early morning walks, that sort of thing. It doesn't sound as if she'd need much more. And you'd have another living being in the house at night. Springers aren't guard dogs as such, but she'll have a good bark.'

Livvy finished her wine. 'You,' she said, pointing to Mark, Lucie and Pete in turn, 'are all incorrigible.'

'Can't speak for the others but I know I am,' Mark agreed without rancour. He saluted her with his beer. 'I'm also very good at getting my own way.'

'Come on, Pete,' Lucie said, as she took the man's arm. 'I'll join you for another drink and we'll share some salty snacking goodliness with Skip. He's welcome to a few crisps but I draw the line at pork scratchings.'

'I'll bring them over,' Livvy said. As she prepared their drinks, she pictured a cute black and white springer sleeping on the end of her bed, snuffling contentedly. Walks on the beach to clear her head would be good too – she couldn't work all the time. He gaze returned to Mark, who was now having an animated discussion with a couple wearing office clothes but who were heavily festooned in tinsel, possibly on their way back from an office party.

He'd offered to help. If he did a few early morning walks and then popped in for something to eat in the evening, she'd see much more of him. For a second her heart lifted with joy at the thought. Then she remembered they were just friends. Friends who might be about to share the responsibility of dog ownership. It could work. Couldn't it?

CHAPTER 23

Gingerbread latte – strongly brewed coffee, warmed milk, added spices and whipped cream. Perfect for warming up chilly guests. Serve with Christmas shortbread.

The letter arrived two days later, enfolded inside an imposing, embossed Christmas card. The card featured a carriage and four horses snorting outside a snow-covered coaching inn. A woman in a Victorian-looking coat and hat, her hands hidden in an enormous fur muff, stood expectantly.

It made Livvy laugh as it reminded her how her mother was always ready for any journey a good twenty minutes too early. She would then stand around nagging her father into a panic induced fluster.

Livvy added the card to the growing collection hung above the bar, making sure it had a prominent central position. She knew her mother would check.

As she unfolded the letter, she thought how typical it was of her parents to write a formal message when a phone call or text would do. Livvy questioned whether they actually knew when their business life ended and family life began. At least they hadn't put it through the office franking system: it bore a proper Christmas stamp with a cheeky red-breasted robin. She tore it off the envelope and popped it in the pot on the bar. The George, along with its support for the RNLI, was collecting used stamps for the hospice in Bridport.

The letter confirmed her parents would be staying the following week before driving over to Southampton to join their cruise. With their usual high-handedness, they hadn't asked, just presumed.

'Well, Dad, if you're staying, you can put in a shift behind the bar,' Livvy murmured.

Whatever her mother's feelings on Livvy running an ordinary local pub, she knew her father would love it. It would take him back to when he began in the business. She read the rest of the letter without a great deal of interest, it mostly concerned the state of the hospitality industry, the expensive repairs on their house in France and their inability to keep a decent cleaner for their pile in the Cotswolds. Then her eye landed on something written nearly at the bottom, just before they'd signed off.

Oh, and we thought you'd like to know we're thinking of letting the Gates go.

This was news. The Olde Gates, the last remaining hotel owned by the family, was going to be sold. Livvy frowned. Her parents were only in their mid-fifties, it seemed far too young to give up the one thing that gave them so much fulfilment. She wondered what they'd find to do with their time. There were only so many cruises you could go on.

Looking around at the pub bar she doubted she'd ever feel like giving The George up. It felt like home now, even though she had to share it with strangers a lot of the time. Scanning the letter again, she supposed, on reflection, it was no surprise to hear her parents were considering retiring. The last few years had been a challenging time for the hospitality trade; a hell of an understatement. Still, it would take some adjusting to.

She pictured the rooms upstairs, trying to decide which one to put her parents in. There were a number of bedrooms but none had been refurbished yet. The only other en suite one would have to do; her mother would baulk at creeping along a cold corridor in search of a loo in the middle of the night. It was a functional but chilly looking room, with white walls, black beams and smear of damp damage on the ceiling. It needed a repaint and some colourful bedding. She didn't have time to repaint, but she could chuck a brightly patterned throw over the bed. It would just have to do.

She wondered what her parents would make of Lullbury Bay. Her father would happily make do but her mother would struggle to find any excitement in a little seaside town in December. What on earth would she do with her? Giggling, Livvy couldn't see her putting in a stint behind the bar.

Banishing her concerns, she went upstairs to check on bedding and have another look at which bedroom to put them in. She'd have to pay Candice some extra shifts to get upstairs looking half decent. Like most pubs, the emphasis and the money was spent on the public rooms and this was certainly the case with The George. Refurbishing the bedrooms was at the very end of a long to-do list.

There was a glowering darkness outside, even though it was ten in the morning. Glancing through the window on the half landing, she could see ominous heavy clouds rolling in over a greeny-grey churning sea. It was one thing which fascinated her about living on the coast; the ever-changing seascape and the fact you could predict the weather by looking out and seeing what would be heading landwards in about five minutes. She stood for a minute watching the clouds roll in and the wind get up. The tree palms in the beer garden began to thrash about.

The garden was yet another project but one which would have to wait for better weather. The smokers would have to put up with the ramshackle wooden pergola for the time being. The beer garden would be a real asset though, when landscaped. It commanded magnificent views across the bay and who didn't like sipping a cool white wine outside on a balmy summer's evening? As the first hit of sleet hurled itself at the window, Livvy shivered. A hot summer seemed a long way off. It was just as well they all had Christmas to look forward to; it was such a dark time of the year.

Her phone buzzed. It was Mark asking her if she was still up for Late Night Shopping that evening. The ensuing conversation warmed her up and completely made her forget all about her parents' impending visit and the horrible weather.

CHAPTER 24

Hot mulled wine – the perfect Christmas drink to get the party started.
Add brandy and cinnamon sticks to spice things up.

'It's so good to get out and indulge in something really Christmassy,' Livvy said, squashing her woolly hat further down her ears and trying not to shiver. Lullbury Bay's main street thronged with people. Shop windows glowed and above them a myriad of lights twinkled. The light shimmered and reflected on the wet street surface and made the whole thing even more magical. It was like being inside a shining, glittering Christmas snow globe.

Mark grinned. 'Even though it's about minus ten?'

'Despite that. At least it's stopped sleeting. That was quite a shower we had this morning. It was white over.'

'How's your mulled wine? Doing the trick?'

'If you mean is it getting me into the Christmas spirit, then yes. If you're asking, is it warming me up? Then sadly no!' Livvy stamped her feet in an attempt to get some feeling in them. 'I like the music,' she added, nodding to the brass band grouped around the Christmas tree and valiantly playing 'Good King Wenceslas'. Each band member wore a bright red Santa hat which matched their noses. 'They must be frozen though. I'm surprised their fingers work. Wonder if they'd like to come and play in the pub one night? It would be really Christmassy.'

'Oi.' Mark nudged her gently. 'It's your night off. No pub talk.'

'Sorry. Force of habit. And how great they've closed off the high street to traffic.' She looked around at the stalls selling candy floss, burgers, falafels, glow sticks, roasted chestnuts, pulled pork rolls, giant gingerbread men on a stick, and Santa hats. Scents of food cooking drifted in the breeze making her stomach growl. 'The stall selling knitted hats and scarves is doing a roaring trade. I can't believe how many people are here in this freezing weather. Oh, and look at the knitted graffiti. On the bollards.'

At the lower end of the high street was a cobbled section of wide pavement. To prevent parking a row of bollards had been erected. Over each was stretched a knitted figure: a penguin, a snowman, a robin and, for some reason, a luridly pink flamingo. Knitted in bright colours, they were all wound round with flickering lights. 'Wonder who went rogue with the flamingo?' Livvy giggled, cupping her mulled wine, enjoying the Christmassy scents and the hot steam.

An elderly man stopped to say hello. It was Austin. Dressed in a forest green coat, topped with a woolly red hat and matching mittens he looked not unlike one of Santa's elves. 'Going to be a cold winter, mark my words,' he said, his breath misting out in the frigid air. 'Reckon there'll be snow before Christmas.'

'Hi, Austin,' Livvy said. 'Happy Christmas. Do you think we'll have a white one?'

'Happy Christmas, my lovely. Wouldn't surprise me one bit. And I'll be up to try your board games afternoon, by the way.'

'Wonderful. I look forward to welcoming you.'

'Told the missus it was a games afternoon, but she got the

wrong end of the stick. Completely.' He giggled and then shivered violently. 'Not standing around in this. I'll maybe see you down at the beach huts. Ta ta now.'

Livvy turned to Mark. 'I don't understand.'

'Aggie, Austin's wife, runs a vlog for erm... sex tips for the elderly. She's a bit of a... how can I put it?... silver swinger. I imagine she thought the games were of a completely different sort.'

'No way!'

'Oh yes.'

'Maybe I'll put a silver swingers' afternoon on? Brings a whole new meaning to community spirit.' She giggled again. 'I didn't think anything would surprise me but Lullbury Bay constantly does.'

Mark laughed, his eyes brimming with mirth. 'It's a unique sort of place,' he agreed. The band stopped playing and, over the sound system rigged up especially, came the blare of Slade. 'It's Christmaaaaaasssssss!'

'Finished your wine?' he asked. 'Here, pass me your cup and I'll pop it in the bin. Just about enough time to get hot chocolate and find a good place to stand. The lantern parade's about to start.' Mark joined a queue at a nearby stall, bought a couple of drinks from a vender dressed as Elsa from *Frozen* and nudged Livvy to some steps outside an imposing building. 'It's the solicitors. I've learned from experience that their top step is sheltered from the worst of the wind and gives a good view.'

'Brilliant.' Livvy took her hot chocolate from him, grateful for its heat. She tucked herself against the Beer stone wall which jutted out. He was right. They were out of the wind and she instantly felt, if not warmer, then no colder. Slade gave way to a jaunty rendition of 'Rudolph the Red-nosed Reindeer' and Livvy watched in amazement as two reindeer pulled Father Christmas down the hill on a sleigh. 'It's a proper sleigh. And real reindeer!' she exclaimed. They were led by a tall, well-built man dressed in jodhpurs and a jerkin, topped with a fur hat. 'And who's that? Kristoff?'

Mark leaned in to explain, over the noise of the music. 'It's Tom Catesby and his reindeers, Elsie and Morag.'

'Of course they are.' Livvy turned to grin at him, aware that he was very near. 'I like their red tartan coats with the flashing lights.' She followed his gaze as it lifted to the stone lintel above them. His eyes crinkled in humour. Someone had hung greenery, dangling with fluttering red ribbons, above the sombre glossy black door of the solicitors. 'Mistletoe. How seasonal.'

Mark waited, brows lifting. 'Well?' He threw a casual arm around her shoulders and pulled her close.

She reached up and kissed him quickly on his cheek. It was cold but he smelled heavenly; something woody, cedar maybe with underlying amber, all mixed up with chocolate and mulled wine. She longed to taste his lips, but he simply grinned and backed away.

Turning her gently back to the parade, he asked, 'Can you guess who Father Christmas is?'

Livvy squinted as the sleigh went past in a cacophony of 'Let it Snow' and flashing lights which clashed with 'Rudolph the Red-nosed Reindeer' which was still playing. 'It's not!'

'It is. He's taken over this year after a rather traumatic experi- ence retired his predecessor. Elsie and Morag did a runner and ruined the bowling green. Think it's only just recovered.'

Darrell, despite the white beard and padding, was instantly recognisable. He waved and chucked a bag of sweets in their direction, which Mark caught with aplomb.

In the sleigh's wake came a procession of children holding handmade lanterns hooked onto long poles. Each lantern was lit and lent the dark skies a warm glow. They inched along in a wiggly line to the soundtrack of 'Oh Come, Oh Come Emmanuel'. The children's excited gleaming faces coupled with the poignant carol made Livvy choke up. She hadn't anticipated being so moved.

'That's Honor at the front,' Mark explained. 'She runs a lantern-making workshop every year for the procession and this year has gone big. She got adults to make one too. See, here they come.'

Livvy gasped. The adults had gone all out. Fantastical creations, some so enormous they had to be held up by a team of four, paraded past. Tropical fish, exotic birds, strange mythical creatures all bobbed and swayed their way down the street to the promenade at the bottom. 'Magical,' she whispered, stamping her feet again to get some blood flowing.

'Hasn't finished yet,' Mark said, putting his arms around her hugging her to him for warmth. 'Here come the floats. Now the fun really begins.'

They'd given in. The freezing weather had driven them into The Ship along with everyone else. Mark squeezed through, leading Livvy by the hand, found them a table in a back room, then went to buy drinks. He returned with a tray laden with two coffees, two mulled wines and two whiskies. Putting them down, he began to take off his coat. Unwinding a striped scarf and hanging his beanie on the corner of his chair, he eventually sat down. 'I make no apology for the purchases. The bar is rammed five deep. Thought I'd stock up. Hang on, is that the choir gearing up?'

'Choir?'

'Community choir.'

'Ding Dong Merrily on High' floated through.

They listened for a moment. 'You know,' Livvy began slowly, 'I've never really thought of myself as a Christmas person. I mean, I like it and everything, but I've never seen why some people go mad about it. With the family being in hospitality, it was always a working holiday, putting the guests first, squeezing in any celebration where we could. But tonight, with the lanterns and the brass band and now this, I totally get it. And this Christmas really isn't turning out as I expected. I thought I'd be working all the time and have a few days off on my own.' She bit her lip, worried about how much she'd exposed. 'I suppose I thought I'd be lonely.'

Mark reached over and squeezed her hand. 'I hear you on the being lonely part. Why do you think I'm in The George so much?'

'Just as well we've got our friendship then,' she said brightly, removing her hand because it made her want to kiss him. 'And, by the way,' she nodded to the tray, 'right choice with the drinks.' She picked up her coffee and sipped. 'It's been such a good night, Mark. Thank you.'

He swallowed his whisky down in one. 'Whatever for?'

'For showing me the best place to stand to see the parade. I can't believe some of those floats.'

He grinned. 'They were really good this year.'

Livvy relaxed. Conversation about the Christmas carnival parade was a whole lot safer than revealing how vulnerable she sometimes felt. 'That Van Helsing one with the moving horses! And the Fab Four float! I can't get over how loud the music was.' She shrugged, mystified. 'Not entirely sure how Christmassy some of them were but they were still extraordinary.'

'I take your point. Think I mentioned before, Carnival is huge down here. The same floats get displayed all around the local carnival circuit and that usually begins in September. Suppose they thought they may as well trot them out for Christmas. The Polar Express one was good.'

'It was *amazing*. Those little boys in dressing gowns and slippers and hanging off the sides. And the front made to look like a steam train, all lit up and blowing steam. How are they made?'

'I'm not entirely sure,' Mark admitted. 'Think the base is a flatbed lorry and then they build the float on and around it and add the trailers at the back. A lot of hard work. Glad you enjoyed it, maybe we'll make it to the Bridgewater Carnival? That's the big one, with loads of street entertainment.'

'You're on.' Livvy finished her coffee and started on her mulled wine. She inhaled the scents of hot wine, orange, cloves and cinnamon. 'Mm. Christmas in a glass,' she said as she sipped. 'And thank you for leading me down to the seafront to look at the decorated beach huts. It's shocking. I've been in Lullbury Bay three months now and I've only got to the sea once. That's where I met Austin.'

'That is truly shocking. Did you enjoy the beach huts? And the window display competition?'

'I'm glad Bee's Books won. Good old Bee. The dancing penguins with their little reading specs all holding a children's Christmas book were a joy. The beach huts were,' Livvy paused to find the right words, 'let's just say I've never seen anything quite like it ever. I mean, one had a model railway running all round it and onto the outside. And one had a swimming pool with real water, and polar bears. And what was the knitted one all about?'

Mark laughed. 'Lullbury Bay's resident Ninja Knitters. They're responsible for the bollard coverings too. Last year was Santa's Grotto, this year they dedicated their entry to the RNLI.'

'I know but who knits a lifeboat? It was nearly life-sized! Did it win?'

'Think so.'

'Mad.'

The choir's carol came to an end to thunderous applause, after which they began to sing 'Silent Night'.

'Oh,' Livvy said, on a sigh. 'This is my favourite although I like it sung in German best.' She closed her eyes and listened. The hectically busy pub hushed, the magic of the words casting a spell. Opening her eyes as the carol finished, she was aware of Mark's gaze on her. 'What?'

'Nothing. Only sometimes you surprise me. You surprise me a great deal.'

Livvy blushed at the intensity of his statement. 'You know what?' she blurted out, in an attempt to diffuse the heat building between them.

'What?'

'It's a Late Night Shopping Event, and we've not done any shopping!'

Mark pulled a regretful face. 'I was going to buy you the life-sized knitted lifeboat, but you didn't sound very keen.'

'It would make an excellent talking point in the bar.'

'It would.'

'But…'

'But?'

'I'd bet good money that Skip would cock his leg all over it.'

For some reason, they both found this the funniest thing ever and laughed like drains.

CHAPTER 25

Glühwein – the perfect drink for after-ski. Use chianti and the juice of a fresh orange. A cinnamon stick and brandy make it extra warming.

Mark picked Livvy up to view Angel the following morning. The sleet of the previous day had hardened into a hoar-frost, coating trees and hedges into a sparkling icy white. The sky, a vibrant blue, dazzled.

'This is very good of you,' she said as he indicated to turn the Mercedes onto the A35.

'No problem. If she's going to be half my dog, I need to like her too,' he answered.

'We seem to be spending a lot of time together.'

He smiled easily. 'I've no complaints.'

'Me neither. And I really did enjoy last night.'

'It was fun, wasn't it? I enjoyed it too. Who's looking after the pub today?'

'I'm turning into an absentee landlady. Karl's doing an extra shift. Said he could do with the money. It's such a relief to have him around. I trust him absolutely.'

A frown flickered. 'You mean you don't trust the others?'

'I do, but I never feel it's risky leaving the pub in Karl's hands. I've got a good team around me but he's the best. What about you? You mentioned you were extra busy in the run-up to Christmas?'

'My turn to play hooky. I mean, look at the weather. It's glorious. Didn't want to be sat in front of a computer screen in a stuffy old office on a morning like today.'

Livvy rummaged in her bag for her sunglasses. 'It's a skiing day. On days like this I miss the slopes.'

'Have you skied much?'

'Most winters. From a child. Do you?'

'I do.' He risked a quick look away from the road. 'Great sunnies. They suit you.'

'Thank you. Eyes back on the road,' she instructed sternly.

'Yes, miss.'

'Where are we headed to?'

'Inland. Just beyond Uploders.'

She sat back and let him drive. Independent woman that she was, sometimes, just sometimes, there was real joy to be found in letting the man take control.

Eventually, having bumped their way along some narrow Dorset lanes only wide enough for one car and with grass growing along the middle, they turned into a rutted drive leading to a red brick farmhouse.

Norman, the beater, brought Angel into the yard. He let her off the lead and she sniffed curiously around them all, not showing any fear, stumpy tail wagging.

For Livvy, it was love at first sight. She knew it would be. She even softened towards the gruff Norman, as he spoke about the dog with affection and with the glimmer of a tear in his eye. He wanted her to go to a home where she could live out her retirement lazing by a warm fire and being spoiled.

Livvy thought, as long as she got on with Skip, it wouldn't be a problem. She crouched down and the springer came to sniff, cautiously at first and then rewarding her patience with a lick, accepting the treat she offered. Livvy caressed the spaniel's silky ears and watched as the dog's body wagged along with her tail.

'Think you'll do,' growled Norman, coughing to clear his throat, or maybe hide the emotion. 'You want to take her for a walk, like? Let her off in the fields yonder. She'll come back on the whistle.' He handed Mark an Acme Thunderer on a frayed blue rope. 'She's livestock trained so don't bother about them sheep.'

They walked through the gate in the furthest corner of the farmyard which led to a muddy field. A small flock of sheep eyed them and then scampered uphill where the frost clung white.

Livvy, with some trepidation, bent down and released Angel. The dog bounded off, nose to earth in true spaniel style. She stopped, gave a short bark as if to say, 'Come on,' and then began following a scent trail along the hedge, her tail wagging furiously again.

'Oh my goodness, Mark,' Livvy said, as her welly sank ankle deep into something pungent and sticky. 'I'm so sorry about your car. I've brought shoes to change into but we can't take Angel's muddy paws off.'

'Don't worry. I've a towel in the boot. We can clean her off a bit.' He shoved his hands into the pockets of his moleskin jacket. 'It's good though, isn't it? Being outdoors on a day like this? Walking a dog in the countryside.' The short vowels were becoming apparent. He sucked in a deep breath. 'Reminds me of home.'

'Yorkshire?'

He nodded. 'Warmer down here though.'

'You're joking. It can't be much above zero today.'

'Thought you were the experienced skier?'

'I am. But I'm dressed for it then. Thermal silk underwear, lined salopettes, furry hat. The works.'

'Silk underwear? Soft southerner.'

Livvy giggled. 'I'll claim that. With my childhood, I've never felt I belonged anywhere until now.' Angel raced back to them, and she put a hand down to the dog. 'Hello, girl. Would you like to be a pub doggie?' Angel snickered in return and walked obediently to heel. 'Someone's trained you well.'

'Decided then?'

Livvy looked at Mark, a broad grin splitting her face. She didn't know if it was the crisp weather, the blue skies, or the simple pleasure of being with a man she liked, but a rush of joy radiated through her. 'What do you think? Come on, Angel, let's get to the top of the field and enjoy the view.'

After another half hour walking Angel around the field and returning to explain their decision, Norman's goodbye was cursory. He almost ran back into the farmhouse and slammed the door.

'Oh,' Livvy said as Angel whimpered after him. 'I was going to tell him to come over and see her any time.' She looked down at the distressed dog. Angel's tail had gone between her legs, and she was straining at the lead to follow her old owner. 'Is he going to be alright, do you think? Will Angel be okay?'

Mark put a comforting hand on her shoulder. 'Pete will have his number. You can ring him. I think it was easier for him to just go. He must have been very attached to her.'

'Am I doing the right thing?' Livvy turned to him, suddenly unsure. 'I just want them both to be happy with the decision.'

'Absolutely.' He cupped her cheek and said tenderly, 'Angel's too old to work at full capacity. Norman knows that. He also knows she's going to have a splendid retirement. He just can't bear to say goodbye.'

'How did you get to be so kind?'

'I don't think I'm all that kind.'

'Oh you are. The kindest man I've ever known.'

Their lips hovered near, tantalisingly close, in search of a kiss and then Angel pawed at Livvy's leg.

'Think she's impatient to go,' Livvy said, her voice trembling.

'Best get her in the car then. Hope she fits alongside all the other stuff.'

To Livvy's surprise, earlier that morning, Mark had gone to a pet superstore in Axminster. He'd bought the basics: food and bowls, a cosy bed, a few toys. One in the shape of a Christmas pudding complete with smiley face and squeak. He'd shown it to her with glee. Norman insisted they keep Angel's slip lead and had loaned them a crate for the journey. The purchases were crammed onto the back seat, leaving the boot for the dog.

Angel obligingly hopped up into her travelling crate, turned round three times and settled.

After changing out of their filthy boots and squeezing them in next to Angel, Livvy and Mark got in for the journey home.

'I hope she's okay,' Livvy worried. 'She must wonder what's going on.'

Mark switched the engine on and 'Driving Home for Christmas' flooded the car making Angel bark. 'Obviously not a Chris Rea fan,' Livvy said, as she clipped on her seatbelt.

Mark eased the car down the drive, trying to avoid the potholes. 'She's not the only one.' He joined the lane, driving gently so as not to alarm the dog. He glanced into the rear-view mirror at the crate. 'She's obviously used to travelling by car, or in the back of Norman's van: she's lying down now.' He flicked a look at Livvy. 'She'll be absolutely fine. She'll adapt. Dogs do. And I'm on hand to help out. Although I haven't got a dog now, we always had them when Nats and I were kids. I'm not a complete novice.'

'Just as well as I don't have a clue.'

'Tell you what, why don't we stop off at Burton Bradstock? If you've got time? We can take her on the beach. Wear her out a bit. We can give her lots of fuss and treats – there's enough on the back seat to keep her going until the next millennium. We can grab a coffee at the Hive. I might even treat you to a scone and clotted cream.'

Livvy peered out at the weather. It was still a blue and white magnificently crisp December day, but it hadn't warmed up at all and she was appreciating the car's heated seats. It wasn't the cold that was bothering her though. 'Do you think she'll come back to us if we let her off the lead somewhere strange?'

'She should do. She's trained to the whistle and she was pretty good to heel back in the field. Or we can keep her on the lead until she's got used to us.'

Livvy watched as the frozen hedges blurred past. There was a lot of *us* and *we* in those sentences. Part of her was hugely relieved that Mark was helping her out with the dog, part of her wondered why. And part of her queried what was in it for him.

It was developing into an odd relationship. A friendship but with an edge of sexual attraction, with the promise of something more and something far more complex. But it was all so uncertain. She was pretty sure he saw her as a friend and nothing more. Whereas her feelings were veering in another direction entirely. Was it ever possible for a man and a woman to have a purely platonic relationship?

She eyed him surreptitiously as he concentrated on driving. He really was very good-looking. Strong nose, lovely warm intelligent eyes and that glorious hair which swooped over his face and which caught the light from the sky. It was most unfair that a man should have such shiny, thick hair. Her own dark blonde was suffering from a serious lack of attention; she hadn't visited a salon for months and it was usually tied back for work. Making a mental note to ask Simona where the best one was, her mouth quirked; she doubted she could afford to go where Simona frequented.

Mark picked up her humour. 'What's so funny?'

'I was admiring your hair and thinking how terribly unfair it is that you have such gorgeous locks.'

Mark grinned. 'Nats thinks so too. She inherited our mother's blonde hair. Lovely ash-blonde but on the thin side. I have my father's genes to thank for mine, although it's darkened a lot from when I was a little boy. Must be the Viking blood. There's a lot of us in Yorkshire.' He glanced at her. 'Nats would kill for your honey blonde. It's the colour she always asks her stylist to do and never quite achieves it.'

Livvy ran a self-conscious hand through her hair. 'I was also thinking of asking Simona for a recommendation for a hair-dresser. If I can afford it.'

'Ah, that might be the problem. Simona's not short of a bob or two. She'll certainly be able to recommend one, but it won't be cheap.'

'Do you know her well?' Livvy almost didn't want to know the answer. The image of them looking cosy in Simona's sports car flew into her vision.

'I was friends with both Simona and Terence when he was alive. She was incredibly cut up when he died. I suppose I was a shoulder to cry on. When she felt up to it, she went to their house in Italy. It's good to have her back. We're good friends but, of course, the town gossips wouldn't have it. The rumour was we were having a torrid affair. As if.' He laughed. 'I could never afford Simona!' He indicated right to go down a suburban-looking lane flanked by bungalows. 'I got really fed-up batting off the tittle-tattle. Gossip is the one thing I can't stand about Lullbury.'

Livvy was amazed at the relief which poured through her. 'Do you think men and women can have a friendship? Without anything else rearing its head, I mean?'

'Certainly is with me and Simona. I love her as a friend, but she'd drive me bananas as a lover. Do you?' His quick look was intense.

'I'm not sure,' Livvy said slowly. 'Sometimes. Oh!' Her sentence was cut off as the dull bungalows gave way and the road dipped down to rolling fields with a great expanse of shingle, with the sparkling sapphire-blue sea beyond. Everything felt huge and open, with wide skies and a sea which stretched forever. The sun bounced off the water with such a bright, metallic force it had her reaching for her sunglasses again. She leaned forward. 'What a place!'

Mark pulled onto a car park next to a marquee. 'It's lovely here at any time of the year but it's even better in the summer. When the weather's hot I always think it's a little bit Greek.'

'Or Italian?' She shot him a look.

He grinned. 'Or Italian.' He gestured to the marquee, festooned with heavy white lights which swayed in the sea breeze. 'That's the Hive Beach Café. Seafood second to none and the chips are to die for. Maybe it's being close to the sea that makes the food taste extra-good? We could come back one day to sample it?'

'I'd like that.' She smiled, recognising she was getting more and more attracted to Mark. Was it too soon after Gavin? His abandonment had cut deep. He'd been her only serious boyfriend. They'd made plans, had envisioned a life stretching ahead of them together. His sudden departure still had her raw and hurting. She supposed it was almost a grieving process. Could she open herself up to trust another man and so soon? For a second she wondered what Gavin was doing now; she'd blocked all his contacts and hadn't spoken to him since. It had been too painful. Strange. She'd been so busy setting up the pub she hadn't given him much thought until now.

'What's wrong? You look sad.' Mark reached out and feathered a touch down her cheek. 'You and Angel will get on like a house on fire, I promise you. Don't worry.'

On cue the dog rattled impatiently at her crate.

'Think someone is keen to get out for a walk.' He glanced at the waves racing to the shore. 'Might be bracing. You up for it? Think Angel is.'

Livvy forced herself back to the Gavin-less present. 'As long as there's a hot latte at the end of it.'

Mark pulled a face. 'You really don't know much about dogs, do you? They don't drink coffee.'

She thumped him lightly on the arm. 'For that, the first round is on you.'

He grinned and opened the car door, letting in a blast of freezing briny air. 'You're on.'

She followed him, hoping the stiff sea wind would blow her introspection away.

CHAPTER 26

*Caffè all'americana – espresso with hot water. Good for
steeling the nerves*

ngel settled in, as if born, to pub life. She and Skip had a few days sniffing around one another suspiciously and then decided to ignore one another. She found her spot on the opposite side of the wood burner to him and spent most of her time snoozing unless she heard the rustle of a packet of crisps, at which point did the mournful spaniel act and begged a few. Livvy kept a watchful eye out. Not everyone appreciated a springer drooling at their knee and she was only let into the bar when food wasn't being served.

For the rest of the time she seemed content to lie in her bed in the back corridor next to the kitchen, reaping the odd scrap of meat or carrot from Fabio. Although slightly subdued, she seemed to be taking her change of accommodation in her stride.

Good to his word, Mark had walked her early in the mornings. However, as he'd now gone to collect his sister from

London before they travelled to York for Christmas, Livvy was forcing herself out of bed in the chilly early hours for a quick run on the beach. The walk back up the steep hill to The George almost killed her at first but her thighs were getting used to it. Eli was besotted and often took Angel out when his lunchtime shift ended. The springer endured it all with a stoical acceptance.

At night, Livvy allowed the dog to sleep on the end of her bed. She was grateful for the warm weight on her feet and put up with the odd snorting snore. Thankfully, the icy cold weather was putting paid to any nocturnal teenage action in the car park and Angel's guard dog prowess was so far untested.

The pictures of Livvy clambering out of the cherry picker after putting up the Christmas lights had hit the front page of the *Lullbury Bay Echo*. The community Facebook pages were a buzz of chatter. The George and its intrepid new landlady had even been given a double-page feature spread in the newspaper, its headline, 'Lights Go Up, Up, Upmarket and Away'. Livvy hadn't been too happy about the emphasis on her family background, but publicity was publicity and, along with the December frosts and the town's love for all things Christmas, had brought welcome extra trade to the pub. They were almost always fully booked for food and, for the first time, Livvy felt she might be making serious money.

She was puzzled, however, when examining the accounts, to see profits not as solid as expected. 'Must ask Mark to take a look,' she murmured, worried she was coming to rely on him a little too much. She pinned the photograph of her in manure smeared jeans and with Gerry's hand splayed on her bottom, to the newly installed noticeboard in the entrance hall. It made her giggle. The cuttings were framed by more cards from customers and a cheery border of frothy silver tinsel.

The bar, with its lavishly decorated tree in the corner, and reams of white and silver tinsel looked happy and festive. The walls remained bare, but Dave Wiscombe had brought up three of Vivienne Little's seascapes which hung in pride of place in the restaurant. It now had its own tree, and with sprigs of ivy, and holly gleaming with bright red berries, in bud vases on each table. The George was gearing up for its first Christmas.

However, if Livvy felt as prepared as she could be for her first hectic Christmas season in the pub, she was less equipped for her parents' visit.

'Well it's rather basic, darling,' Penny Smith-Lygott announced as she came downstairs from unpacking. She gazed dismissively around the bar. 'It's going to take an awful lot of work.'

Livvy fumed silently. It was just as well her mother hadn't seen the pub before its refurb.

'I like the bar,' her father said.

'Thanks, Dad. It's cosy, isn't it?'

Penny flicked a finger over one of the scrubbed pine tables. 'Homely, I suppose.'

'Mum, it's a pub bar, not The Ritz and I plan on doing up the restaurant a little more luxuriously when I can. The place has already had quite a lot of work done but I've more planned for the future. I'll get the B&B side of things up and running and I'll land-scape the beer garden and then tackle the outbuildings.' Sticking up for her little empire, even though her heart was hammering against her ribcage at the predictable criticism from her mother, she added, 'But I can't do everything at once. Not until I'm established.'

'Well, it's a shame not to have the bedrooms done,' Penny sniffed.

'Oh, do give it a rest,' Brian Smith-Lygott groaned. He winked at his daughter. 'Ever since we decided to properly retire, your mother has been channelling the Hotel Inspector.'

'Nothing wrong in having standards, Brian,' Penny responded, crisply. She narrowed her eyes at her daughter. 'If something is worth doing, it's worth doing well.'

Livvy wondered how she was going to get through the next week. 'What about a coffee?' she suggested brightly. 'Before you have lunch. Fabio's made a delicious *cataplana* as a special today. The fish is from the wet fish shop in Lullbury Bay's harbour. Can't get much fresher than that.'

Penny's nose twitched. 'Fish stew?' She tweaked a carefully blonded hair back into place. 'Oh, Olivia!'

'Yes, with local mussels too and home-made bread.' Livvy winced at how defensive she sounded. She resented how her mother always brought that out.

'Sounds delicious.' Her father beamed. 'And we'll go for two Americanos if that's possible. Might have a quick snifter with mine, darling, as it's so cold.'

'Brandy, Dad, or a whisky?'

'Single malt if you've got it.'

'Of course. Go and warm yourselves up.' As Livvy made the coffee, a familiar slow-gaited shuffle alerted her to an arrival. 'Usual, Pete?'

'Ar. Reckon a cider would go down a treat. And a packet of cheese and onion. Buggerin' freezing out there.'

'You do look cold.' The old man's face and knuckles were reddened by the chill wind. 'Go and get yourself warmed up. I'll bring it over.' She turned and her smile faltered. 'Oh. Looks like your seat's has been taken.' Her parents had bagged the table by the wood burner. Skip, taking no notice, had slumped in his usual spot on the rug in front.

'What a jolly gorgeous collie,' her father exclaimed, not giving Livvy time to warn him Skip wasn't friendly. She watched, open-mouthed, as Brian rubbed Skip's tummy, and the dog rolled over in ecstasy.

At the bar Pete narrowed his eyes and harrumphed. 'Who's that then, taking liberties with my Skip?'

'It's my dad. My parents have come to stay for a few days. Looks like he's joined the exclusive and very short list of humans Skip tolerates.'

'Where's our Angel today?'

'Eli took her for a run on the beach. They'll be back for the lunchtime service.'

'Reckon I'll go and join your folks, then.'

Livvy winced and then shrugged. If her father could win over Skip, he could cope with Old Pete. And her mother would just have to put up with it. 'Fancy today's special, Pete? On the house,' she whispered. He looked as if he could do with a hot meal.

The old man brightened. 'Don't mind if I do, young Livvy.' He fished in his greasy tweed coat. 'And here you are, my lovely.' Handing over a battered Christmas card, he added, 'Place has come alive since you took over.' There was a suspicious glitter in his rheumy eyes. 'The boys have really appreciated you keeping the skittles alley open. And those burgers were the business.'

She took the card, feeling her throat close with emotion. 'Oh, Pete, thank you.' After all the hard work of the last few months, it was good to hear she was doing something right. 'I'll put it up in pride of place.' Sniffling, she said, 'I'll go and find out how Fabio is doing with those specials.'

CHAPTER 27

Beer – an alcoholic beverage produced by the brewing and fermentation of malted barley and other cereal crops. Lullbury Bay Micro Brewery's Good Elf is a strong, dark beer with sweet top notes and a bitter chocolatey finish.

'Just as well we let folk have a table in the restaurant,' Karl said, drying a glass with a tea towel and holding it to the light for inspection. 'Quiz is fully booked. There was even a waiting list.'

It was Sunday and the night of the Christmas Quiz. Karl and Livvy were in the bar doing some last-minute tweaking and it most definitely felt like the calm before the storm.

'Do you think Lucie will cope with the mike?' she asked, as she distributed the picture quiz sheets around tables. They'd had to rig up a sound system to make everything heard through into the restaurant and bar where all tables were booked for teams of six.

'No worries there. Got a voice like a foghorn when she wants.

She'll sort them out and, if there are any problems, she can come in the bar and repeat the questions.'

'She's done a great job writing the questions.'

'She has.'

'And everyone's rallied round with the raffle prizes. Not sure if Brittany used thumb screws or her natural charm but we've got some amazing things to give away.' Livvy ticked them off using her fingers. 'Christmas wreaths and greenery from Daisy, a meal at the Old School Kitchen, a bundle of children's books from Bee's Books, a bottomless brunch at The Station House and, can you believe it, Christmas lunch at The Henville in Berecombe. I want to win that one for myself.'

'You're not alone there, my lovely. Scoreboard set up?'

Livvy nodded. 'Mark's in charge. He's the numbers man.'

'Marking team ready?'

'Darrell, Dave Wiscombe, and Austin and his wife Aggie.'

Karl hooked the glass onto the rack above him and picked up another to polish. 'Uh-oh. Aggie's like Lucie. Don't take no prisoners. Shame Pete's missing it.'

Livvy grimaced. 'Think it might be too hectic for him and certainly for Skip. Same is true for Angel. I've put her in her bed in my room. Apparently, Pete and Skip are having a quiet night down at The Old Harbour.'

'Lucky Claude.' Karl grinned.

'And Stewie's in charge of the kitchen. Light snacks only tonight: sausages wrapped in bacon, brie and cranberry mini tarts, filled turkey and gravy Yorkshire puddings and deep fried halloumi fingers with a sweet chilli dip. Oh, and mince pies and clotted cream, or Christmas pudding ice cream if anyone fancies dessert.'

'Cracking. Fabio not coming?'

'Not his scene I imagine, and it is his night off. Eli and Brittany will be manning the bar, along with you and my good self, so that should be covered. It'll be rammed before it starts and, in the interval, but should be fairly steady trade during the actual quiz. Think we're all set.'

'Got your fancy dress sorted?'

'Yeah, Karl.' Livvy gave him an old-fashioned look. 'I don't normally go around dressed as an elf.' She pirouetted, showing off her green miniskirt and stripey red tights. 'I've a hat to go with this lot too.'

He chuckled. 'Very fetching on you. You should show your legs off more often.' He caught her look. 'I'm not allowed to say things like that, am I?'

She went behind the bar, took his arm and hugged it. 'Not really but from you I'll take it as the compliment it was meant.'

He looked relieved. 'Jen, the wife, is always on at me for being not PC.' He began polishing another glass. 'So, what are your parents doing tonight?'

'Think Mum's staying in her room watching TV, but Dad might come down and join in.'

'Been a bit of a trial, having them around?'

Livvy sighed. 'It's such a busy time, Karl, that's the issue, and they demand entertainment, especially my mother. I packed them off to the Henville for Sunday lunch today. That kept them busy for a few hours.'

'Nice.'

'Think Mum appreciated the luxury. Simona went along. Those two have forged a rather worrying alliance.' Livvy rested her hands on her velvet-covered hips and contemplated her bar. 'Right. Think we're ready.'

An hour later, the bar was five deep in assorted Father Christmases, reindeer and the odd penguin. Karl was cool and unflustered, Brittany quelled anyone getting impatient with a withering look and Eli was just about coping. Livvy, returning from showing a group dressed as Telly Tubbies to their quiz table in the restaurant, saw that Gerry and his entourage had turned up. They weren't in the requested fancy dress and didn't look as if they were taking part in the quiz, so she assumed they were in to drink. Eli looked uncomfortable; he was trying to deal with them, but the group was already getting rowdy. To her relief, her father had appeared and was making his way over to lend a hand.

Against the soundtrack of 'Fairy Tale of New York' blasting out, as Eli had, once again, cranked up the volume, her father yelled across, 'This is good fun, Liv. Just like the old days when I had my first bar. Just love the Christmas madness.' He adjusted his Santa hat and began pulling pints of lager for Gerry's mob.

Diving behind the bar herself, she took an order for three mulled wines, a pint of cider, a gin and tonic and a pint of Santa's Sauce Ale. Putting them on a tray, she asked, 'Contactless?' and handed the machine to the man waiting. 'Oh, Jason. I didn't recognise you. Great fancy dress. Very Johnny Depp.'

He raised a sardonic brow from under his Captain Jack Sparrow hat. 'Expressing my inner pirate. Just hope I don't have to make anyone walk the plank tonight.' He leaned closer. 'I have to express surprise at seeing Gerry Wiscombe in here. Is he the sort of customer you want to attract?'

She gave him a thin smile. She was beginning to dislike Jason intensely. Pompous didn't gel with lookalike Jack Sparrow sexy eyeliner. 'I'm keeping an eye on them. Enjoy your night and good luck with the quiz. Now, who's next? Hi, Daisy. What can I get you? Great fairy costume!'

Risking a glance across to her father, she could see he was in his element. However, an argument was breaking out between a blustering, red-faced Gerry and one of his friends. Livvy winced. It would be awkward if she had to eject them but if they caused any trouble she'd have no choice. Keeping a wary eye out, she decided to let Eli handle it. He didn't have an awful lot of confidence, and she didn't want to undermine him in front of his family.

'Darling, what a crush!' Simona, dressed as Jessica Rabbit in a slinky red number appeared, wriggling her way through. 'Good to see the old place busy though. Ooh, I see you have the delectable silver fox helping you out.'

Livvy laughed. 'My dad?'

'I can see where you get your good looks from, darling. He's a honey! You look swamped, sweetie. Want a hand?'

Livvy blinked. 'You want to serve behind the bar?'

Simona pushed a perfectly manicured hand through her immaculate peek-a-boo wig. 'Don't let this glossy appearance deceive you, kitten. I worked in many a bar and club before I married Terence. I'm sure it can't have changed all that much. And I take it the prices are all on the till?'

'Yes. I–'

'Oh go on. It would be fun.'

'Be my guest. Actually, that would be brilliant. I could concentrate on getting the teams to their tables, everyone seems to want to stay in this crush at the bar for some reason and Brittany's just popped into the kitchen to give Stewie a hand. Ask Karl or Dad if you need any help.'

Simona gave a ridiculously camp wink. 'I shall make sure I ask Brian, don't you worry.' She clapped her hands together in glee and lifted the bar hatch. Turning to a group of three men dressed from top to toe in red and white stripes, she said, 'Hello, my darlings. What wonderful candy canes you make. What can I get you all? Pints of our craft ale or some of our home-made mulled wine. It's absolutely delish on a cold night like tonight.'

Livvy watched her for a second and grinned. She would do fine. She turned to attempt to usher a quiz team, all dressed as Scrooge, to their table. 'Hello there. What's your team name? What the Dickens. Great name. You're over here on this table. Follow me, I'll get you seated and then get you some drinks. Yes, it is a crush at the bar!'

Things calmed down once the quiz actually began. Lucie proved an excellent quiz master and everyone was charmed by the brass band turning up at the halfway point to play carols.

Jonquil had volunteered with a collection bucket for the RNLI and was making her way round the tables. People were giving generously, possibly as Jonquil was employing her very own 'special' brand of charm.

To the accompaniment of the band thumping out 'I Saw Three Ships', Livvy carried two platters groaning with food to Daisy and Rick's table. She said hello to Jan, Daisy's mum, and her boyfriend Colin and then headed back to the kitchen. The snacking plates were proving popular. As she did so she became aware of raised voices coming from Gerry's group. Going over, she asked brightly, 'Everything all right, gents? Having a good evening? Love the tinsel crowns. Very Christmassy.'

'We'd have a better night if Eli would serve us what we asked for,' Gerry slurred.

Livvy faced Eli. He looked miserable. 'Is there a problem Eli?'

'No, Livvy.'

Once again, she wondered if Gerry was making life difficult for him in some way. She looked at the group of men. There were seven of them, all sweating and drunk. They'd only been in the pub for an hour so it was puzzling how they'd become inebriated so quickly. She caught sight of a shot glass. Ah, so it had been pints and chasers. 'Well, tell you what, chaps, we'll make this pint your last and then you can get home to your families. You don't want to sit through the rest of the quiz if you're not taking part. I mean, how boring would that be?'

They started to look militant.

'How about, to show you how much we appreciate your loyal custom, I'll get you a couple of plates of snacks. No charge. Get you in the mood for Christmas. And your first pint the next time you're in will be on the house.'

The group's grumblings turned to appreciative cheers. Gerry swayed a little, slopping his beer onto the stone flags. 'You're a game girl, babe.'

'I am indeed. But I'll hold you to a promise that after this one you'll go home. I won't serve you anymore tonight.' She smiled. 'More than my licence is worth.'

Gerry saluted her with his glass.

She squeezed behind the bar and whispered into Eli's ear. 'I'll get them their food, hopefully it'll mop up a bit of alcohol but don't serve them anymore. If they start getting stroppy, get backup from Dad.'

He nodded, looking relieved.

'Back with their food in a mo and then we'll gently encourage them out. Before the rest of the quiz gets going. Okay?'

'Thanks, Livvy.'

She patted him on the shoulder. 'No problem.' She just hoped the strategy would work. It was either that or bring her father in; he had a lifetime's experience of dealing with difficult customers. She didn't want to do that though. It wasn't just Eli's self-confidence that would be undermined if that happened.

CHAPTER 28

Cognac – eau de vie! For celebration and to be shared with friends.
To be savoured

Livvy closed the main door and bolted it behind the last customer. Turning, she let out an enormous sigh of relief. The Christmas Quiz had been a raging success. Gerry's group had, with one or two amiable grumbles, dispersed as requested. Karl had gone home to his wife, Lucie had given Brittany and Eli a lift and Stewie, having cleaned up the kitchen and brought out some leftover snack plates, had disappeared into the night. It was midnight and the only people left were her father, Simona and Mark.

She collapsed onto a chair. 'That went well. It was manic! Lucie was brilliant and the raffle prizes were all well-received; I was so glad Jan and Colin won the Christmas lunch at The Henville. Such nice people. And I can't believe the vicar won the bottomless brunch. She seemed pleased.' She lifted up her green suede pixie boots and wiggled them. 'My feet are killing me, though. Oh hello, Angel,' she said, as the dog nuzzled her drooping hand. 'Did you mind missing all the fun? It was a little too crazy for you, my love.' The springer, having been released from the bedroom and, having had a quick shuffle round outside, now settled in front of the dying embers of the wood burner.

'I thought it was all marvellous.' Brian brought over the bottle of Delamain Pleiade cognac, and glasses. 'Haven't had so much fun in ages.' He sat down and lifted the bottle to the light. 'I say, someone's been giving this a hammering.' Pouring them all a measure, he added, 'And I was full of admiration at how you handled that group at the bar, Liv, darling. The ones with Gerry Wiscombe? No need for me to intervene.'

'Thanks, Dad.' Livvy sipped her brandy. 'Just hope they were too drunk to remember I promised their next round was on the house.' She frowned. 'We do good business from them in wet sales on a Sunday night but I don't want to encourage a crowd like that.'

'No indeed.' He turned to Simona. 'And we are very grateful for your help, my dear. You were an absolute angel behind the bar.'

Angel, at hearing her name, lifted her head and whined.

Simona giggled. 'Not you, my little darling doggie. It quite took me back to my working days. I was fortunate to marry a rich man, Brian, and gave up any idea of working for my living but sometimes I miss it.' She lifted her glass to his and they clinked them together.

Livvy glanced over at Mark. He was still dressed in the bottom half of his costume, a thick pair of brown corduroys. He'd taken off the brown jumper with the enormous flashing red nose on it and the antlers. His hair stuck up in sweaty spikes and his cheeks were flushed. His white T-shirt showed off surprising biceps; she'd never seen him in so little clothing. It made Livvy go hot all over. Tortoiseshell specs on, he was engrossed in his phone so she didn't want to disturb him.

His sister, Natalie, had gone out with friends, so he'd come along to the quiz alone and had manned the scoreboard. Santa's Little Helpers, who for some reason had come dressed as flamingos, had come in a close second, so had demanded a recount. Livvy wondered a) why some people took quizzes so seriously, and b) just what the fascination Lullbury Bay had with big pink birds. The marking team conducted a recount and the What the Dickens team was proclaimed the winners. It had been a stressful half hour, but he'd handled it all with calm efficiency. That was the key to his personality, Livvy realised. Nothing seemed to ruffle him.

'Oh my feet though,' Simona echoed Livvy's moan. 'Had I known I was to become mine host I would have worn my Crocs.'

Livvy smiled. 'I can't believe you have any Crocs, Simona.'

'Of course, sweetness. One can't wear Manolos all the time.'

Livvy giggled. 'Help yourself to food. Think you've all earned some. Plates!' she exclaimed. 'I'll go and get some.' She began to haul herself off the chair but her father rose, pushing her down by the shoulder.

'I'll go.'

Simona watched him go through narrowed eyes. 'He is simply dreamy, your father. I've had an absolutely heavenly time, Livvy. Any chance of letting me do it again?'

Livvy surveyed her over the rim of the brandy glass. 'You really want to work in a pub, Simona?' she asked disbelievingly.

'Well, only this pub. I can't tell you what a fabby time I've had. And maybe I could choose my shifts? Give you a hand when you're really busy like tonight?' Simona cocked her head on one side and Livvy thought she detected wistfulness. 'I wouldn't expect a salary. Maybe a gin and tonic every now and again.'

'But why would you want to work unpaid at a job which can be really hard work?'

'Christmas is coming up, darling. It's when I miss my Terence the most. He loved the season, you see. We'd hole up somewhere beautiful and snowy, eat wonderful food, just be together, the two of us, cocooned against the world. And then in the new year, we'd go skiing.' Simona bit her lip, her eyes dewy. 'Being busy would take my mind off him a little.' She brightened. 'So you see, darling, it would be you doing me a favour, not the other way round.'

Livvy was touched. 'Of course you can. It would be lovely.' She meant it. Simona was fun to be around. The customers thought so too.

Brian brought the plates through and dragged over another table to give them more space to eat.

'Don't feed her too many sausages, Simona,' Livvy warned as the woman fed Angel a treat. 'She's getting tubby now she's retired. I wouldn't have you down as a doggie person.'

'Darling, the least said about my past sex life the better.' Simona giggled, back on form. 'Oh, I see what you mean! I absolutely adore dogs. Just couldn't have one. Terence and I were never in one place long enough and the yacht never seemed the right place.'

'No, I can imagine,' Livvy said drily. Her parents were wealthy, but Simona's lifestyle was something else. She took a brie and cranberry tart. It was the first time she'd had a chance to eat all evening. Closing her eyes in bliss, she chewed.

She heard Simona give a silvery giggle. 'Seeing as your daughter has checked out, I'll do the honours. Would you care for a sausage, Brian? They're delicious.'

He chortled. 'I don't mind if I do.'

'And do you cook, Brian? I can quite see you in a frilly apron.'

'It's usually me who cooks Christmas lunch. Off to the Caribbean this year. Jolly good fun.' He lowered his voice conspiratorially. 'Just as well The George has Fabio and Stewie. I wouldn't trust Livvy with a turkey baster.'

'I heard that!' Livvy said, not bothering to open her eyes.

'What are you doing for Christmas Day, Simona?'

'I'll be all on my own. I was going back to Italy to stay with friends, but travel is so tedious at Christmas. I have a Marks and Sparks feast and am going to enjoy cuddling up in a blanket in front of some mindless Christmas specials on the TV.'

Livvy heard the pout.

'We can't have that,' Brian blustered. 'You must come here. Seeing as we're off on the water for Christmas, we're having an early celebratory lunch here tomorrow before we go. Don't worry, I'm cooking.'

Livvy opened half an eye. They looked to be getting very cosy. She smiled and closed her eyes again, exhausted.

She wondered what her mother would think of the exquisite Simona getting so pally with her husband. To her amazement, Penny had been lured downstairs by the brass band and had stayed for the second half of the quiz. She'd joined Daisy and Rick's team and actually looked to be having a reasonable time. Livvy stifled a groan, silently thanking her father for landing her with a guest for their early Christmas lunch. Their family dynamics could be tricky at the best of times. Still, maybe having Simona there would dilute things?

'Gotcha!'

Mark's shout had them all jumping a foot.

'God, Mark,' Livvy gasped. 'You gave me a heart attack. What is it?'

He waved his phone at her. 'You're on *South West News and Views*.'

'What's that?' Brian asked.

'It's the premier website for restaurants and pubs down here. Reviews, recommendations, where to eat suggestions. Incredibly influential.'

This made Livvy sit up. Reaching over, she took his phone. 'We are! Look, everyone, we're featured. They've even included a review. They must have been in to eat, and we didn't notice.'

'What, like a secret shopper?' Simona said. 'I've always fancied myself as one of those. I think I'd be rather good.'

'You would,' Livvy agreed. 'And they've included the pic of me in the cherry picker. Look, Dad.'

Brian slid his reading glasses down off his forehead and squinted. 'Oh I say, Liv. Was that safe?'

'Probably not. And there's a write-up of the bonfire party and they like the fact we stick to local produce. It's all fantastic promo. About as positive as you could get. More so!'

'Brilliant, Livvy,' Mark said, his face glowing with pride. 'It might be why it was so busy tonight. Looks like the feature went live two days ago.'

'This calls for a celebration.' Brian emptied the last of the cognac into their glasses. 'Well done, my darling. Proud of you!'

'Thanks, Dad.' Livvy was taken aback. He'd never been so blatantly complimentary before and this was twice he'd praised her tonight.

'It's all rather marvellous, isn't it?' Simona put in. 'How much have we made for the RNLI, Mark?'

Mark took his phone back. 'I was totting it all up before I spotted the feature on the South West site and got distracted. One thousand and fifty-three pounds but I haven't counted the bucket donations yet.'

'How wonderful. Well done, Livvy.'

'And that should reflect in a tidy profit too,' Brian said.

'Wasn't the point of the evening, Dad.'

'Can't make a profit, can't keep going, darling girl. That's the reality. You've staff you're responsible for now. Can't let them down.'

Livvy gulped. She hadn't thought about that before. Had been so fixated on the risks she was making, hadn't considered how her staff would feel if it all went tits up. Stewie and Brittany were young; they'd find similar jobs, as would Eli, although she was beginning to feel protective of the boy; she'd rather he worked at

The George than fall into his uncle's clutches. And people were always looking for good cleaners, so Candice would be fine. It wouldn't be as easy for Karl and Fabio. Karl had already been made redundant once and Fabio would be fussy, even though he was keen to stay in the area while his mother was ill. She couldn't deny they were all depending on her, in some way. She loved the team she'd built up; she didn't want anything to change that.

Her mood sobered. Trust her dad to prick her bubble. Staring into the wood burner, she murmured, 'The fire's dying down. Shall I put another log on?'

'It's late. It won't hurt to let it die out,' Mark said kindly, perhaps sensing her shift in mood. 'The evening's been a resounding success and all thanks to your hard work. Didn't you say the chimney sweep found something up there?'

'She did,' Livvy answered, thankful for his change of subject. 'Jonquil was at the quiz tonight. It was her collecting donations with menaces. Her team came dressed as wrapped Christmas presents.'

'It was a super idea,' Simona said, 'until they tried sitting down. Had to take their boxes off.' She gave a peal of laughter. 'Just as well they had something on underneath and the place was nice and cosy. They had to sit the evening out in T-shirts and shorts. What did Jonquil find in the chimney, darling? She sweeps mine next door too. I find her rather,' she paused, 'abrasive, shall we say?'

'It's why I gave her team second prize in the fancy dress comp. Felt sorry for them. They've won a bar meal for four.' Livvy ignored her father's tut. 'She found a cat.'

'Oh, my goodness. A stray?'

'No, it was dead. Long dead and horribly mummified. Jonquil said she finds all sorts of things up chimneys. The cat was supposed to ward off evil.'

'Hell's bells, kitten,' Simona said with feeling. 'Wish I'd never asked.' She glanced at her dainty gold wristwatch. 'Goodness, is that the time, darling? This Cinderella needs her beauty sleep. Walk me home, my gallant?' she asked Mark.

'Delighted to just as soon as I can find my reindeer jumper and antlers.'

Costume found and thank yous and hugs exchanged, Brian and Livvy saw their guests out. Illuminated by The George's Christmas lights, the pub car park was white over, a gleaming, sparkling frost covered every surface, the windscreen of her parents' BMW opaque. Stars glimmered in an inky, cold sky. Below them, in the quiet, the sea shifted and sshed.

'What a perfect night.' Simona shivered as her breath misted out into the frigid night. 'So romantic.'

'Night, Livvy.' Mark hugged her to him and kissed her cheek. His lips felt very hot on her frozen face. 'Been a great evening.'

At that moment, the security lights blazed on.

'What the–' Brian exhaled in shock.

Livvy gasped and Mark's arm tightened around her shoulders. Her van, discreetly parked out of the way in the far corner and next to the old stable block, had the word BITCH painted clearly in white paint on its side.

CHAPTER 29

Champagne – a sparkling wine for celebrations and to cheer the spirit

It was just as well The George closed on a Monday. Livvy spent most of the day organising a respray for the van and talking to the police. In the end, after she'd added the other incidents onto the online form, two uniformed officers came round, took photographs and noted her concerns.

When they'd gone she followed the aroma of roasting meat and found her father in a hot and steamy kitchen. He was wearing a Santa hat and an apron emblazoned with *Ho Ho Ho!* and was basting an enormous turkey. The work surfaces were crammed with saucepans of vegetables, potatoes and sauces. Carols blasted out from Bay Radio.

'Oh,' she said surprised. 'Are we still having Christmas lunch?' Going over to the radio, she turned the volume down on 'The Holly and the Ivy'.

'Thought we'd battle on. Simona's coming round, don't forget.'

'We have these things called phones, Dad. I'm sure she would have understood if we'd rung to cancel.' Livvy knew she was coming over shrewish and ungrateful but last night's incident had unsettled her. Night-time teenage pranks were one thing but painting the word bitch on her work van, on the vehicle she depended upon to do her job, felt intensely spiteful.

Brian returned the turkey to the oven, washed his hands and came over. 'Your mother and I want to have this as our Christmas day with you, darling girl, because we won't see you on the actual day. We haven't seen you for months, you've holed yourself up in this money pit and we want to have a nice family meal together. Besides, some good food and drink might cheer you up after what happened last night.' Unexpectedly, he hugged her. 'Can't get over my big grown-up girl owning her very own business.'

Livvy relaxed into the hug. Her father hardly ever showed her any physical affection; they simply weren't that sort of family. When she'd been young her parents had always been too busy running the hotels to have much time for her. To her chagrin, she began to cry. She'd tried to be independent and resilient for so long, the hug had crumpled through her defences.

'Hey, hey, what's all this?' Releasing her, he thumbed the tears away. 'Don't let it get to you. I could tell you some tales of what disgruntled staff did to us. Hands in the till, giving free drinks to their buddies, all sorts of rubbish. You learn to develop a thick skin. It's not personal.'

Fishing out a tissue from her pocket, she croaked, 'Trouble is, it feels personal. The word bitch feels very personal. And there's been other stuff. Nothing major. Kids in the car park at night,' she nodded to the kitchen door, 'rattling that. It's as if someone has something against me. And it can't be a member of staff, I've got a great team who I trust.'

'Even Eli?'

Livvy's brow wrinkled as she dismissed the idea. 'Eli's a good kid.'

'With some interesting relatives.'

'And a loving family. I don't think it was Gerry's lot who did that. I saw them off the premises and they all ambled down to the bus stop. They were drunk but not belligerent and unless they doubled back carrying a can of white paint, I'm pretty sure it wasn't them.'

'Then who do you think it might be?'

'That's just it, Dad. I don't know. The town has welcomed me with open arms. Even the other pub owners. I'm not a direct threat to anyone. If anything, it's me who can't compete with The Old Harbour's setting or the established trade in The Ship. There's room enough for all of us.'

'I can see it's unnerved you.' He turned his attention to the stuffing. 'Spiced chestnut and apple,' he declared. 'My favourite.'

Livvy managed a watery smile as she watched him work. She hoped Fabio wouldn't mind his kitchen being used. 'It's made me nervous, I'll admit. It's a big building to be in on your own. That's why I adopted Angel. Doubt she'd be any good as a guard dog but she's company. And it's good knowing Simona is right next door. When I first bought the pub she was away.'

'And it looks as if Mark is a good friend? Your mother approves.'

Livvy refused to be drawn. 'He is. And Lucie, Daisy and Rick. Karl, Pete and Austin too.'

'Ah yes. I met Austin last night. Quite the character. His wife is rather alarming.'

'I gather she is.' It was possibly not the moment to reveal what Aggie was really like.

'I'm so proud of you, you know, Liv.' Brian's voice broke. He turned to her, wiping his hands on a tea towel. 'Your mother and I still don't understand why you didn't want to stay in the family business but we're proud of you. Of what you're trying to do here. I could see from last night how much it means to you.'

'I wanted something of my own, Dad. Something I'd built up myself.' Tears were flowing again.

He nodded curtly. 'Understood. I can see why you'd want to set this place up. Penny's proud of you too, you know, but your mother doesn't show her feelings. Sometimes the more she feels, the less she shows. You're very like her in that.'

'Am I?' Livvy was surprised. She didn't think she and her mother were at all similar.

'She frets, darling. She was very fond of Gavin. She worries, Liv, that you're doing this all on your own. When we started out it was difficult but we had each other to see us through the tricky bits. You haven't got anyone.'

Livvy blew her nose and gave a wan smile. 'Well, the plan wasn't for me to do this alone but in the end I didn't have much choice.' Straightening her shoulders, she forced a grin. 'And I'll be fine.' Sucking in a frustrated breath she hated to admit it, but she needed his advice. 'Speaking of which, I'm concerned that, even though we've been really busy, I'm not making as much profit as expected.'

Brian gave her an appraising look. 'Pilfering?'

'Hope not but it might explain the discrepancy. An objective eye on things might be helpful. Can you give me the number for the stock taker you used?'

'Bernie? Of course. He'll be absolutely straight with you. Busy chap though.'

'If he can squeeze me in, I'd be grateful.'

Brian gave his daughter another quick hug. 'You know, if you want anything, any advice, help, contacts, you only have to ask.' He backed off at her look. 'I know, I know,' he said, putting up his hands in mock surrender. 'You want to be Miss Independent.'

'I'm trying to be, although Bernie's number would be a help. And, ignore the weepy moment. I'm knackered, Dad, and stressed after this morning's encounter with two of Dorset's finest police.'

She pinned on a smile. 'I'm determined to make this place a success.'

'Righty-o then. Jolly good.' Her father's tone was gruff, but tears sparkled in his eyes. 'So, seeing as I've got to get lunch on for three o'clock, and I appear to be completely without any sous chefs, I'll have to rope you in to peel the carrots.' He threw over another *Ho Ho Ho!* apron. 'Get prepping, Olivia!'

'Christmas' lunch was splendid. And her father was right, it did take Livvy's mind off things.

If she was expecting a bitch-fest between her mother and Simona, she was disappointed; the women got on like a house on fire. Simona waxed lyrical about one of the Smith-Lygott hotels she'd stayed at, and they swapped hair tips and dress shopping stories until Livvy gave up listening out of sheer boredom and concentrated on drinking champagne. They ate late but, by that time had drunk so much bubbly and were in such good spirits, nothing mattered. Crackers pulled, they wore the paper hats and giggled over the dreadful jokes. Livvy got them to pose for a group selfie which she pinged over to Yolanda, captioning it: *Early Xmas with the Folks. Actually good fun! Love to Cosmo and the Bumps x.*

Penny loved her glass light catcher and the earrings, and Brian flushed pink at the cummerbund and said it would be perfect for formal nights on the cruise. To her embarrassment Simona had bought her a present.

'Oh, Simona, I haven't got you anything.'

'Well, darling, it's not actually Christmas yet, so I'll forgive you. And I'll let you into a secret, kitten, I didn't actually buy it as your present.' She gave her trademark silvery giggle. 'It's a dress I bought some time ago, hung in the wardrobe and forgot all about. With your gorgeous colouring I thought it would be perfect.'

Livvy shook it out of its tissue paper and gasped. 'Oh, Simona, it's beautiful.' She stood up and held it against her.

'Oh, very nice, darling.' Even her mother approved.

She ran into the kitchen corridor where there was a long mirror at the bottom of the stairs. Holding it against her she gasped. It would have been mid-calf length on Simona but, as she was much taller, it skimmed her knees. Spaghetti straps, low-cut over the breasts and dipping to nothingness at the back, it was dark olive in colour and made of some glittery fabric. Livvy knew it would cling like a second skin. 'It's so gorgeous,' she murmured to Angel who had followed. 'Although there's not an awful lot to it!' The springer gave a sharp bark of agreement. Livvy's phone vibrated in the back pocket of her jeans so, flicking the dress over her shoulder, she slid it out. It was a text from Mark:

> So sorry. Couldn't get over today. Christmas
> shopping with Nats. Nightmare! Hope you're ok?
> Take care xxx

She hoped she'd have an opportunity to wear the dress for him. Holding the dress to her again, she waltzed solo back into the restaurant to the soundtrack of Bing Crosby crooning 'White Christmas' and thanked Simona profusely.

'Thought you could wear it on Christmas Eve, sweetie. I assume we're having a party?'

'We are now, if it means an excuse to wear this wonderful dress!'

'What a shame we won't be there.' Penny pouted. Livvy suspected too much champagne. Her mother adjusted her paper hat which sat drunkenly. 'We'll be halfway across the Atlantic by then.' And then she launched into another conversation with Simona, this time about cruise wear and the captain's table.

Brian winked at his daughter and poured them all another glass of fizz.

CHAPTER 30

Whisky – single malt. Singular and complex on the tongue

In the end, Livvy was sad to say goodbye to her parents. She loved her father, even though he, inadvertently, pricked at any confidence she built up in herself. He'd said they were proud of what she was doing. It was enough. He'd been a huge asset behind the bar and seemed to thoroughly enjoy himself. She had a more complicated relationship with her mother; she never felt she had ever measured up but could never work out in what way. To her surprise Penny had given her a swift hard hug before leaving, seemed to be on the brink of saying something and then began nagging Brian that they'd be late and would miss their embarkation slot.

The George was now in full Christmas mode. They were busy. Maybe word was spreading or the feature in *South West News and Views* was having its effect, but the restaurant was fully booked each night and tables were scarce in the bar. It was slightly quieter during the day, Livvy reckoned this was a good thing; it enabled them to catch their breath.

It was an evening in the week before Christmas and everyone in Lullbury Bay seemed to have braved the icy weather (the local news reported the month was heading to be the coldest Dorset December on record) and had made their way to The George. The place was packed. Livvy overheard a couple in the restaurant saying everywhere in town had been fully booked for months so maybe her pub was reaping the benefit of being new and with available tables. She didn't have much time to question it.

Brittany was flat-out serving food in the restaurant, with spillover diners eating in the bar. Livvy, wishing her dad was still around, had called in Simona to help. With everyone in the Christmas spirit and 'It's the Most Wonderful Time of the Year' blasting out – Eli would insist on turning the volume up – the place was buzzing.

She emerged, flush-faced from emptying the glass washer, to see Jason Lemmon standing at the bar. He was wrapped up against the cold, his nose and chin an unbecoming red.

'I never know how to greet people at this time of year,' he said with uncharacteristic joviality. 'Is it too early to wish you Happy Christmas? I've just come from the RNLI carol concert on the seafront. It was far too cold to stand around.' He looked about him. 'Seems the rest of Lullbury has had the same idea. Still,' he raised one pale brow, 'good for business.'

Did she detect an edge to the comment? She still couldn't put her finger on why he was so unlikeable. 'Of course it's not too early to say Happy Christmas. What can I get you? Gin and tonic?'

'Actually, as it's rather chilly out there tonight, make it a whisky.'

'Which would you prefer?'

'A single malt if you have one.'

'We do.'

'Make it a double. Doubt I'll get near the bar again for a while.'

Definitely an edge. Why hadn't he stayed in town to drink, or better still, gone home? 'Ice?' Livvy didn't think he needed any. His personality was chilly enough.

He shook his head. 'Wouldn't dream of diluting a good Scotch. Tell me, are you still intent on keeping the skittle alley?'

Livvy poured a double measure of Glenfiddich. 'Yes. Why?'

'Don't you think it would be better to get rid? Extend the outside space. Makes sense for the summer season.'

He had a point, but she'd rather die than admit it. Besides, what business was it of his how she ran her pub? 'Well, it's certainly a consideration. Enjoy your whisky.' She turned away, not trusting herself to keep up the pretence of being polite.

The skittle alley was a sore subject. It was costing her a fortune to heat for minimal return. Glancing over at Pete in his corner sipping his cider, one hand on Skip's head, she softened. How could she get rid of something that meant so much to him and her more traditional clientele? *No room for sentimentality in this business,* she could hear her mother say. *It's all about the profit.* Livvy looked around. Profit *was* important – how could it not be? But she wanted more for The George. She wanted it to have its place at the heart of its community, not to rely solely on summer season trade. She also wanted to become a food destination. Seeing Pete give the dead eye to someone who dared move a chair from his table she wondered if it was going to be possible to meet everyone's needs.

She wished she'd had time to sit down with her father and discuss branding and marketing strategies. She sighed and pulled a pint of Santa's Sauce for Jonquil's husband, who was the next customer. Pinning on a professional smile, she listened as he made small talk about how well the carol concert had gone.

'Penny for them?' Simona asked, sidling alongside and beginning to slice lemon. 'Don't let Jason wind you up. Thinks he owns this town, darling. Men, eh? Can never resist telling a woman how to do things.'

'He thinks I ought to tear down the skittle alley.'

'What does he know about owning a pub? He's a bloody property developer!'

'Maybe he was touting for business? If I got anyone to do it, it wouldn't be him, it would be The Three Ds.' She poured a glass of red wine and took the payment. 'He's right though. I need to make some decisions. I've been fudging it ever since I took over. I need to develop a definite image for the place. I need to decide what sort of place I want to run. But there can be a clash between community needs which don't necessarily make much money and turning over a profit.'

'Looks like you've got it right to me, kitten. Lots of locals in tonight, a smattering of visitors. Is the restaurant booked out?'

'Gosh yes. Fabio's champing at the bit to try them out with his sprouts with peas and cashews, and honey-roasted ham.'

Simona giggled. 'What I wouldn't do to honey-roast him! Why not get The Three Ds to do a quick job on the alley? Nothing fancy, make it watertight, insulated. See how that goes. You can always do a complete refit when funds allow, if you decide to keep it going.' She handed over the gin and tonic she'd just made. 'And a mulled wine and a mineral water? Coming right up, darling.'

'You know that's not a bad idea. Wonder if I could use it for other things? Valentine's disco maybe? It would need some kind of floor though, to temporarily cover the skittles run.'

'Marvellous.' Simona popped the lemon slices into a glass of sparkling water and added a generous amount of ice. 'A function room could be a real asset. But I have to make it crystal clear, kitten, I'll only come along to the Valentine's do if Fabio is on the menu!'

Livvy giggled and turned to serve the next customer. It was the vicar. 'Verity, how lovely to see you.' The tiny woman, swamped in a full-length black padded coat, was shivering violently.

'Jago, Honor and I have sneaked away from the carol concert. Think God will forgive us just this once. I have completely lost all feeling in my feet.'

'It's really cold out there tonight,' Livvy agreed. 'I have mulled wine. Might warm you up?'

Verity's eyes brightened. 'Make that two. I expect Jago will have a pint of Gnat's Brew or whatever the real ale is called.'

Livvy laughed. 'You're not far off. This week we have Santa's Sauce or Good Elf.'

'Good Elf then, I suppose.' Verity rolled her eyes. 'Hope it's more promising than its name. Are you still planning on running the board game afternoon?'

'I am. Sunday. Three 'til five. As much tea and coffee as people can drink, or anything from the bar of course, a roaring wood burner and Fabio's mince pies.' Livvy poured two steaming mulled wines into glass beakers and added a cinnamon stick to each. 'We're trying it out. If it's a success, we'll make it a regular event after Christmas and maybe charge a small entrance fee. Think it might be needed more then. January can be such a lonely month.'

'I do think it's a wonderful idea, Livvy. It'll be another brilliant community asset.'

Livvy began to pull the pint of beer. It foamed, dark and pungent into the glass. 'Come along, you'd be very welcome.'

Verity grimaced. 'If I can, I will. Busy time of the year, is Jesus's birthday. I really don't know why he wasn't born at another, less hectic time.' She paid for the drinks. 'And may I offer an invitation to St Winifred's Christmas service? It's truly magical, even though I say so myself. Would advise wrapping up warm. In December the church is even colder than it is outside.'

'I would but,' Livvy hesitated, 'I'm not really a church goer.'

'Oh, nobody else is who comes,' Verity said gaily, passing the pint to Jago behind her. 'I don't fool myself about that but it's a time when the town comes together. It's very special.'

'I'll try my best. It's my busy time too.'

Verity tutted. 'If you ask me, JC has a lot to answer for. Happy Christmas, Livvy.'

'Happy Christmas, Verity.' Livvy smiled fondly as the woman squeezed her way through the crowd in the wake of Jago's towering presence. If anyone could persuade her to go to church, it would be this vicar.

'You're doing well. Looks like you've got God's blessing now.'

'Mark!' Livvy beamed at him. He was looking positively edible in a thick navy sweater. 'A pint of your usual?'

He grinned back and flicked a heavy lock of hair off his face. 'And that's what makes having a local such a pleasure. A pint of your finest ale is absolutely what's needed. Can I introduce my sister? Natalie, this is Livvy.'

They shook hands. 'Lovely to meet you, Natalie.' Livvy observed Mark's sister. Fair hair, a creamy complexion and startlingly green eyes, not Mark's warm hazel. And tinier than she remembered from seeing her on the television. 'I've heard a lot about you.'

'I've heard very little about you, so I aim to interrogate you later when you've a moment.' Natalie giggled, softening the words. 'And it's Nats to my friends.'

'Okay,' Livvy said, a little nonplussed.

Mark scrubbed a fist over his sister's hair. 'Take no notice of her, she's protective of me. And is incurably nosy.'

'Ow! Beast!' Nats cried, ducking away. 'For that, the first round is on you.'

'It always is,' he said good-naturedly. 'You never have any money, you poor starving actor. And in answer to your question, Livvy, I'll have a pint of Good Elf for a change, Nats will have mulled wine and crisps. We definitely need crisps. Don't suppose you've room for two to eat tonight?'

'Sorry.' Livvy grimaced. 'Might be a chance later but there'll be a wait.'

'Make it four packets of crisps then, those posh ones.' He handed Nats her mulled wine. When she'd gone to find a seat, he leaned nearer and asked, 'Everything okay after the other night? I'm sorry I've not been around. Nats has taken up all of my time and then I had to whizz back to London for meetings. Are you sure you're all right, Livvy?'

'I'm fine. Nothing else has happened and I had my parents for company.' She felt herself blush. 'It's good to see you though.'

Mark nodded sharply. 'I felt guilty not being here.'

'No need.'

He seemed to be on the verge of saying something but shivered instead. 'It was surprisingly cold in London, but it feels even icier down here. Maybe the damp's getting in my bones. Mind you, standing on the harbourside singing carols for an hour is hardly likely to help. I reckon we're in for snow.'

'Snow in Dorset? Hardly likely. Go and sit by the wood burner and annoy Pete. He's scared everyone else away so there are two chairs free. I'll check with the kitchen. See if they can rustle you up something to eat. Might only be burgers though.'

'Burgers would be great. Thanks, Livvy.' He went to go and then turned back to her. 'It's good to see you again too.'

She smiled at him and something warm gladdened her heart.

CHAPTER 31

*Ratafia – a sweet, fortified wine with the flavour of bitter almonds.
Popular in the nineteenth century.*

'I hear you're interested in Ada Lovelace,' Nats said.

The pub was emptying. Pete had shuffled off, with Skip at his heels, refusing the offer of a lift from Verity. Mark, Nats and Simona were lounging in front of the wood burner. Livvy had poured the remains of the mulled wine into a jug and had joined them. Michael Bublé crooned in the background and it all felt very mellow.

'Good night, Livvy,' Jason called from the door. He'd spent the evening talking to Jonquil and her husband.

'Night, Jason,' she responded. He swept them with what she thought was an odd look, speculative, not jealous exactly but more the look the boy with no friends in the playground gives to the cool crowd. The mask had slipped but she still couldn't fathom what lay beneath. Livvy shrugged him off, turning back to Nats to answer her question. 'Not sure if I'm interested in her especially but Mark and I came across someone in the museum who might have known her. Adela Dickson. Her family owned the house which the museum is in. The display mentioned she may have known Ada, maybe met her in London. Then your brother here waxed lyrical about Ada Lovelace.'

Nats rolled her eyes, her face flushed from the heat of the fire. 'Caught that off his ex-father-in-law.'

'Yes apparently, he's very interested in her?'

'Obsessed more like. But she is a fascinating character. Byron's daughter, brought up by her mother to ignore anything arty in case she took after her wicked father. Trained to be a scientist. Gambler. Two children and dead by thirty-six.' Nats sat back looking slightly smug. 'I'm auditioning to play her in a new biopic, so I've had to do some research. She was an amazing woman. Just imagine what she could have achieved had she not married and died young.'

'I don't have a clue about computers beyond how to use them, but didn't she have something to do with programming?'

Nats nodded enthusiastically. 'Don't know the deets but she wrote some notes on this counting machine Charles Babbage invented. Credited with writing the first computer program.'

'It'll be exciting to play her.'

'You bet! There's this scene in her London house where she hosts Babbage and Charles Dickens! At Christmas. Can you imagine it all? Huge Christmas tree, those gorgeous, gorgeous silk dresses, all the men in those sexy tight trousers and side-burns. Snow. Horses and carriages. Just like something off a Christmas card. Maybe your Adela was there too?'

Livvy smiled. Nats was garrulous and slightly drunk. 'Not sure if Adela packed quite as much into her life as Ada Lovelace. Did a Grand Tour, owned a big house, lived a long time.'

'Amazing women at a time when women's only role was to marry and bear children. You and I wouldn't be tolerated, Livvy,' Nats said, her glass of mulled wine slopping dangerously. 'No man in sight, no marriage, no children, careers of our own.' She giggled. 'We'd be considered wanton, you the owner of an inn, me an actress! One step short of being scarlet women.'

'Stop boring Livvy,' Mark put in.

'She's not,' Livvy answered. 'You're really not, Nats. It's just that your world is so different from the one I inhabit, that it's hard to imagine.'

'You can say that again, sweetie,' Simona piped up. She slid her shoes off and massaged Angel's furry flank with her toes. The dog huffed out a sigh of ecstasy. 'I wouldn't mind being in the glam world of acting. The parties, darling, the delicious men!'

'Now you've gone and done it, Simona,' Mark groaned.

'What have I said?'

'Actors,' Nats tutted. 'Every last one of them self-obsessed and narcissistic. How long have you got, Simona? I will give out divers schedules.'

'You what, sweetie?'

'Stop being pompous, Nats,' Mark scolded. 'She's quoting *Twelfth Night*,' he explained. 'And misquoting it at that.'

Nats shot him a look. '"She never told her love, but conceal-ment, like a worm i th' bud, feed on her damask cheek." More accurate, bro?'

He narrowed his eyes. 'Shut it, Nats.'

Simona emptied the jug of mulled wine into their glasses. 'Do tell, darling. I mean about the self-obsessed and narcissistic actors.'

'Well, I had one actor boyfriend who lived his role. *All* the time,' Nats began, lurching closer to Simona. She giggled. 'Which was okay except he was playing a bloke who got his sexual kicks out of pretending to be a cat. He even coughed up fur balls…'

As Nats began to confide in Simona, Mark shifted towards Livvy. 'How's everything been? Have the police been helpful?'

'Not a lot they could do,' Livvy admitted. 'They logged it, told me to keep an eye out for anyone who might have a grudge against me. That sort of thing.'

'It's such a weird thing to happen. Lullbury is practically crime free. I mean, there are the odd waves of mindless vandalism, but we seem to have escaped the stuff that other seaside towns suffer from.'

'I'll put it down to that, then. Mindless vandalism. Dad told me it might not be the last thing to happen. He said pubs can attract behaviour like that.'

'Not pleasant though. How was it, having your parents around?'

'Actually, it was nice.'

'Nice?' One of Mark's brows lifted. 'That good eh?'

She laughed. 'It was good,' she amended. 'We had Simona as a guest for Christmas lunch and she helped ease the tension.'

'Don't you get on with your parents?'

'I get on well with my dad and, in fact, he was a godsend behind the bar. I love him very much. But Mum…'

'It's more complicated. I get it. Nats is the same with our mother whereas she's a real Daddy's girl. Mum can never understand why she threw away her degree and went into a profession with a ninety-eight per cent unemployment rate. And she hates that we're both so far away.'

'I get that. They all want the best for their children, don't they? Can't imagine an acting life being an easy one.'

'Nope.' Mark sat back, easing his shoulders. 'But you've gone into the same profession as your parents. Your mother must have more of an understanding.'

'To some extent. She married Dad when he'd already worked in the hotel trade for yonks. They started with a pub much like this one and then expanded into hotels but I think she's forgotten their humble beginnings. Mum is brilliant at the hard-nosed, facts and figures side of things. She loved having her little office empire. I haven't inherited her business sense; she always says

I'm too sentimental. Dad was always happiest front of house and even when they owned seven hotels, he'd often find time to pop in and chat to guests and staff. Couldn't keep away. I think his stint behind the bar here took him straight back to how he started out. Whereas Mum seems happy to put it all behind her and embrace retired life.'

'Have they retired completely then?'

'As good as. They still have The Olde Gates in the Cotswolds. Once they sell that they'll be fancy-free. It'll suit Mum but I can't see Dad being content with lunch at the golf club and five cruises a year.'

'Still puzzles me why your mother can't understand you taking this place on.'

Livvy sipped her wine thoughtfully. 'Sometimes, I don't understand why I've done it either. The responsibility is immense.' She shrugged. 'And I live on a knife edge. The George's reputation lies entirely with Fabio at the moment. If he decides to go, I'm up the proverbial creek.'

'How did you find him?'

'Funnily enough, Jason suggested him. No idea of the connection between them but I trust Fab whereas Jason Lemmon, I'm not so sure.'

'Wise not to trust that one.'

'How do you know him? I mean, apart from living in the same town.'

'Just that. It's a small town, you get to know most people, or of most people. Jason's well known for his property developing. His company built the estate on the edge of town. Wasn't universally popular. He obtained planning permission by promising some affordable and rented properties and when it came to it, wriggled out of providing any.'

'Ouch. Houses are so expensive here. That must have really hurt. How did he get away with it?'

'Usual way I expect. Backhanders. It's the sort of thing that makes me enraged.' Mark frowned. 'I can't bear corruption and deceit like that.'

Livvy waited for Mark to elaborate but he gazed silently into his glass. He was usually so laid-back; it was odd to see the flush of anger on his cheeks.

'Speaking of finances, can I repeat my offer of looking over the books? I'd be happy to.'

'Thanks, Mark. I'm concerned about one or two things, mostly why I don't seem to be making as much profit as I'm expecting. But I've a stock taker booked in and he'll see if there's anything obvious amiss.'

'I'll say night then, Livvy,' Karl called over. 'Dropping Eli, Stewie and Brittany home, seeing as it's so cold.'

'Thanks so much, Karl,' Livvy called back. 'Thanks, everyone, for all your hard work. Been a busy one tonight. Drive safely. See you all tomorrow.' Watching, as her team disappeared, a wave of fondness for them washed over her. Or maybe it was the mulled wine talking. Turning back to Mark, she asked, 'Will you be around for the Christmas Eve party? Simona has bullied me into having one.'

'I don't remember you being all that hard to persuade, kitten,' Simona said indignantly.

'A party?' Nats exclaimed. 'A Christmas Eve party? Way to go, Livvy. I'm in.'

'We're driving up to Yorkshire on Christmas Eve,' Mark reminded her. 'Sorry, Livvy.' He pulled a regretful face. 'We won't be around, otherwise I would have loved to come.'

Nats pouted. 'And here's me, having heard about the luscious-ness that is the fabulous Fabio the Italian chef. I wanted to check him out.'

'Oh, darling, I am sorry,' Simona put in, not sounding sorry at all. 'He'll just have to put up with little old me, then.'

CHAPTER 32

Schnapps – a distilled fruit brandy or herbal infusion. Perfect in a hip flask and to stave off chilly weather.

'Do you think there'll be many there?' Livvy asked Mark as they walked briskly down the hill to the church service. She burrowed her face into the upturned collar of her coat.

'It'll be packed.'

'No Natalie tonight?' It was proving too cold to have a conversation. Her teeth were chattering too much.

'Wrapping presents.' He gave a short laugh. 'Always leaves it until the last minute, does Nats.'

'When are you driving up to York?'

'Tomorrow. Traffic's usually fairly quiet on Christmas Eve and we'll leave first thing.'

'We'll miss you at the party. Perhaps we'll have a rerun on New Year's Eve?'

'I'll be there.' He gave her a warm look.

Livvy felt herself blush crimson but was covered in confusion. She'd noticed the furtive conversations he and Simona had been having. Heads together, whispering urgently. Worse, it stopped when she approached. She'd tried to shrug it off. Mark was a free agent. She couldn't blame him for falling for Simona's charms and, much as she liked the woman, she flirted with any man going. But it hurt to think he may have lied to her on the day they'd collected Angel, about the true nature of his relationship with Simona. She suppressed a sigh. The vibe between her and Mark had been strictly friendly, nothing romantic, and friendship was what she wanted. Wasn't it? But, risking a sideways glance at him now, as he strode along beside her, she knew she was falling for him.

The realisation of her true feelings for the man made her babble with unaccustomed nerves. 'Glad the service landed on the day The George is closed so I could make it. I'd thought about opening up today but it didn't seem fair. I know Karl wants to come tonight and Stewie said he always goes with his family. Even Brittany's getting dragged along by her mum.'

Mark scanned the dense black sky above them, his nose pink with the cold. 'It's amazing how the service draws people in each year. The church will be full even if they're forecasting The Beast from the East Mark II. It's freezing tonight.'

'Thought you were the tough northerner?' Livvy teased, smiling at his beanie which he'd pulled down as far as it would go.

'So did I but even I'm freezing tonight.' Mark thrust his hands into the pockets of his long black coat.

'Too cold for snow, Austin said. He came to the board games afternoon with Pete. He also said it hardly ever snows at the seaside.' She lifted her face out of her collar. Condensation from her breath was making her chin damp and even colder. The pavement was already shimmering with frost. Some of the windows in the Victorian cottages which faced onto the street had their curtains open and had been decorated. A magnificent white tree glistened in one, a lit-up Father Christmas face dominated another, complete with *Santa Stop Here* sign and another had an enchanting nativity scene lit with coloured fairy lights. With the chilly, sparkling weather it couldn't feel more Christmassy. Or romantic. Livvy suppressed another sigh. *I need to get a grip. He sees me as a friend. Remember that, Liv!*

'No snow at the seaside you say? Oh yes, except for 2018 when we were snowed in. I've rarely seen snow like it and I'm a Yorkshireman don't forget. We had eight inches up on the top of the hill going out of Lullbury. People were skiing down the main road and the beach was covered. Before it began you could see it coming in from out at sea. Very weird.'

'Sounds fun though. I've had my fair share of snowy winters in the Cotswolds but nothing that bad. Oops.' Livvy clutched onto Mark's elbow as she skidded on some ice. 'Knew these boots were a mistake. I've been in flats for so long, I've forgotten how to walk in heels.'

He tucked her arm through his. 'Better? No guarantee of me not slipping but at least it'll be the two of us going down and you can break my fall.'

Livvy giggled.

'Thing is,' he continued, 'because we so rarely get snow on the coast, we're not prepared for it. There are no grit bins. It caught the gritter lorries out and drivers were stranded for hours on the high bit of the A35.'

'Less fun. What time of year was this?'

'March.'

'Oh well, we hardly ever get proper snow in December, except on Christmas cards so I think we'll survive the service and the walk back.'

They reached the bottom of the hill and turned right along the narrow lane which led to the old town and St Winifred's. In the distance the sea roared and the streetlights glowed softly orange in the cold damp air.

'How did your board games afternoon go?'

Mark had released her arm now they were on the flat. Livvy battled the urge to grab it back. She longed to grab *him* back and, in the intimacy of the dark evening, kiss the life out of him, but resisted. She was fond of Simona and she'd never been the sort to go after another woman's man. She couldn't help thinking they made an odd couple, though. Hadn't Mark himself said Simona would be too much for him as a girlfriend? Still, they'd been friends for a long time and friendship often ran into love. Mark had hinted he could be lonely, and Simona missed Trevor. A relationship could grow from such roots. The thoughts chased relentlessly around her brain.

'I said, how did the board games afternoon go?'

Livvy forced herself to focus. 'Sorry. Concentrating on where I was walking.'

'You can have my arm again. Keep me warm.' There was a definite twinkle in his eyes.

'No, I'm good thanks.' Was it her imagination, or did he look disappointed? Was he flirting with Simona *and* her? *Not on, Mark. I didn't have you down as a player.* 'The board games afternoon was great,' she began matter-of-factly. 'We had about fifteen there. A lot brought their own games which helped as I've only managed to accrue a few, Fabio's mince pies went down a treat, they drank us out of tea and we even sold a few gin and tonics and a pint or two. Brenda somebody and Avril – that's Jago's mum – even brought books and settled by the wood burner and read. I made the mistake of making up some mulled wine and Aggie got tipsy and began singing.'

Mark snorted. 'Good old Aggie. What did she sing? "White Christmas"?'

'Nothing so sedate. She brought an old-fashioned record

player in and some vinyl. It was great, I'm keeping it to get out another time. Going to get customers to bring their own records along. We could have seventies nights, eighties nights.' She laughed. 'Although I can't see Fabio willing to make cheese and pineapple hedgehogs and Black Forest gateau. Aggie treated us to "Christmas Wrapping" – which, according to her, was a big hit for The Waitresses back in the eighties – and "Run Rudolph Run".' At Mark's bemused expression, Livvy explained, 'Old Chuck Berry track. I was streaming a Michael Bublé Christmas collection thinking it would be restful and she completely drowned it out. What was worse, she got everyone else joining in! It was a riot and I had trouble booting them all out for evening opening.'

'Will you do another?'

Livvy nodded. 'Absolutely. I'll be more organised next time though. I need to figure out a way of getting people in who don't know anyone. That's who it's aimed at really. I really need to resurrect the darts board too. I never got around to putting that back up after the refurb.'

'Good idea.'

'I'd like to develop the pub's community feel more.'

'Okay.'

'But I'm not sure it's a good fit with a foodie place.'

'Don't see why not.'

'Sorry. Going on about work again. Oh look,' Livvy added, 'we're here.' Mark's responses had become stilted. She was sure it had been the mention of Fabio which had changed the atmosphere between them. Lapsing into silence, they turned off the road and began to ascend the steep slope which led to the church. 'Quite a queue to get in,' she said. 'I like the knitted Christmas post boxes. The Ninja Knitters have obviously been at it again. They've covered the bollards. Look, one's even got knitted letters sticking out of it.' She peered closer. 'And is that really knitted *tinsel?*'

'Livvy, I wanted to–'

'Livvy! Mark!' Daisy ran up to them, giving Livvy a kiss. 'Can I hang with you guys? Rick's working at the restaurant and Mum and Colin are on a date so I'm Billy-No-Mates.' She thrust her arm through Livvy's. 'Good to see you having a night off. You won't regret it. Verity's Christmas service is always wonderful. And, of course, you get to admire my magnificent flower arrangements. I supplied them. Oh, and the tree, of course. Verity loves to dress St Winifred's at Christmas. I'm particularly proud of the colour theme this year, white and gold with the biggest star you've ever seen on top of the tree.'

'Hi, Daisy,' Livvy greeted her. 'We must get together in the new year and discuss a regular flower order for The George.'

'Absolutely. Let's do it over a January glass of wine. We'll have more time then. Like you, now is my busy time.'

'Thank you for the Christmas wreaths you sent over and my tree is fabulous. I meant to say on the night of the quiz, but it was manic.'

'No worries. It was a good night. Made a change for me to dress up. I'm usually in jeans.'

'I feel like that about tonight. Feels most odd to wear a dress.'

'Not to mention a bit draughty.' Daisy giggled. 'It's freezing tonight. Austin says–'

'It'll snow!' they chorused, shuffling forwards in the queue.

'Doesn't St Winifred's look beautiful all lit up?' Daisy added. 'I love how the stained-glass windows glow. We need some welcoming light at this time of year, as Honor often says.' She cocked an ear. 'And is Lexie bashing out "Joy to the World" on the organ?' She chuckled. 'It will have made her Christmas. She's the music teacher at the primary school,' she explained. 'Usually only gets to tinkle the ivories on the school's ancient upright.'

They found seats in a pew halfway back. There was room for two on the end so Daisy and Livvy squeezed in next to Brittany, Avril Pengethley and her little girl. By the time Livvy had said hello to them all she missed where Mark had gone to sit.

The church gradually filled. Livvy recognised many of those coming in. Austin and Aggie walked purposefully to the front, she saw Honor in charge of a group of school children, Bee said a quick hello as she went by and Lucie and her enormous Wiscombe clan chattered noisily three pews ahead. Verity climbed to stand behind the massive eagle-shaped lectern which dwarfed her, and a hush descended. With the decorated tree glowing next to the altar and a full congregation it felt magically Christmassy.

The service was lovely, even to Livvy who was no church goer. The carols were traditional: 'I Saw Three Ships' and 'In the Bleak Midwinter', which, given the weather outside, was mournfully appropriate. Verity's sermon was a simple but heartfelt message about hope bringing light to the world at its darkest time, and forgiveness.

'For when we forgive others,' she said, 'we forgive ourselves. And I am currently forgiving myself for eating three mince pies this afternoon.'

Everyone laughed but the message hit Livvy hard. The solid nub of resentment she'd held towards Gavin began to ease away. It was time to forgive him, to move on. Better to find out his heart wasn't in the business right at the beginning. Running the pub hadn't been easy on her own but she'd made a go of it. Allowing herself a little pride in her achievements, she tuned back into the service. Honor led the children to the front, where they grouped around a knitted life-sized nativity scene, complete with a donkey and camel. Singing along to their rendition of 'Away in a Manger', Livvy didn't know whether to laugh or cry.

And then it was over.

'That was so lovely,' she said to Daisy. 'I'm glad I came in the end. It's fantastic to see the town turn out like this.'

'Always a highlight. Always think it feels as if Christmas has really begun.' Daisy shivered. 'Wish they'd get the heating sorted out though. It's never warm in here but tonight it's positively arctic.'

'I know. I haven't even taken my coat off. And I can't feel my nose. My posh frock has gone completely unappreciated. Mark and I are walking back up to The George. Would you like to come? Pub's closed tonight so we can have a quiet drink in front of the wood burner.'

'I'd love that. Sure I wouldn't be a gooseberry though?'

They stood up and joined those drifting out.

'Don't worry about that. Mark and I are just friends. Ah, Mark, there you are,' Livvy said as he joined them on the path outside. 'Daisy's going to come up to the pub. Would you like to join us for a night cap? I can guarantee heat.'

'Heat sounds good.' He looked frozen and miserable and had the collar of his black coat turned up. 'Can't stay too long though. Early start in the morning, that's if I can get Nats out of bed.'

Once the crowds had dispersed, they picked up the pace and began the climb back up the hill to The George. It left them little breath to talk.

'We'll go in via the kitchen door,' Livvy explained, as she led them under the carriage arch and into the car park. Feeling something delicate settle on her nose she looked up. 'Guys, I think it's snowing!'

It was. From a heavy black sky flurries drifted down.

'Amazing,' Daisy yelled in glee. She grabbed Mark's arm and began to dosey-doe with him. 'Come on, Mark, dance with me. It's the only way I'm going to warm up. We might be in for a white Christmas, after all.'

The security lights flooded on. Daisy and Mark were too engrossed in dancing to notice at first but, when Livvy's eyes adjusted to the glare, she saw.

'Oh my God,' she said. 'Look.'

Daisy and Mark stopped abruptly at her distressed voice.

'Fuck,' Mark said.

Livvy ran to the far end of the car park. Mark and Daisy followed. In the harsh white light the damage was clear. Once again Livvy's work van had been daubed with paint. This time it looked as if an entire pot had been thrown over the windscreen. But it was worse this time. The vandal hadn't been content with daubing paint. All four tyres were slashed too.

'Oh, Mark,' Livvy whispered, horrified. 'They've done the same to your car!'

CHAPTER 33

Tea – an aromatic and comforting beverage, best made with loose leaf tea and freshly boiled water in a warmed pot. Ideal for a crisis.

As they went into the kitchen a distressed springer greeted them, jumping up and whining, her tail between her legs.

'Oh, Angel. Did you sense someone outside, girl?' Livvy bent to comfort her.

'I'll put the kettle on.' Daisy shrugged, 'I can't think of anything more productive to suggest. I'm so sorry, Livvy. This is awful and really unlike Lullbury. I promise you, usually nothing ever happens here.'

'I'll take Angel out. She'll need a wee and I'll have a look around,' Mark said. 'You'd best report it.'

Livvy nodded, grateful. She couldn't help but be relieved that he was the one going out in the cold and dark when someone with ill-intent was around. She went through to the bar, put on the wall lights, stoked up the fire and went online to report.

To her surprise, a PC Khan rang back almost immediately. No one was available to get out tonight, he said, but, should she wish it, someone could attend in the morning. The advice would be to fit security cameras.

'Is there anything else I can do?' Daisy bustled through, bringing a tray. 'Hope you don't mind but I found some biscuits.'

Livvy started. Her nerves were shot. 'Thanks. Think they're what's left over from the board games afternoon.'

Daisy put the tray on the bar and began to pour. 'I heard it went really well.' She brought Livvy a steaming mug. Looking around she added, 'Funny being in here when the last time it was packed. Places have a different atmosphere when empty, don't they?' Putting her hand to her mouth, she said, appalled, 'Sorry. Not the most tactful of things to say after what's just happened.'

Livvy forced a laugh. 'Don't worry. I'm used to being here on my own. Having Angel around has helped. Speaking of which, here she comes.' The springer scurried into the bar and nose-butted her knees. 'You can be always sure of a warm welcome when Angel's around.' She buried her hands in the dog's thick fur. 'Ooh, you feel cold.'

Mark followed, clapping his hands together. 'It's freezing out there and I mean literally. Thanks, Daisy,' he said, as she handed him a mug. He toed a chair nearer the wood burner and sat down.

'Is it still snowing?' Livvy asked.

'No, it's stopped. Just a hard frost.'

'Could you see anything,' Livvy paused, 'or anyone?'

He shook his head. 'Angel ran round in circles, nose to the ground. She could obviously smell someone had been out there but I'm pretty sure they've gone now. Whoever has done this is far away. They won't hang around.' He sipped his tea. 'What did the police say?'

Livvy repeated what she'd been told. 'I'm not sure what the police could do if they did come round tomorrow.'

'They wouldn't take fingerprints or anything?' Daisy asked.

'Don't think vandalism, however distressing, is high enough up the agenda.'

'That's shocking.' Daisy drank her tea thoughtfully. 'I can't think of anyone in town who would do something like this and it's a definite escalation of what happened before, isn't it? Almost as if it's personal.'

'Oh it's personal all right,' Mark put in grimly. 'Have you any idea who it might be, Livvy?'

She shook her head, exhaling heavily. 'I can't think of anyone who dislikes me enough.' She shuddered.

'The ex-boyfriend?' he suggested.

'Gavin?' Livvy went silent for a moment. 'Can't see what motive he'd have. He made it abundantly clear he wasn't interested in running the pub with me.'

'Take it from me, ex-boyfriends can go weird,' Daisy said, bitterly.

'But, as far as I know, Gavin's still working in the midlands. Why would he drive all the way down here just to do some petty vandalism? It doesn't make sense. And I haven't annoyed any local pub owners, or anyone else as far as I know, so it's a complete mystery.'

Daisy shook her head vehemently. 'Everyone I've talked to has said what a great job you're doing and that they're happy the pub is open again.' She pointed a shortbread finger. 'There's trade enough for everyone. Rick says the same thing.'

'So, do we think it's bored teenagers?' Mark asked. 'There was a spate of vandalism going on a while back.'

'You mean Eli?' Daisy asked.

He nodded.

'That was a while ago,' Daisy said, 'and it was led by a kid who came from Axminster. He was the one who pinched the cars; Eli was stupid enough to get in them. Idiot. And I know my cousin's no angel but he's grown out of all that now.'

'I really don't want to think of Eli doing it.' Livvy sighed. 'He seems happy working here, wants to prove that he's put all that behind him.'

Daisy sat up suddenly, putting her tea in peril. 'Besides, he was at the service tonight. He was with Lucie.'

'He was, although he came in late,' Livvy agreed. 'I remember seeing him sneak in. Who else can we eliminate?'

'Half the town,' Mark said. 'The church was packed. I had to sit right at the back. Squashed in with Tracy from The Sea Spray.' He mustered a grin. 'Kept me warm. And the bonus was she had a hip flask.'

They lapsed into a heavy silence, only punctuated by the hiss and crackle of the fire. The rap on the kitchen door had them all jumping a foot. Angel ran to it, barking furiously.

'I'm so sorry,' Daisy said. 'That'll be Rick. I rang him to collect me when he'd finished work. Didn't fancy walking home in the dark on my own. Not after what's happened.'

'I hate how this is making us all feel,' Livvy muttered through clenched teeth.

Daisy put a hand to her shoulder as Mark went to let Rick in. 'Me too. I love living in a town where I feel safe enough to walk around on my own whatever the time. I just got a bit spooked tonight.'

Rick came in, looking concerned. 'Livvy, I'm so sorry this has happened. Is there anything I can do?' He ran a hand through his dark hair and swore. 'This just shouldn't happen in Lullbury Bay!'

Daisy went to him and cuddled into his side. Livvy watched on with envy. She could really do with a hug right now. 'Look, Livvy, if there's anything we can do, just ask. If you want to borrow Primrose – that's my work van – until yours is back up and running, then please do.'

Livvy stood up, shaken at how wobbly her legs felt. 'Thanks, both. Thank you, Mark. You've all been so kind keeping me company. Oh and, Daisy, we didn't even have that drink.'

Daisy came to her and kissed her on the cheek. 'There'll be other times. Night, my lovely. Stay safe.'

'I'll see you out,' Mark offered.

Livvy collapsed onto her chair, turning her mug of tea round in her fingers. She looked up as he returned. 'You should be getting off home too. I suppose you'll have to ring a taxi?'

He shook his head and sat back down. 'I'm staying here tonight.' Putting up a hand to deflect her protestations, he added, 'I've rung Nats. She's fine and sends her love by the way. Neither of us would dream of you being here alone when this has happened. Besides,' he grinned, 'taxis are hard to come by at this hour in this town and I really don't want to walk all that way in the cold. Call me a wuss.'

'I wouldn't dream of it, but honestly wouldn't you rather be in your own bed? Oh, Mark,' her hand flew to her mouth. 'Will you be able to get your car fixed in time to drive up to York?'

'I'll have a ring round tomorrow but it's Christmas Eve, it'll be a bit tight.'

'I'm so sorry,' Livvy said in a small voice. 'That's your Christmas ruined.'

'Not at all. I'm sure I'll be able to find somewhere open to replace the tyres.'

'What about the paint?'

'That might take a little more sorting. Tell you what,' he said briskly, 'how about that drink? Think we could both do with one.'

'Absolutely.' Livvy rose but her legs gave way, everything crowded in on her and she staggered. Her face crumpled and, putting her hands up to cover her distress, she began to sob.

Mark surged to his feet, wrapped his arms around her and held her tight. He crooned comforting nonsensical phrases until she'd stopped shaking. Leading her to the settle under where the darts board used to be, he arranged the cushions around her. 'Back in a mo.' He returned with two tumblers brimming with whisky. 'You're in shock. I'm not entirely sure this is the right remedy, but it was the only thing I could think of seeing as we've done tea and biscuits.' Putting the glasses down on the table in front of them, he slid in beside her, putting an arm around and pulling her close. He rested his chin on top of her head. 'I'm so sorry this is happening to you, Livvy.'

'It's not your fault.'

'I just wish I could find out who's done it. I'm fucking furious.'

It was so unlike him to swear, Livvy almost giggled. Squashing down the building hysteria, she said, 'I'm so sorry about your car.'

'Oh, Livvy.' He sighed and swore some more under his breath. 'I don't mean about my car, that's fixable. I mean this targeted campaign, because that's what it's beginning to look like.'

Much as she'd loved the feel of his arms around her, Livvy sat up and moved away. Picking up the whisky, she took a mouthful. Feeling the liquid run a fiery path inside brought her back to herself. 'Sorry.'

'You keep apologising. There's no need.' Mark pointed his tumbler. '*You* haven't done anything.'

'It's just not the way I envisaged the evening turning out,' she said sadly. 'I loved the Christmas service, felt all warm and glowy inside. Was looking forward to a quiet drink here with friends and then it all went wrong.'

'And, as I say, you've done nothing to deserve any of this. For all we know it could well be bored kids.'

'I'd rather it was, than a focused campaign.' She swallowed another mouthful of whisky. 'Makes about as much sense but makes me feel far less hated.'

He took her hand and held it. 'You're not hated, Livvy. Far from it.'

She sucked in a breath. 'Good. Right then,' she added decisively, needing to do something practical. 'We'd better get you sorted with some bedding. And go to bed. I've an early start tomorrow. Loads to do. Got the stock taker coming round, got to prep for the party and there'll be the visit from the police of course.'

'I'll be okay. I'll sleep down here in front of the fire.'

'Oh no you won't,' Livvy said, horrified. 'Not when I've a spare bedroom. My mother may not have approved but it's decent enough. And I might even be able to find you a toothbrush. Could you, would you mind–' she let the question trail off, embarrassed.

'Anything.'

Livvy winced. She hated asking. Hated being so dependent. 'Would you mind coming round with me making sure it's all locked up down here before we go up to bed?'

'No problem.'

'Thank you, Mark.' She let out a breath in relief. 'Thank you so much.'

He leaned in and kissed her swiftly on the top of the head. 'It's the least I can do.'

CHAPTER 34

*Tequila – distilled from the blue agave plant. Strong, earthy flavour.
High alcohol content*

Livvy was only too aware of Mark sleeping a few doors away and it gave her a restless night. She got up early to see him out. 'Thanks for staying over,' she said, as he unlocked the kitchen door. 'Are you sure I can't make you breakfast?'

'No, best be off. Get on the phone to find someone to sort the car.'

Both studiously avoided looking at the wrecked vehicles.

'I hope Nats was okay on her own.'

'Bingeing on a *Downton Abbey* box set was the last message. And drinking her way through my wine stocks. She'll be fine.' He glanced at his watch. 'And won't be in the land of the living yet. It'll give me time to get ringing round.'

'Walk safely.' Livvy peered at the sullen grey sky. 'They might be right about The Beast from the East Mark II. And the frost hasn't lifted. Don't slip and break a leg to add to the bill I owe you.'

'You don't owe me anything, Livvy.'

'I'll say Happy Christmas then. If you do get to York, I won't see you until afterwards.' Livvy tried to keep the desolation from her voice. She was trying hard to be the independent woman but, at the moment, all she really wanted was for him to be around.

Mark hovered on the kitchen doorstep. 'I suppose. Can't believe you're still going ahead with the Christmas Eve party.'

She shrugged. 'Everyone's expecting one and besides, I don't want to let the events of last night defeat me. I'll be damned if he scares me off.'

'Attagirl.'

They stood awkwardly facing one another.

'I suppose I'd better get off then,' Mark said, not moving.

'I suppose you better had. Give my love to Nats and wish her Happy Christmas.'

'Will do.' He reached forward, smelling of her toothpaste. It made the gesture feel intimate and familiar, as if they were an established married couple. Kissing her cheek, he whispered, 'Happy Christmas, Livvy. Keep safe.'

She watched him walk gingerly away over the icy surface of the car park until he reached the carriage arch and then turn uphill and disappear. For a second, she was alone. It was horrible. She felt naked and vulnerable, and as if someone was watching. At her whistle, Angel came bounding in from the beer garden just as a black Range Rover turned in off the main road.

'Bernie' Winters was an old family friend, trusted and reliable. Her father, just before he'd left on holiday, had ignored Livvy's plea that she could ring and had called him himself. Today was the only time Bernie could conduct a stock take. He got out of his car, looked curiously at the van and at Mark's Mercedes and inched warily over to her. A solid man with sandy-coloured hair and on the verge of retiring, he was exactly the fatherly sort she wanted about her today.

'Looks like you've had a wee spot of bother,' he said, in his soft Edinburgh accent.

'Hi, Bernie. I'll explain later. Get yourself in. It's icy out here. What are the roads like?'

'Och. Not too bad for the moment.'

'Thanks for coming.'

'Not a bother. I told your dad I'd do what I could to help.'

Livvy bit her lip. First Mark, now Bernie. She was calling in so many favours, it was making a mockery of her going it alone.

Bernie bent to pet an ecstatic spaniel. 'Now, who's this wee girlie?'

'This is Angel. Let Bernie in, will you,' she said to the dog, grabbing her collar. 'We haven't all got a fur coat.' Livvy bustled them all into the kitchen. 'Bacon sandwich and a mug of tea do you?' The springer barked in approval.

'Grand. Then, if you don't mind, I'll crack on. Weather forecast's looking lively and I'll want to get home.'

The teapot was doing overtime. She made Bernie breakfast and pointed him in the direction of the bar. PC Khan arrived thirty minutes later. He simply repeated what had been said the night before but, having drunk his tea, promised to have a good look around the car park before he left. 'And, in the new year, I seriously recommend getting CCTV fitted,' was his parting shot.

When Fabio and Stewie arrived, Livvy left them in the kitchen prepping for the day's lunch service. Going through to the bar she switched on all the Christmas lights and busied herself carting a load of logs in and stoking up the fire. Keeping active was a way of stopping herself thinking. And, although it was good to have people around her again, she needed light and warmth too. The post took another half hour to sift through. The first bills were in and made her heart sink. She sat for a moment, breathing in and out, calming herself, trying to instil some confidence. Taking another deep breath, she coughed. The logs were damp and the wood burner was all smoke and no flames. It didn't seem a good omen.

Two hours later Bernie perched on a bar stool and picked up the turkey and stuffing roll Stewie had made for him. 'Livvy,' he said heavily, 'from what I can see – and I've been through all your itemised till readings, all your dispensed spirits and your real ale barrels – accounting for wastage, you've got three bottles of vodka, one of gin and two bottles of tequila unaccounted for. You always note down any drinks for your own use, don't you, and those given out on the house?'

Livvy nodded, feeling slightly sick. She put down her own sandwich, her appetite gone.

'Seeing as it's you, I'll go through everything one more time but it looks very much as if one reason for your lack of profit is–'

'Someone's pilfering.'

'Och, it's not uncommon, Liv. Your father's had it happen more than once in his hotel bars. It's rife in the hospitality industry.'

'I just hoped it wouldn't happen in my part of it.'

'Obviously, talk to your accountant about any other issues. It's been a nightmare of a time for pubs. It's nigh on impossible to predict any profit margins, what with the unpredictability of the last five years. Look at what you're charging, lassie, what you can cut down on.' He took a swig of coffee. 'But remember, you need to look at it long term. My advice, if you want it, is to increase your food covers. That's where the profitability will lie.'

'Thanks, Bernie,' Livvy said slowly. 'Lots to think about.'

'First thing you need to do is sort who's taking the unaccounted-for spirits. You got anyone working for you with a wee drink problem? It's also common in our world.'

'I'll have to have a think about it.'

'Then you'll have to catch them at it to prove it. Not easy.' He picked up his sandwich and continued eating.

'I'll leave you to your lunch. Thanks, Bernie, I appreciate it. And huge thanks for coming out on Christmas Eve. Happy Christmas and give my love to Moira and the kids. Safe drive back.'

She took her own coffee to Pete's favourite chair and table in front of the wood burner. She couldn't seem to get warm and hugged the mug to her chest, her mood low. No one said running a pub would be easy and she should have anticipated problems of this kind. As Bernie said, it was a common occurrence in the pub trade, but she'd thought her little team was bomb-proof. Letting a sigh escape, she wondered what else could go wrong.

She watched, through the many-paned window, as traffic inched down the narrow hill into town. It was a bottleneck outside The George and when two busses met it caused chaos. It would be fun when the tourist season began. The roads were slick with wet and no longer icy, but drivers were obviously erring on the cautious side. *Is any of this worth all the stress? I could be out, like everyone else, doing last-minute Christmas shopping.* Not only had she a malicious vandal to contend with, but she also had someone working for her who was stealing. Screwing her eyes shut, she forced herself to think calmly and rationally. She wasn't the first landlady to face this problem, she wouldn't be the last. She had to deal with it logically, remove the emotion.

Sipping her coffee, she thought through each member of the team one by one. Despite her attempt to be professional, it hurt her personally to think one of them was pilfering and in such quantities.

Candice the cleaner was an unlikely suspect; she didn't work when the pub was open, plus Livvy was usually around when she was in cleaning. She supposed the woman could have helped herself to a sneaky spirit but was hard-pressed to fit all the cleaning in as it was. And in those quantities? Surely Livvy would have noticed the optics getting low before opening times.

Brittany was a health nut, lapsing with the occasional burger and didn't touch spirits. The most she ever drank was the odd glass of white wine, or champagne.

Young Karl she'd trust with her life, besides he was a beer man through and through and loved his real ale. It couldn't be him; if it was, she'd be horrified.

It was unlikely to be Stewie as he rarely ventured out of the kitchen, Fabio kept him too busy.

Could it be Fabio? He wouldn't be the first chef to have a drinking problem. But surely, as he had to drive all the way back to Honiton after each shift, he wouldn't risk drink-driving? With his mother being sick he'd need his driving licence for any emergency. Livvy drained her mug. That is, of course, if what he'd told her was the truth. *No!* She prided herself on being a good judge of character; she couldn't believe it was Fabio; he invested so much of himself into making The George a success. Surely, he wouldn't jeopardise that? And hadn't Jason mentioned Fabio's ill mother?

Her thoughts twisted and turned. Alcohol was a desperate addiction, though. For those who suffered, it took over their lives and they cared for little else. She put her mug down with a bang. It wasn't possible. She refused to think it was Fabio.

And what of Simona and Eli? What would Simona's motive be? She wasn't short of money, had generously given up her own time, didn't drink a great deal and ate even less. Besides, Livvy considered her a good friend now; she'd made the busy run-up to Christmas great fun.

It left Eli. Of all her team he was the one she felt she knew the least. He was mostly monosyllabic, crucified by shyness, then came across sullen. It meant he didn't always go down well with some customers but was efficient unless it was hectic when he got flustered. And that was improving, along with his confidence. The only time he seemed scared of his own shadow was when his family were in; he was especially wary of Gerry. She'd never seen Eli drink while at work; like Stewie, he was another young person who was happier with a pint of cola or orange squash.

She couldn't see him having the guts to work out he could take a measure and not put it through the till. And she'd never seen him even mildly tipsy let alone drunk.

Livvy ground her teeth. This was all her own fault; she should have kept a closer eye on everyone. She let an enormous sigh escape.

'Ooh, kitten, sounds as if you have the weight of the world on your shoulders. Missing your Mark? Or is it that awful scene out there in the car park? Darling, I can't believe it's happened again. How awful. There was a rather nice Scot getting into a new plate Range Rover out there. He said bye-bye and Happy Christmas. I do rather like a man in a kilt.' Simona giggled. 'Shame he was in a boring old suit.'

Livvy twisted round to see Simona come into the bar. As she chattered nonsense, took off her fur hat, shook out her hair and went behind the bar to make herself a latte. Livvy watched as she found the little black book and wrote down that she'd had one. She never expected staff to pay for tea and coffee, or soft drinks within reason but expected them to record what they'd had. Surely, if Simona automatically noted down a latte, she wouldn't bother snaffling a shot for free – and she certainly wouldn't touch tequila.

Simona sat in Pete's chair and stretched her feet out to the wood burner. 'Brr. Cold as murder out there. Now, sweetness, tell me all about it. What's up, kitten? Can't be just the vandalism, although awful as that may be. You look really forlorn.'

'Oh, work stuff. You know.'

Simona pulled a face. 'Grim. But come on, angel, let me take your mind off things, spill the goss about you and Mark.'

'There's nothing between me and Mark. No goss.'

Simona tapped the side of her nose. 'Do pull the other one. A girl has eyes. I can see when the sparks are...' she waved her hands around, desperately seeking for the right word and failing, '...sparking.'

'We're just friends, Simona.' Livvy said it more forcefully than she meant but she couldn't deal with this today.

'Oh. Soz, darling. Didn't mean to offend.' Simona picked up her mug and hugged it to her.

'No offence taken.' Livvy rubbed an exhausted hand over her face. 'Sorry, Simona. I didn't mean to snap. It's one of those days and I'm knackered.'

'Well, I think it's a damn shame. About you and Mark. There's you, all glossy honey-blonde hair and endless legs and our luscious Mark. He's terribly keen on you, you know.'

'Is he?' Livvy thought back over all the things he'd done for her since she'd taken over the pub. 'He's a very kind man. As I said, I think he's just being a good friend.'

Simona snorted delicately. 'Believe that if you will, my angel. I'd jump him like a shot. Good men are hard to come by, trust me.' She sighed. 'But maybe I'm simply jealous of you having a man hang off your every word.'

Livvy's head reared up. She'd suspected Simona had feelings for Mark. And that it was mutual.

'Don't look at me like that, sweetness. Mark only has eyes for you. I gave up on that ship long ago.' She shrugged her thin shoulders. 'I mean, if he was offered up on a plate, I wouldn't kick him out of bed–'

'Simona!'

'I know, darling. I'm awful, aren't I? But you love me anyway, you simply can't help it. If only our fabulous Fabio felt the same about me.'

'Fabio?'

'Don't look so startled. I thought I'd rather made my feelings for that man clear.'

'I always thought you were joking around, you know, flirting. I mean, you flirt with most men. Even Old Pete on occasion.'

Simona gave her silvery laugh. 'I do love Pete. So deliciously and determinedly grumpy. Ah but Fabio. Hormones will out with that one. It's just that I do rather like him, but he insists on remaining distant. Comes in, cooks his divine food, and then off he goes back to Mummy. He's such an unknown, don't you think? Such an enigma. Do you think Mummy exists or do you think he has a wifelet and a whole brood of stunning, dark-eyed children secreted in some hovel in Honiton?'

Livvy laughed, she couldn't help it. 'I've no idea. When I interviewed him he said his ill mother was what had brought him back here to the UK. I've no reason to disbelieve him.'

'Really, haven't you?'

Livvy looked at her. 'I didn't think I had.' She glanced quickly to the door. It was firmly shut; they couldn't be overheard. Taking a deep breath, she launched into an explanation of the problem Bernie had discovered.

CHAPTER 35

Prosecco – an Italian sparkling or semi-sparkling wine,
perfect for parties

Simona wouldn't hear of the party being cancelled. She agreed with Livvy that it was a way of sticking up two metaphorical fingers at whoever was doing the vandalising. She also promised to keep a close eye on who might have a hand in the till. 'Trust me,' she'd said, tapping the side of her nose. 'Everyone writes me off as a dumb blonde. It has its advantages to be thought stupid. No one takes any notice of me.' Giggling, she'd added, 'I get to see all sorts of things!'

At six thirty Livvy and Simona were shivering in Livvy's frigid bedroom, high up in The George, primping their party outfits.

It had taken Livvy some soul-searching to decide what to wear. For a working day she stuck to black trousers, a white shirt and comfortable shoes, a legacy of her time working in hotels. Dull but practical when you spent the whole time on your feet.

She was desperate to wear the dress Simona had given her but part of her longed to wear it for the first time when Mark would have a chance to see it. He'd never really seen her dressed up. Even at the church service, she'd had her close-fitting wool dress covered up by a coat. Then she decided. It went against her beliefs to dress up for a man; she'd dress for her own satisfaction and wear her new, gorgeous, glittering gown for herself. Having washed and deep conditioned her hair, she let Simona help her put it into a messy, sophisticated updo with casual tendrils escaping onto her neck. It certainly made a change from her usual ponytail. Simona had also, over a couple of glasses of Prosecco, painted her nails a deep velvety red.

'It's so lovely to have some girly time,' she whispered, as she admired Livvy's nails. 'You're going to be the belle of the ball, kitten. You look like a real diva!'

'That's what I'll do then. Embrace my inner diva.' Livvy giggled.

'You, a diva? Darling, that's about as far from you as could possibly be.'

Livvy grinned. 'That's the point. And, may I say how glam you look in your white dress.'

Simona preened. 'Always wanted to be Marilyn.' She patted her hair, backcombed sixties style. 'It looks good, doesn't it? Might regret these heels come midnight, though.'

'You and me both.' Livvy stuck out her stilettoed foot. 'These bad boys are going to be agony. But, you know what they say, you haven't had a good night if you can't wait to get the shoes off.'

Simona suddenly caught Livvy's hand and clutched it to her chiffon-coated bosom. 'I'm so glad you've come to town, Liv. I feel I've made a really good friend and I've had such fun working in the pub. It's made me feel alive again and I haven't felt that for a long time.'

Livvy hugged her. 'I can't tell you how much you mean to me too,' she said realising it for the first time. 'I've never had many women friends. Never kept many friends full stop. My parents were always moving onto somewhere new, then they sent me to boarding school and most of my classmates lived abroad.' She released her. 'It's good to have a mate. My bestie's moved to the US and, now she's pregnant with twins, I can feel us drifting apart.'

'Goodness. Twins. And yes, it happened to me when my girl-friends had their children. We grew apart, had little in common. But they've come back.' Simona giggled impishly. 'Rounder and with bags under their eyes but looking for a bit of fun again. I'm off to Klosters in the new year skiing with a couple of them, actually. It'll be good to reconnect.'

'Just don't tell them they look bigger and older,' Livvy said, aghast.

Simona made a face and zipped a finger across her lips. 'I shall concentrate on having some girly time and stay silent.'

Livvy laughed. Simona was outrageously naughty and quite possibly completely amoral, but she was good fun. She was a good distraction and she needed that tonight. 'I'm enjoying this girly time.'

'Oh so am I. So am I.' Simona enveloped her in another scented embrace. 'And I have a feeling all your worries will come to nothing, kitten,' she whispered.

'I hope so. God, Simona, I need to let rip tonight. I need to party.'

Standing up decisively and straightening her dress, teetering ever so slightly on her heels, Simona added, 'And now, are you ready, wingman?'

Livvy allowed herself to be pulled up. 'I most certainly am!'

The party was proving a roaring success. The Christmas spirit was alive and well and being thoroughly celebrated. Even

Norman turned up. Ostensibly to see Angel, he stayed on to drink cider. Eli had the soundtrack sorted and played it loud. A succession of Christmas bangers got people on their feet. Someone had spread the rumour that it was fancy dress, and Livvy was astonished at how many people had embraced the concept.

'This town loves any excuse to dress up, even when they're not supposed to. Actually, *especially* when they're not supposed to!' Simona trilled, as she began to drag Darrell to the middle of the crowd to dance to 'Step into Christmas'.

'Maybe I should have opened up the restaurant and cleared a space,' Livvy yelled back. 'It's awfully crowded in here.'

Simona batted off her concerns. 'Use it as an excuse to get up close and personal, kitten.' She blew a kiss at Darrell. 'I am.'

Despite being desperate to enjoy herself, Livvy felt a wave of despondency overcome her. The one person she craved to get up close and personal with wasn't here and, despite what Simona had said earlier, she still wasn't sure how Mark felt about her. He was nice to her but he was nice to everyone and his behaviour had given her nothing but friendship vibes. Finding a space at the bar, which was serving as party snack central, she leaned against it and observed. Popping a crab vol-au-vent into her mouth, she chewed thoughtfully. Despite the return of her low mood, she couldn't help her lips twitching into a smile at the sight before her.

Jonquil and her husband were bopping away. The chimney sweep was dressed as a fairy complete with wand. 'Always wanted to be Tinkerbell,' Livvy heard her shout. 'Ooh, Little Saint Nick,' she yelled as the Beach Boys replaced Elton John. 'Got to love the old ones.'

Brittany was doing some too cool for school moves, along with Jen, Karl's wife. Stewie, having a rare night off from the kitchen was dancing with Candice and even Gerry's group, dressed up as cowboys, were strutting their stuff and seemed to be behaving themselves. The Happy Christmas banners, balloons and flashing lights all added to the slightly frenetic mood.

Livvy laughed out loud as a crowd of dinosaurs – Barbara and her colleagues from the museum – turned up. If she and the pub got through next year, she vowed to make this an annual event. She took another vol-au-vent, this time turkey in a white sauce.

'Bit retro but always go down well at parties.' It was Fabio. Wearing a navy velvet dinner jacket and bow tie he looked devilishly handsome.

'Hi, Fab. Glad you could make it.'

'Only popped in to see how it's going. Have to get back to Mama. You know, babe, you should do this for a New Year's party. Clear the restaurant for dancing. Get in a proper sound system. Charge for entry. Have fireworks.'

'Great idea. Too short notice for this New Year's Eve though.' She gazed at Fabio. He looked tense, a pucker of worry playing about his beautiful dark eyes. 'You look very dashing. James Bond?'

He shrugged. 'Whatevs.'

'Do you know who spread the rumour it was fancy dress?'

'No idea. Fun though.'

She plucked at her dress. 'I didn't get the memo but Simona says I pass muster as a diva.'

He turned to her, took her hand and lifted it to his mouth. '*Bella,*' he whispered, staring into her eyes and kissing her fingers.

The compliment silenced her. Livvy snatched her hand away, worried it must smell of crab vol-au-vent.

They watched as Austin and Aggie, dressed as Fred and Wilma Flintstone, berate Eli for not having the music up loud enough.

'That outfit is going to do nothing for Austin's arthritis in this weather.' Livvy giggled trying to take the heat out of Fabio's gesture.

Fabio didn't join in with the laughter. He caught her hand

again. 'Livvy, it's probably not the time or place but I need to talk to you about something–'

'Livvy! Stop standing there like a melon. Come and dance.' Daisy dragged her away.

As Livvy looked back, she could see Fabio staring down, unseeing, at a tray of pigs in blankets and her heart went cold. Surely he wasn't leaving?

She'd been dancing with Daisy and Lucie for about twenty minutes when a pair of hands encircled her waist, long narrow fingers digging in.

'Olivia, may I say how delicious you look?' It was Jason, his breath hot on her neck. Twisting her round, he pulled her into him. He was dressed in a Father Christmas outfit. With his thin-rimmed black specs jutting out beneath a frizzy white wig, he looked the antithesis of a man bringing good cheer. He was too lean and predatory. It was disconcerting.

'Oh hello.' Taken aback, she resented how he always managed to unnerve her. 'Have you got yourself a drink?'

'Had one earlier.' He nodded. 'Dance with me.' He slid an arm around her back, his hand cold on the exposed bare skin where her dress dipped down low. He pulled her close. It all felt very sixth form disco dancing like this to Bob Dylan's 'Here Comes Santa'.

She moved away from him a little. 'Are you having a good time?'

'I am now.' His smile glittered down at her.

He reminded her of a black cat, all pale-eyed and watchful. A shiver of revulsion ran through her. 'Are you staying long?'

'That rather depends.'

The music changed. David Essex's mournful 'A Winter's Tale' came on. Some guests moaned but others took the opportunity for a slow dance. Jason put a hand on her bottom and pressed her into his groin.

'If you'll excuse me, I rather think it's time to go and check on how the bar is doing.' Removing his hand in a deliberate gesture she stepped away from him.

As she went to go Jason gripped her upper arm. His fingers dug in. It was painful. 'Always working,' he sneered. 'Makes Livvy a very dull girl.'

'But I *am* working, Jason. This is my pub.' She gave him a tight smile, wondering how drunk he was. 'I need to go and check on Angel too.'

'Angel?'

'My dog. She might not like all this noise.'

He made a moue of disgust. It told her all she needed to know of his opinion on dogs.

The pale eyes were almost hypnotising. And filled with a strange mixture of lust and, could it be hate? But why would he hate her? She walked away, checked that Karl and Eli were okay at the bar and fled into the kitchen. Angel was fast asleep in her bed, unbothered by the music, but she'd been the ideal excuse to get away. Pouring a long cold glass of water, Livvy was annoyed to find her hands shaking. *Bastard.* She should tell the man where to go. It was difficult though; he was a customer. *Tact needed, Livvy old girl. Tact.*

The springer stirred in her bed, rolling over for a tummy rub. As Livvy bent down to the dog, she forced a laugh. 'Wonder if Dad has ever been hit on, Angel, girl? Bet he has. What did he do about it, eh?' She promised to message him to ask. Maybe it was finally time to admit there were some things she needed help with. In the meantime, she'd do all she could to keep away from Jason Lemmon.

CHAPTER 36

Mineral water – a refreshing, natural water filtered through rock and containing beneficial minerals. An excellent choice to maintain a clear head.

It was getting late but the party showed no signs of flagging. Most of the food had gone, the mulled wine had finished an hour ago and people were still dancing. Livvy had to admit the good folk of Lullbury Bay had stamina.

Going behind the bar she poured herself some mineral water and added a chunky slice of lemon. Dougie and Duncan were dancing with their wives and mum but there was no sign of Number One D. Norman, wearing pair of reindeer antlers, chased a shrieking Aggie around with a bunch of mistletoe. Livvy looked for Simona as it was just the sort of thing that would make her squeal with laughter but realised she hadn't seen her for the last thirty minutes or so. A lump of disappointment fell into her gut. Simona and Darrell had been slow dancing earlier, but it had all looked jokey. Surely they hadn't gone off somewhere together? She hadn't thought Simona's immorality would stretch as far as messing about with a married man. And she'd thought more of Darrell too.

Fabio was at the bar talking to Eli and Stewie. Karl was twirling Jen around with abandon and Jason sat in Old Pete's seat, glaring. He'd removed his Father Christmas wig and beard and was nursing a whisky. His face looked curiously flushed and his hair was awry. Too much booze, or possibly too much cheap red and white polyester dressing-up outfit. Pete had been collected to spend Christmas with his niece and Livvy was glad. The old man didn't have much time for Jason – she couldn't say she blamed him – and Skip definitely wouldn't have tolerated the man sitting in their spot.

As Norman emerged from the crowd of dancers again, this time with Aggie chasing him, a wave of familiar loneliness sweep over her. It would have been so good to have Mark here. He would have found it funny too.

Suddenly she'd had enough. Desperately seeking fresh air, she tiptoed through the kitchen so as not to wake Angel and opened the door. The freezing air hit her like a sledgehammer, but she was glad of it. Mark's Mercedes sat where it had been parked the night before, its tyres still ruined. Her van, tucked away in its corner, was the same. She doubted anything much could be done for either until after Boxing Day. Wistfully, she wondered why Mark hadn't come to the party. Maybe he'd hired a car to drive to York.

The car park wasn't too full, with people preferring taxis or a lift so they could drink and not worry. Snowflakes danced about in the dark skies but not settling, just drifting on the wind and, against the background of party noise, the sea murmured relentlessly below. The office block opposite was now empty, and on the market and, despite the fifty or so people partying behind her, the car park felt a very lonely place. Better security lights and cameras were definitely needed.

Livvy pulled out her phone and sent a text wishing Yolanda Happy Christmas. She added:

> Miss you. Must find time to visit you in new year.

It was never easy to take holidays as a publican, but she must be able to find time for a long weekend in Washington in January? Scrolling through the messages on her phone, she was pleased to see one from her parents. They'd managed to connect to the ship's wi-fi. Apparently, her father had spent most of his days at sea checking out all the bars. Livvy giggled. The man was obsessed.

Shivering, she'd just decided to go back in when the security lights flared on. Against the furthest most wall, the one which bordered the steep drop to the cliffs and the sea below, a figure emerged. Female, dressed in white and tottering on vertiginous heels. Simona.

Livvy reared back in disgust. Snogging in a freezing cold December car park with a married man was sordid. How could they? As her eyes adjusted to the harsh light, she saw a man appear. Her stomach heaved. It would have been one thing for it to be Darrell. But the man wasn't the burly builder.

It was Mark.

Running back into the kitchen, she slammed the door shut, leaning against it. The noise woke Angel who began to bark and who then scrabbled at the door as it was pushed open to let in Simona and Mark. One look at their flushed, triumphant faces had Livvy reeling.

'What's the matter, Livvy? Don't look at us like that, kitten. Oh angel, wait, it's not what it looks like, darling.'

'Livvy, wait, we've got something to tell you–'

She ran back to the sanctuary of the bar and poured herself a whisky, her hand shaking so much she couldn't hold the tumbler to the optic.

'Livvy, *bella*, are you okay?' Fabio asked.

She shook her head and downed the spirit in one, hardly noticing as Mark ordered Eli to cut the music.

'What's going on, Mark?' Karl asked. 'It's not kicking out time yet.' There were one or two confused grumbles but some took the opportunity to sit down, hoover up some party food and finish drinks. Aggie sat down on Norman's lap and Gerry lurched to the bar and ordered lager. Livvy found herself unable to move so Fabio flipped the bar hatch open and pulled him his pint.

Livvy watched through narrowed eyes and could barely breathe as Simona went to stand next to Mark. She clutched his arm to her, looking impossibly pleased with herself.

'We've an announcement,' Mark declared.

A few oohs and ahs and knowing chuckles rumbled through the party goers. He had their full attention.

Livvy covered her face with her hands, aware of Fabio's arm coming round her shoulders. She shrugged his embrace off, desperate to get away from him, to get away from everything. She got as far as the end of the bar, her fingers biting into its wooden edge.

'Wait, Livvy. Please wait,' Mark said. 'You need to hear this.'

'I can't.' Distraught, she stared at him, shaking her head violently. 'I can't listen to this.'

'Livvy, we know who's been doing the vandalism.' The sentence came out in a rush. White-faced, Mark waited for her reaction.

Livvy's mouth fell open, Fabio gasped and someone, she thought it was Daisy, squealed. In Pete's corner, Jason stood up.

'Who? Who is it?' Livvy could barely utter the words.

'Darling, we've been out keeping watch on the odd occasion when we've been able, over the last week or so,' Simona squeaked, bouncing up and down in excitement. 'Your lovely

Mark and me. Tonight we got evidence on our phones. It's a bit hazy and my hands were shaking so much due to the cold, but we've got a photo of a man carrying a pot of white paint.'

'And one of him hiding it in the skip that Darrell's left out there,' Mark added. 'Darrell's putting the pot of paint somewhere safe right now. It's evidence. Probably circumstantial but evidence.'

'Then who is it?' Livvy's voice was hoarse and barely more than a whisper. Too much was coming at her. Mark and Simona weren't out there having an illicit tryst; they'd been stalking the vandal! She glanced at Eli who was shifting uneasily.

Mark turned towards Pete's seat and the lean man standing there. 'He was dressed as Father Christmas. It's you, Jason. Isn't it?'

More gasps from the crowd.

'Jason?' All the breath left Livvy's body. She grabbed the edge of the bar again, this time to keep herself upright. To her left, she felt Fabio vibrate in shock. 'I thought it was teenagers. I thought it was stupid, mindless vandalism.'

'Oh no, Livvy,' Mark said. 'I'm afraid there's been an orchestrated campaign of intimidation. And it's all been led by Jason Lemmon here.' He was his usual unruffled self, but Livvy sensed the fury which bubbled beneath. She'd never seen him so angry.

The silence in the bar was profound. Jason was tolerated by most and disliked by many, but this still came as a shock.

Livvy was bewildered. 'Why?' She turned to Jason. 'Why would you do that to me?'

'I can tell you why,' Mark put in, his voice terse.

'Yes, Mark, pray enlighten us.' Jason spread his hands to the room, his light eyes glittering. He was now stone-cold sober and seemed all the more dangerous. 'If you're going to fire accusations that serious then you better have the evidence to back up your claim. Even a man as wealthy as you may find a lawsuit a tad expensive.' Taking off his Father Christmas jacket, he folded it with careful precision and laid it over the back of the chair. In his white polo neck, he resembled a Bond villain.

'You put in a bid at the auction to buy The George, didn't you? You've also shown interest in buying the office block next door.'

'So?'

'With the intent of redeveloping the site. I should imagine luxury apartments with sea views would make you millions.'

'Dear boy, I'm a property developer, that's what I do. Making a healthy profit isn't against the law.' Jason's voice dripped scorn.

'You should build affordable houses for local people,' Aggie yelled. Jason ignored her.

'No,' Mark continued, fury making white lines appear around his mouth and his words clipped. 'It isn't against the law, but your plans were partially thwarted when Livvy was successful in purchasing the pub. The George has a massive footprint. Added to the office block, it would have enormous development potential. But you missed out on buying it, didn't you, so the first part of your plan was foiled.'

He shifted nearer and his icy rage surfaced from beneath the calm surface. 'But if you could get Livvy out, she'd sell up and you could proceed.' Mark bit the words out. 'You didn't have much hope of Livvy making a success of this place, did you? Except she has. Look at all these people here, supporting her. The last thing you wanted was for her to make a go of it. It's been done many times before. Run down a pub so it can be sold cheaply, then the council agrees on a planning change from business to residential as it can be proved the pub isn't a viable business. You lost the first chance to redevelop the site when Livvy bought the pub and so you thought you'd intimidate her enough to drive her out, then you could have a second chance to buy it. And at a rock-bottom price.'

Angel had crept to Livvy's side, snuggling into her knee and giving her courage. She found her voice. 'It was *you* rattling the kitchen door in the middle of the night. You slashed the tyres. It was you who painted the word "bitch" on my van? I thought… I thought if we weren't exactly friends then at least you liked coming here.' She put a hand to her mouth. 'And you kept giving me unwanted advice. Confusing me. And I listened because you were a local business owner. A bloody man who knew everything. Oh,' she spat, in furious indignation. 'You wanted me to close the skittles alley!'

Angry and astonished murmurings rippled through the party crowd.

'Old Pete wouldn't be happy about the alley closing down,' Austin huffed.

'He wouldn't be alone there,' one of the Ds added. 'It's the only one round here for miles.'

'I can't believe it was Jason who was scaring our lovely Livvy,' said an appalled Daisy. 'What an absolute arse!'

A slightly drunk Tinkerbell stood up and pointed her wand. 'You stuffed that cat up the chimmley, didn't you?' Jonquil shook her head in disbelief, dislodging her sparkly tiara. 'I knew it! I knew there weren't summat right about it when I came and swept this old chimmley here. It weren't nearly far enough up there. You *killed* a cat to shove up a chimmley?'

There were horrified gasps.

Jason laughed derisively. 'It was roadkill, dear woman. Long since dead.'

'It was someone's pet,' Jonquil roared, she was being held back by her husband. 'Decent folk would have taken it to the vet to have the chip checked. You bollocking bastard!'

'That really upset me, Jason.' Livvy reached for Angel, taking comfort in the dog's nose nuzzling into her hand. 'That poor, poor cat. It preyed on my mind for ages.'

'As it was meant to,' Jason snorted.

Mark swallowed his anger, his fists balled. He shot her a concerned look. 'It's worse than that, I'm afraid. As well as the vandalism and the campaign to unnerve you, I suspect Jason's been orchestrating other things.' He wheeled round to Gerry who was swaying slightly, pint in hand. Mark fixed his gaze on a red-faced Eli. 'It's only a hunch but I think Jason has been encouraging Gerry's lot to come in here. And, Eli, they've been extorting you to give them drinks on the house, haven't they? It's only a guess but that looked to be the case. It's why your profits haven't matched up, Livvy.'

'I'm so sorry, Livvy,' Eli began to shake, tears not far off. Lucie went to him and put an arm round his shoulders. 'They threatened to do me over if I didn't give them what they wanted.' His face crumpled. 'I didn't know Jason was behind it, I swear.'

'You got a bunch of middle-aged men to bully a teenaged boy?' Lucie hissed at Jason. 'And you, Gerry. How could you?'

Gerry shrugged drunkenly. 'Didn't mean no harm. Put in a few shifts on Jason's building site and he said was I interested in another little earner on the side. Paid to drink for free in a pub? No brainer.'

'It's stealing, Gerry,' Livvy said quietly. 'You were not only intimidating a member of my staff, but you were also stealing from me.'

'Ah, Livvy, babe. Wouldn't have done anything to the boy. He's me own flesh and blood.'

'I'd like you and your friends to leave my pub now,' Livvy hissed. 'I will tolerate no one, *no one* you understand, intimidating and bullying any member of my staff. You're barred. For life.'

'Get out,' Karl roared. 'Get out now.'

'I'll just finish me pint,' Gerry slurred. He didn't have time, his feet lifted off the ground as Karl took one arm and the newly arrived Darrell took the other.

'You heard what Livvy said. You're barred,' Karl yelled. 'We don't want your sort in Lullbury Bay.' To boos and applause, Gerry was 'escorted' out, his pals following on.

Livvy shook her head at Jason. 'Why? Why would you do that?'

He raised one pale brow, shrugging carelessly. 'Fun. Because I could. Because if word spread that you were serving obnoxious drunks other customers would stay away.' He turned on Mark. 'You'd better have firm evidence of all you've accused me of. You'll be hearing from my solicitor first thing in the new year.'

Mark made a violent movement towards him but was blocked by Simona. 'I'm not sure it'll get that far, Jason sweetie,' she said, gesturing to the room. 'We have fifty or so witnesses to Gerry's confession. As for the rest of it, we'll hand over the evidence to the police and they'll take it from there.' She shrugged her thin shoulders. 'And if it doesn't reach court, I rather think it won't matter. Your reputation in this town is shot, isn't it, darling? I don't think you'll ever work in Lullbury Bay again.'

'And the customers didn't stay away, did they?' Fabio suddenly spoke up. 'We've been more or less solidly booked since we opened. People like what we do here, they like Livvy and the food and the welcome.'

'We do!' Austin yelled. 'We liked the board games afternoon too.' There were cheers.

'The mince pies were delicious.' This was from Aggie. 'I had twelve.'

'Oh, so our much-lauded chef speaks. Got anything else to add, Fabio, or should I say, Fred?' Jason sneered. 'About your role in my little scheme? I mean, after all, if we're in the mood for confessions, we may as well have yours. Don't you think your boss has a right to know who she employed?'

'Fabio?' Livvy turned to him. She wasn't sure how much more she could take.

Fabio let loose a violent-sounding stream of Italian. '*Bastardo. Si,* I'll come clean.' He nodded urgently, then sucked in a breath, his nostrils flaring. He took Livvy's hands. 'It's what I was trying to tell you earlier. Jason wants everyone evicted from the flats where my mama lives. It's another of his redevelopment schemes. Only she's refusing to leave. He said if I took this job, he'd hold off until she…' he paused and swallowed, unable to say the words.

'Oh, Fabio, that's awful. But I don't get it,' Livvy was baffled. 'I mean that's a truly horrible, vile thing for him to say but–' she let the sentence trail as understanding dawned. 'You promised to sabotage the restaurant in return.' Her eyes widened in shock and she felt her gorge rise. At her side, Angel sensed her distress and whimpered.

Fabio nodded hopelessly. 'But, when it came to it, I couldn't do it.'

'Professional pride?' Livvy couldn't hide the derision. She didn't believe him. She snatched her hands from his.

'Of course. Livvy, I beg you to believe me. I couldn't risk my reputation.' He shrugged hopelessly. 'I had ideas, made plans but I couldn't see them through. I had my status as a chef to protect, yes, but it was more than that. Right from the start, I came to admire what you were trying to do here.' He looked at her from under thick dark lashes. 'I came to admire… you.'

Livvy heard Simona give a little hiccough of distress.

'Think it's time you went, Jason,' Mark said, hard steel in his voice. 'Because if you don't,' at this he gazed speculatively at those behind him, the partygoers looked murderous, 'I may not be able to guarantee your safety.' Somehow Mark's words, uttered with quiet warning, held more menace than if he'd yelled.

'A lynch mob?' Jason sneered.

Karl and Darrell took an arm each, ready to march him out, just as they had done with Gerry.

'Get your hands off me,' Jason bit out. 'Or–'

'Or what, Jason?' Mark asked. 'You'll call the police? I think they'd be very interested in what we have to say.'

Muttering, Jason grabbed his Father Christmas coat and

strode out. Karl and Darrell followed. The pub erupted into jeers and boos.

Livvy's throat constricted with tears. It was too much. It was all too much. Her vision dimmed and she swayed. Vaguely aware of supporting hands leading her, she sank into a chair. In the distance she heard Brittany snap into action and say, 'Party's over, darlings. No more drama. Off you go. Time to go home. Oh look at the snow! Get home safe and Happy Christmas!'

CHAPTER 37

Hot strong tea with sugar – good for shock

Someone had made Livvy a cup of tea which she clutched to her. Angel was a heavy weight on her feet as they sat in front of the wood burner soaking up its comfort. Michael Bublé crooned in the background about it being a cold December night and the team, with a few stragglers, were tidying up the paper streamers and discarded party hats.

It felt as if Christmas had been and gone, had been a tremendous disappointment, and with only the emptiness of the in-between days to come. Livvy struggled to remember it was still actually only Christmas Eve. So much had happened.

'Well, that was quite the night, kitten.' Simona was keeping her company, nursing her own mug of tea. She gave her silvery laugh, but it came out high-pitched and brittle. 'What a truly odious man. And there he was, dressed as Father Christmas too. Don't think he'd recognise the Christmas spirit even if it jumped up and slapped him in the face like a wet haddock.'

Livvy managed a weak giggle.

'I mean, I only know the story from the Muppet Christmas Carol, and Scrooge was the baddie in that, but at least *he* came good in the end. Don't think the same will ever be said of Jason Lemmon.'

'Verity's message in her church service was to forgive but I think it'll be a long time before I even think about forgiving him.' Livvy blew out a breath, beginning to feel more like herself.

'Quite right too, sweetie. Don't think the man deserves it. And Verity would agree, she's realistic like that.' Simona leaned forward. 'Tell you what though, darling. What did demonstrate the meaning of Christmas was how much everyone was supporting you. They were backing you to the hilt tonight. When Mark ordered Jason to leave, he hesitated, took one look at the crowd and then legged it. He was lucky to get out alive.'

'And that definitely wouldn't have been very Christmassy.'

Simona tittered. 'Hardly.'

'Can't say there's been a dull moment since I took over The George. But, Simona, how can I thank you? Staking out the car park. It must have been freezing.'

Simona gave her trademark silvery giggle again, this time sounding more normal. 'It was tonight, sweetie.' She indicated her Marilyn Monroe dress. 'I wasn't quite dressed for sub-zero temperatures. Have you seen the snow out there? It's really coming down now. Think we might have The Beast from the East Mark II after all.'

'It was brilliant what you and Mark did. I'm so grateful, Si, or I will be when this has all sunk in.' Livvy shook her head. 'I can't believe the lengths Jason was prepared to go to.'

'Lot of money at stake. Don't get me wrong, kitten, I'm rather a fan of the filthy lucre myself but there are limits as to what I'll do to get it.' Simona sipped her tea thoughtfully. 'And in my opinion, I think he rather gets off tormenting folk. I expect he pulled wings off butterflies as a child. He's the sort. Ugh!'

'I just hope that's the last we see of him.' Livvy shuddered. 'Hateful man.'

'I don't think we'll see him in town again. The good folk of Lullbury Bay may be, on the whole, an unsophisticated lot, but they're loyal and on your side. His line of business depends on networking. Word will soon get round, darling. And, as I said to him, even if it doesn't get as far as anything legal, it'll affect his business and that's where it'll hit him where it hurts most.'

Livvy sucked in a breath. 'And I'm sorry about, you know, what Fabio said. I had no idea that's how he felt about me.'

'Didn't you, angel? It had crossed my mind. I often wondered how he felt about you, whether it went above and beyond how a chef should feel about his boss. The fabulous Fabio always seemed more authentic, somehow, when he was around you. The excitable Italian chef act wasn't as quite to the fore.'

'I'm not sure what I'm going to do about him.' Livvy blew out a regretful sigh. 'I mean, he's gorgeous and, in anyone's eyes, someone you–'

'–wouldn't kick out of bed,' Simona finished.

'Sorry. Didn't mean to rub it in.'

'You're not, darling. I suggest you talk to the man. Thrash it all out, so to speak. And I'm not surprised you didn't notice how he was around you. You've been so engrossed in your lovely Mark. No room for anyone else.'

'And I need to apologise about that too.' Livvy winced. 'I spent the best part of this evening thinking really dreadful things about you. First, I thought you'd hit on Darrell and then I thought you'd been snogging in the car park with Mark like teenagers. I'm so sorry. I feel awful.'

'Oh, darling,' Simona roared. 'Chance would be a fine thing. No one notices me when you're around. I think the entire male population of Lullbury Bay is in love with you. And who can blame them? You might even be successful in turning me!' She blew a kiss with her still perfectly glossed lips to soften the words. 'But onwards and upwards. I did like… I *do* like Fabio,' she corrected herself. 'But maybe it's for the best. He's far younger and it would only have been a flingette sort of thing. Probably not what I need right now.' She pulled a comical face. 'But, then again, maybe I'll chance upon a hot ski instructor in Klosters?'

Livvy laughed. 'I hope so.'

'Although no one will ever replace my Terence.' Simona lapsed into silence, her mouth working, trying to control the emotion.

'I know.' Livvy reached for her hand. 'Come round tomorrow. Can't promise any food but we can have a drink. I don't want you to be on your own.'

Simona patted her hand, her eyes tearful. 'I will, darling. Thank you.'

'Oh my goodness,' Livvy was suddenly aware of the mess. 'I'd better help with the clearing up. Look at the state of this place!'

'You stay there, sweetie. I'll go.' Simona gazed ruefully at her manicure. 'I've managed to break a nail tonight, so it won't matter about the others.' Bending down to tickle Angel's ears, she said, 'Look after your mistress, darling doggie. She needs TLC.'

Livvy wasn't alone long. Eli hovered, shifting his weight from foot to foot. 'I wanted to say sorry,' he said on a gulping breath.

Livvy looked up. His face still bore the lumpy, reddened marks of distress. Even though Eli was heading to nineteen, he was still such a child. 'Eli, I'm the one who's sorry. I've been so preoccupied with everything I didn't notice how unhappy you've been. I knew Gerry and his lot were causing you problems, but I mistakenly thought you were handling them. I should have checked up on you. Sit down here for a minute.'

He perched on the very edge of the chair. Angel stretched. Going to him, she nuzzled into his hand until he gave in and scratched her ears. 'I'll pay you back what they owe.'

'Oh, Eli, that won't be necessary. I'm just thankful to have found what was causing the discrepancy. We've been so busy I just couldn't understand how we weren't making a bigger profit. My bad. I need to be more on top of things.'

'No! You're brilliant. It was my fault. I should never have given in to them.'

'They're playground bullies,' Livvy said gently. 'They know what to say to get what they want. And stupid too. I can't believe Gerry confessed straight away about what Jason made him do. If I hadn't been in shock I would have found it almost funny.'

Eli's mouth twisted. 'I suppose I'll be getting the sack now.'

'Do you want to carry on working here?'

He nodded violently. 'I love it here. I mean I know I've got a lot to learn but I really like it. It's well cool.' His eyes strayed to Brittany who was laughing at something Simona said.

Livvy's lips twitched. Eli would have to get a whole load more world weary before he tackled Brittany. 'Then you can keep your job—'

'Oh, Livvy, that's so great!'

'Hold on, before you get too excited, you have to promise me something.'

Eli nodded eagerly. 'What?'

'That, if you're unsure about anyone, or someone makes you feel uncomfortable or puts pressure on you, you come straight to me. Understood?'

'Understood. I promise you, Liv, I won't let you down again. And it's way cool, I mean, really good of you.'

'Well, Verity the vicar drummed the message of forgiveness into me at the church service so I'm trying to put it into practice.'

Eli leaped up, went with an impulse and kissed her cheek, blushed furiously and went.

Livvy stared into the flames for a moment, bone-weary. Eli made her feel old. Gathering what was left of her strength, she stood up. That was the Eli problem sorted and she'd apologised and thanked Simona so that left one more person. Collecting their discarded mugs, she went into the kitchen where, as expected, Fabio and Stewie were cleaning up. Bay Radio played 'Happy Xmas, War is Over' softly in the background.

They really ought to update their playlist. The inconsequential thought came out of nowhere. *But it's the season for cheesy Christmas songs and this one's weirdly appropriate for a night like this.* She hoped whatever war Jason had waged on her was truly over. 'Stewie, would you mind going into the bar and collecting some glasses? And shove the first lot in the washer, will you? Oh, and don't forget to pick up your envelope with your Christmas tips. It's behind the till.'

'Sweet. Will do. Cheers, Livvy. Happy Christmas.'

'Happy Christmas, Stewie, and thanks for all your hard work.'

She waited until he'd gone through to the bar. Outside, the car park was in blackness. The security lights came on, making her flinch, but it was only Karl putting the empties into the bottle recycling bank. The noise thundered through the tension as she faced Fabio. 'Fabio?' she began.

He put up his hands in defence. 'No, let me start. I have much to say. I promise you, even though the intent was to sabotage the restaurant, over order stock, incorrectly charge, mess about with the invoices, that sort of thing–'

Livvy's eyes widened. 'I had no idea.'

'I did nothing.' Fabio stabbed the air. 'Nothing. *Niente.* Not even right at the start.' He agitated his head from side to side. 'Well, I admit to a tiny bit of over-ordering at first, but I soon stopped that.' He threw a cleaning cloth onto the aluminium prep surface. 'Even though that man,' he pointed an aggressive finger towards the bar, 'harassed and bullied me, just as he has been doing to Mama. I couldn't do it. I couldn't serve substandard food or send out service lukewarm or badly seasoned. I have too much pride in what I do. In my art.'

Livvy sank down onto a stool. Flailing for a response, she opened her mouth, but his torrent of words continued.

'From the first, from the very first, when I cooked you that tasting menu, I knew I could make this place a success. I believed in you.' This time the finger stabbed towards Livvy. 'So I vowed I would never compromise my cooking or this restaurant. Never!'

'I can't believe Jason asked you to do all that,' she murmured. 'The man is despicable.'

Fabio's response was to flick his thumb from his teeth, which Livvy was pretty sure was his definitive judgement on Jason Lemmon. She could but wholly agree. 'In which case, I must thank you for not bowing down to the bullying. You could have ruined The George all too easily. I'm so grateful, Fabio, you must believe that.'

'I did nothing. I cooked, I created, but I would never sabotage what we have here. I wouldn't do that to you. I knew you had the vision for it. I knew The George would be superb. With my cooking and your vision.'

'I'm not sure I agree with that.' Livvy sighed. 'The vision bit, I mean. I've spent the last three months agonising over exactly what I wanted to achieve with The George.'

'You're too close to it. It's evolved organically.' He gave an Italian shrug. 'You have somewhere people want to come to drink and socialise, a community base,' Fabio's voice was heated. 'Even a thriving skittle alley, although I'm mystified by the appeal.' He paused, then added with emphasis, 'And a restaurant everyone is talking about.'

'And that's down to you.'

Fabio ignored the comment, continuing passionately. 'In three months you have achieved all of this! You're too modest, you don't believe in yourself enough. You don't see yourself,' he prodded his chest with a thumb, 'how I see you.'

Livvy bit her lip. He was getting more Italian with every sentence. 'Can I... Can I rely on you to stay? Do you want to continue here?'

'Of course.' Fabio looked surprised. 'Unless you feel it's not right. It's true I have to earn back your trust, I appreciate that.'

'I don't think you ever lost it, Fabio,' Livvy said softly. 'You haven't done anything wrong. I didn't mean that though. Earlier on you said, you hinted you–'

'I have feelings for you.' He sucked in a great breath, staring down at the gleaming work surface. A muscle in his cheek worked violently. 'I fell for you when we drank cognac and renamed the pub. Yes, that long ago.' He lifted his gaze to meet hers. 'But I see how Mark looks at you. I see how you light up when he's near. I know when it's hopeless. That there can never be a me and you.'

For the second time Livvy was silenced. 'Then how can you work here feeling like that?'

'Because I'm a professional. And I think too much of you to leave you without a chef. Stewie will be good once he's trained but he's not anywhere near my standard yet.'

That ego again. Livvy felt a smile twitch about her lips. 'You'll stay then?'

Fabio nodded. 'I'll stay. Same as before. I'm here while my mama is sick.' He sucked his teeth. 'And when the worst happens, I'll work out as much notice as you need to find a replacement. That is my promise. My word.'

The relief was enormous. 'No one could replace you, Fab.'

'This is true.'

'What's going to happen about your mum's flat?'

'She's got tenant's rights but doesn't want to stay there knowing that man is around. Mark's looking into finding her somewhere, maybe in an assisted care unit.'

'He's a good kind man.'

'A good man, full stop. Don't let him get away, Livvy.'

'Trouble is, Fab, I think we're destined to be just friends. I don't think he feels any other way about me. I think Mark and me are friends. Nothing more.'

CHAPTER 38

Flat white – espresso based coffee made with steamed milk,
deceptively strong

'You taking my name in vain?'

Livvy ran to Mark, like an arrow seeking its target. She felt his arms enfold her as he hugged her to him. He smelled of the cold, of snow and Christmas. It didn't matter how he felt about her. At this precise moment in time the only embrace she wanted was his.

Above her head she heard him say, 'Oh, you off, Fabio? Well, yes, it's been quite the evening. Thank you for everything. Night, mate.'

And then Mark led her back to the stool where she sat feeling exhausted, self-conscious, overwhelmed and about a hundred other emotions. She watched as he expertly made coffee on Fabio's new machine. They didn't talk until he put a mug in front of her. He sat on another stool on the opposite side of the work prep station. Far too far away. 'Happy Xmas, War is Over' had finished long ago and was replaced by 'It'll Be Lonely This Christmas'. She really hoped it wasn't an omen. Could she risk telling him how she felt? What if he just wanted friendship? An awkward one-sided relationship was a sure way to misery; she wasn't sure she could be as pragmatic as Fabio.

'Karl's taken the kids home,' the love of her life said matter-of-factly.

'Kids?'

'Sorry. I think of them as the kids. Shouldn't really. I mean Stewie, Brittany and Eli. And I walked Simona round to her door. She said she'd be back tomorrow. Everything's tidied and locked up. Even Austin helped out although I got an eyeful when he bent over to pick up some party popper streamers. I don't think I'll ever recover.'

'Why?'

'He'd gone commando tonight. There was nothing under that Fred Flintstone costume apart from what nature endowed. It's put me off pickled eggs for life.'

Livvy managed a giggle.

'Oh, and Angel's been taken out for her late-night visit to the garden. Absolutely nothing out of the ordinary to report from the car park. Well, apart from the snow, of course.'

'Thank you. That was kind.' God, this was stilted. Why couldn't she look at him? She was like a teenager with a crush. But this was worse. Far worse. With the same hollow dropping out of the stomach you get when you miss the last step running downstairs, she grasped she was hopelessly, irrevocably, deeply in love with him. After a long pause, she said, 'Shouldn't you be getting back to Nats?'

'She's gone to our neighbour's. They were doing Christmas cocktails. Heavy on the schnapps knowing Vince and Queenie.'

'And you've missed it. And you won't be able to get to your parents for Christmas. And it's all my fault.'

A smile played about his mouth. 'Vince and Queenie are

lovely people but are best savoured in small doses. I can catch up with them on Boxing Day. And, as for driving up to Yorkshire, have you had a proper look outside lately?'

Livvy shook her head.

'We've had about a foot in the last hour. Even if I'd got the tyres fixed and the windscreen replaced, the only way I'm getting up the hill and out of Lullbury Bay is in a 4x4.' He blew on his coffee to cool it. 'And who says I want to get out anyway?' he said neutrally.

'Your parents will be devastated not to have you home for Christmas.'

'They understand. They'd rather I was safe and not there than skidding into a snowdrift. My aunt and uncle and their children will be with them tomorrow, so they won't be on their own.'

'I'm so sorry.'

'You keep apologising, it's turning into a bad habit. Why are you sorry?'

'If I'd kept a closer eye on everything, I could have got the truth out of Eli, communicated better with poor Fab, sussed out Jason bloody Lemmon, avoided getting your lovely car ruined and saved you all the trouble of having to stake out the car park.'

Mark's eyes twinkled. 'It was no trouble,' he said softly. 'Not for you. For what it's worth, I don't think there was anything you could have done. That Jason bloody Lemmon is a smooth operator,' he added, anger warming his voice.

'Did you know Karl caught him snooping around in the bar once?' Livvy began, as the memory flooded back. 'Think it was the night of the fireworks party.' She put a hand to her mouth in horror. 'Must have been the night he put that poor cat up the chimney.' She shook her head. 'I still can't believe he went to such lengths, to be so extreme about it.' She pulled a disgusted face. 'To pick a dead cat up off the road and put it up a chimney! Ugh.'

'Stuff of nightmares, I agree, but he stood to make millions out of redeveloping the two sites. Prime residential land. Fabulous views, not too far out of town.' Mark's lips pursed. 'There would have been no decent pub nearby though. I wouldn't have bought one of his penthouses.' He put his mug down decisively. 'But forgive me, I'd rather not talk about that man anymore.'

'Why?' At the look in his hazel eyes, Livvy's heart leaped into her throat.

'Because, if you didn't mind, I'd very much like to take you to bed.'

'Oh,' she croaked, glancing at the kitchen clock. Elvis had shifted into 'Have Yourself a Merry Little Christmas' and Judy Garland's achingly melancholy voice promised sweetness. 'Yes, it's late. Nearly Christmas Day. I need sleep, especially after what's happened tonight.'

'I hadn't planned on getting much sleep.'

'Oh.' It seemed the only word Livvy could utter. Was he suggesting what she thought he was?

'Look, I'm going to say it because if I don't, I never will.' Mark's words tumbled out. 'And if you feel otherwise then I won't darken your door again, won't ever mention it, won't get in the way of whatever you want to do with your life, be it with Fabio or Eli or Karl or even Silent Ernie, or any of the other men you have trailing after you. Not that I blame them. I mean, you're stunning and kind and hardworking and conscientious and–'

'Karl's married,' Livvy interrupted. 'And very happily. Not sure about Silent Ernie. Think he might be in a deep and profound relationship with his tractor. Eli's far too young and Fabio is–'

'Extremely good-looking, charismatic and talented, and you and he make an amazing team.' Mark gave her a shuttered look from under dark lashes.

'Except.'

'Except what, Livvy?'

'What was that thing you were going to say to me? I'm not sure you ever did actually say it.'

Mark bit his lip. A lock of glossy red-brown hair fell over his face. He flicked it back irritably, a flush staining his cheeks. 'Got nothing to lose now, have I?'

He sounded almost cheerful, but Livvy could tell he was nervous. She realised she knew him better than she'd known anyone. His easy-going, unruffled nature, the way the expressions shifted over his mobile face, that he was sometimes too vain to admit to needing glasses, the innate kindness that ran through him like letters through seaside rock. His were the only hugs she wanted, she craved to be near enough to inhale the delicious way he smelled, to listen out to how his flat northern vowels slipped out occasionally. The way he quietly and effortlessly got on with whatever was needed. Tonight was the first time she'd seen him truly rattled. It had been both shocking and strangely erotic.

'I love you, Livvy. I know this may be pointless, and I have no hopes of you ever reciprocating but, as I just said, if I don't say it now I never will. Maybe it's the drama of the night. Maybe it's because everyone else has been confessing stuff so I thought I'd get mine out there too. And you looking drop-dead gorgeous in that dress. I mean, you're such a beautiful woman, Livvy.' He huffed out a breath. 'But I know you see us as friends, you've said it often enough, and I can promise you that can carry on, if it's what you want. But I'd hoped, maybe... it's just that you're a really difficult person to read sometimes and I keep questioning if I was actually getting friend vibes or,' he looked up and stopped as he realised she'd interrupted. 'What did you say?'

'I said I love you too, Mark. I love you very much. I don't want us to be friends. Well, I do, but as well. As well as being lovers.'

'Oh.' This time it was Mark's turn to go monosyllabic. He cleared his throat. 'Wow. Wasn't expecting that. What are we going to do about it?'

Livvy put her head on one side. 'I think, about three cheesy Christmas songs on Bay Radio ago, you said something about taking me to bed?' She held out her hand, palm uppermost, inviting. 'I can't think of anything I'd like better.'

Mark rose. He came round to her side of the worktable. 'I was chancing my arm when I said that.' He pulled a rueful face. 'Trying to be the alpha male. I thought, with Fabio around and everything, you like that sort of thing. I'm sorry. It was horribly presumptuous.'

Livvy stood up. 'This time it's you who mustn't be sorry.' She put her arms around his neck breathing in his cedar and amber scent, pulling him into her. 'I liked it. But don't be an alpha male.' She pressed herself against him, her breath catching as his hands found her naked back. 'You'll do as you are, believe me. I don't need an alpha male. I need you. You kind, funny, glorious man. Kiss me, Mark Cavanagh.'

Bay Radio began to play The Carpenters' 'Merry Christmas Darling'.

'They *really* ought to update their playlist,' Livvy murmured and then, when Mark's lips met hers, she lost all power of rational thought.

The kiss was everything they wanted, had longed for. And more. To the sound of Karen Carpenter's sultry voice they kissed, mouths and fingers exploring one another... Eventually breaking apart, they stared at one another, amazed at what they'd just created.

'Bloody hell,' Mark said, sounding very Yorkshire.

'I know. Wow.' Livvy answered, barely coherent. 'Now let's go to bed.' She sighed. 'Please.'

CHAPTER 39

*L*ivvy woke early on Christmas Day. Slipping out of bed quietly so as not to disturb a sleeping Mark, she padded downstairs to let Angel out.

Opening the kitchen door the cold, and the pink-streaked dawn sky took her breath away. Angel leaped into the snow and disappeared. The dog emerged shaking her head, gave a joyful bark and bounded around to the beer garden. Livvy watched her, concerned, but the springer played happily.

When it had begun, the unpromising thin flakes of snow hadn't looked as if it would amount to much, but it had fallen steadily. Snow coated the car park turning it into a winter wonderland, magically hiding the reminders of their enemy's work. Her work van was camouflaged against the wall where the wind had blown a four-foot drift and Mark's Mercedes was an unidentifiable white blob. It must have snowed throughout the night, not that she and Mark had noticed. Livvy hugged herself. It had been perfect. Mark had been as kind and thoughtful as a lover as he was as a friend. Only *so* much sexier. She gulped as a little aftershock of pleasure shot through her. He'd surprised her. Easy-going Mark had turned out to be quite something in bed. He had more of the alpha male in him than he thought. She giggled.

Staring at the view beyond the car park, contentment blanketed her. The sun was low but bright, making the snow gleam and sparkle. Tendrils of mist floated low over a denim blue sea and a few gulls wheeled, calling and cackling, joyfully riding a thermal. It was Christmas Day, and the world was at peace. Despite, or perhaps because of, what had happened, Livvy still loved this view. She'd had many moments where she'd doubted herself and her sanity in taking on The George. Staring at this view and its ever-changing beauty, she felt it was a true privilege to live and work here. She sucked in a great breath of fresh salty air and then coughed a little as its frigidity hit her lungs. Her feet were solid blocks of ice. Calling Angel in, she retreated to the warm kitchen and clicked on the kettle.

The springer found Mark before Livvy got to him.

'Ow. Dog. Get off me. I'm not awake!'

Livvy put the tea tray down and hauled Angel off the bed. 'Sorry. She's excited by all the snow. It must be three feet out there and deeper where it's drifted. I've brought tea and toast.'

Mark sat up, his hair ruffled and his hazel eyes gleaming. 'Could you get any more perfect? Come here so I can kiss you.' Pulling her on top of him, he kissed her hungrily. The tea forgotten, Angel taking advantage, stole a slice of toast off the plate and scampered away.

Later, much later, after showering and making fresh tea and toast, they sat in the kitchen listening to Bay Radio. This morning it was wall to wall traditional carols.

'"Silent Night". Your favourite,' Mark said, grinning lovingly at her.

Livvy kissed him. 'I love that you remember things like that.' Then her phone trilled, interrupting them. 'Excuse me,' she said, a crease of worry appearing on her forehead. 'I need to take this.'

'Everything okay?'

'Not sure. It's my mother. Bit odd, it's usually Dad who rings.' She took the phone into the bar. It was cold, they hadn't yet got around to lighting the wood burner. Livvy switched on the Christmas tree and the fairy lights around the bar to brighten the place. From the kitchen she could hear Mark singing along to the carol. From the accompanying clatters and bangs it sounded as if he was washing up.

'Mum. Hi.'

'Olivia, darling. Happy Christmas.'

'Happy Christmas. Are you both okay?'

'We're fine. Having the most marvellous time. In port, so taking advantage of a phone line and wanted to wish you season's greetings.'

'That's lovely. You worried me. I thought something was wrong.'

'I'm sorry, darling. There's really absolutely nothing to worry about. We're both fighting fit and enjoying ourselves. I just wanted to talk to you about something. How's everything at The George?'

Livvy gave a short laugh. 'Eventful but I'll fill you in when we have more time to talk.'

'Are you all right?'

'All good here. In fact,' Livvy paused as she listened to Mark cooing over Angel, 'everything is perfect. Better than perfect.'

'How very intriguing. I sincerely hope the better than perfect involves a man called Mark?'

'I'll fill you in on that later too but yes.' Livvy perched on a bar stool, wishing she'd brought her mug of tea through. This was turning out to be an unusually long call from her mother.

'I'm *so* pleased. I didn't spend much time with him, but your father has been singing his praises. Jolly well done, Olivia. And now, onto the reason I'm calling. Your father and I were so impressed by what you're doing with The George. I know I didn't say much but it was such a busy time and we had to dash off so early to get to Southampton. You know how I despise being late for things and one thing that doesn't wait is a departing cruise ship. Couldn't afford to miss it, darling.'

Her mother sounded nervous. Weird.

'Oh I'm prattling on, I knew your father should have made this call but he did so insist I do it.'

Livvy could hear her take a deep breath.

'We haven't given you a Christmas present because we were thinking over what the right thing was to do and we've decided.'

'Decided what, Mum?'

'We've decided, if you'd like it of course, to give you The Olde Gates.'

Livvy couldn't speak. No matter how hard she tried her mother's last sentence wouldn't compute and no sound would emerge in response.

'We thought about selling it, darling, but decided not to. We want it to go to a family member, Olivia, and, after seeing how successful you're making The George, think you'd be the perfect person to run it. And don't worry, we'd be completely hands off. We realised rather late, or I did I suppose, that you quite rightly wanted to carve your own path in the industry. We were the same when we started up and I was stupid not to grasp you'd be just like us.'

Penny paused. Livvy had the feeling it was to get her breath. The words had come out all in a rush.

'We're so alike, you and I,' her mother continued. 'I think that's why we clash. Although I think you're a far better manager than I ever was. Quicker to praise. That doesn't come easily to me, I'm afraid, my darling. I need to do better at that.'

Livvy still couldn't utter a word. Was her mother on something? As a *volte-face* it was nothing less than a Christmas miracle.

'I promise you The Olde Gates will be yours and yours alone. To sell if that's what you want. But I think, having seen The George, that you'd like to do the same but on a bigger scale. Brian says the only thing he's asking for is an occasional shift behind the bar in your pub. He did so love it when we stayed. You don't have to decide now, of course, but we need to know in the new year. If you don't want it, we'll put it on the open market then. So, my darling, have a very wonderful Christmas. Are you open today?'

Livvy was stunned. Finally finding her voice, she responded. 'I had planned to open for lunchtime drinks, but we've had heavy snow. Looks like the town is snowed in. Even if they wanted to, I don't think any customers will get here.'

'Sounds fun. Sounds very Christmassy. Must go. I'm heading into yoga in a mo. And we're on the Captain's table for dinner tonight so I need to get myself all spruced up for that. The officers are all waiting on us as is the tradition on Christmas Day.'

'Enjoy. Happy Christmas, Mummy.' The childish endearment slipped out. 'And, well, thank you. Send my love to Dad.'

'Will do.'

And then the line went dead.

She was still sitting, open-mouthed, on the bar stool when Mark came through, Angel at his heels. He took one look at Livvy and said, 'Are you all right, love? It wasn't bad news, was it?'

She shook her head, staring at him. Blinking rapidly, she tried to make sense of what her mother had just said. 'Mum and Dad want me to have The Olde Gates,' she began slowly. At his blank look she went on. 'It's their hotel in the Cotswolds. The one they've kept going having sold the ones in Rome, Venice and Berlin.' She paused and said on a long exhale, 'They want me to take it over.'

Mark pulled up a stool next to her. 'What will you do?'

'I have absolutely no idea. They've promised to be completely hands off so I could do anything I like with it.'

'And it's important that you're independent of them, isn't it?'

Livvy nodded, grateful for his understanding.

'No Jason Lemmon interfering either.'

'Thank goodness.' She laughed drily. 'Even his influence doesn't extend that far north. It would be a lot to take on though, Mark. Eighteen rooms, and a restaurant with a hundred covers. Not to mention the function suite. I could do weddings. Fabio would really be in his element. He could re-establish his name.'

'Lots to think about.'

'Lots.' She frowned. 'What's that noise? Sounds like an engine. I didn't think any traffic could get up or down the hill.' Angel ran into the kitchen barking furiously. They followed and opened the door.

'Hi, guys,' Nats said. 'I got a ride down on Silent Ernie's tractor. Happy Christmas!'

CHAPTER 40

Snowball – the classic Christmas cocktail made with advocaat, lime and lemonade. Add a glace cherry for retro appeal.

From then on, it was a constant stream of visitors.

Karl popped by with his wife on his way to his in-laws. They'd walked all the way dressed in thick boots, woolly hats and bulky coats. Standing at the kitchen door, he handed over a card saying, 'Happy Christmas, Livvy. We couldn't pass without stopping to wish you season's greetings.' He harrumphed, looking embarrassed. 'And wanted to say I'm sorry for not keeping a closer eye on Eli.'

She flung her arms around him, hugging him tightly. 'Oh, Karl, don't be sorry. It was all my fault.'

'Wasn't your fault,' Jen, Karl's wife, declared fiercely. 'It was that bugger Jason. Just hope it don't put you off running The George. My Karl's been that happy working here.'

'I'm the one who's lucky to have him working for me, Jen.' Livvy ran to the bar to retrieve an envelope. It contained Karl's share of the Christmas tips. 'Thank you for all your hard work. It wouldn't have been the same without you.' She pressed it into his hand. 'Happy Christmas, both. Take care walking down the hill and have a lovely day with your family.'

'We'll be okay,' Karl responded. 'Silent Ernie's giving us a lift into town. He's going to try to clear the worst of the snow on the main road so folk can get in and out. Happy Christmas, Livvy!'

Livvy shoved on some boots, threw on a coat and followed them out. They watched as Silent Ernie manoeuvred his tractor back out of the car park, its enormous tyres leaving three-foot-deep gouges in the snow. She smiled as she saw the cab was festooned with tinsel and fairy lights. It seemed a long time ago, and in another life, that she'd been hoisted up in the cherry picker. Glancing up at the lights, switched on for Christmas Day, she realised it might be the only way to get them back down again. Waving them off she was just about to join in with Mark, Nats and a white fur-coated glamorous Simona who were building a snowman in the beer garden, with Angel dancing around them, when Daisy, and Lucie and Eli Wiscombe staggered over.

'Just come up to wish you Happy Christmas,' they chorused, red-faced from the exertion of climbing up the hill in deep snow.

'It's madness in town,' Lucie added. 'People are skiing down the main street and there's snow on the beach. On the beach!' she repeated incredulously. She tugged off her hat and raked a hand through her bright red hair, fluffing it up. 'Never thought I'd say this but, for once, Austin's weather forecast came true. He said it would be a white Christmas and it is. You coming down to join in the fun?'

Livvy shook her head. 'Maybe tomorrow. Looks like I'm hosting Christmas dinner for four.' She pulled a horrified face. 'Just hope they survive my cooking.'

'We'll maybe see you tomorrow then. Don't think this snow is going anywhere any time soon.' Lucie came closer. 'Thank you for giving Eli another chance. Think he's been through hell and back. I knew something was up with him but couldn't figure out what. I'll give him a good talking to after Christmas.'

'No, don't do that.' Livvy watched as Eli, hampered by the snow drifts in the car park, lurched over to greet a just arrived Brittany and Stewie. 'I think he's learned his lesson.'

Lucie gazed at her. 'It hasn't put you off running this place, has it, Livvy? Lullbury Bay would miss The George if you went. Think the town would miss *you* if you went. I know it's not been long, but you've really become part of the community.'

'Lucie's right,' Daisy piped up. 'We want you to stay in Lullbury Bay. I mean where else can I dress up as a fairy? Don't let Jason ruddy Lemmon drive you out. I'd miss you if you went.'

Livvy didn't have time to answer as Brittany began a vicious snowball fight against the boys. She looked at them. 'Think Eli and Stewie need help. Up for a challenge?'

Screaming a battle cry, they went in on full attack.

'Sweetie, you've got snow all over your coat,' Simona said, as she, Livvy, Mark and Nats made their exhausted way back inside. The others had gone, after a snowball fight which recognised no rules. 'Let me get it off you.' She began to beat snow off Livvy's back. The snowball fight had got out of hand with them all joining in, and with Bee from the bookshop turning up. She'd brought an old-fashioned wooden sledge and, having squeezed Daisy behind her, had whizzed off down the hill.

'Thanks, Si. Ssh, Angel, stop barking. Ugh. My hair's soaking. Is that the landline ringing? Go into the bar everyone and make yourself a drink. I need to get lunch sorted.' Livvy escaped her coat and ran to get the phone.

'*Buon Natale, bella!* I've been trying your mobile but there was no answer.'

'Fabio! Happy Christmas. We've all been outside having a monumental snowball fight. Are you having a good day? Did you get home okay last night? The snow was really bad.'

'Took a while, babe, but got home eventually. Not going anywhere today though. Just me and Mama and a turkey big enough for a football team.'

'I forgot to give out everyone's Christmas tips last night. I was in such a state. Only Stewie picked up his and I've given Karl's his today.'

'It'll keep. I'll be back in the day after Boxing Day.'

'Oh yes, we get a whole two days off and then it all starts again.'

'And you love it,' he accused.

'I do. Have a lovely day. Love to your mum.' She put the phone down only for it to ring again immediately.

'It's Austin and Aggie here wishing The George very warm felicitations. Happy Christmas, Livvy. Hello? Is there anyone there, or am I speaking to an answerphone?'

'Hello, Austin. It's Livvy. A real live person here. Happy Christmas to you both and thank you for supporting The George. And you were absolutely right about the snow.'

'I was.'

'Always a first time,' Aggie cackled in the background.

'Forgive my good lady wife, we're on our second bottle of champagne.'

'Way to go.' Livvy giggled. 'Enjoy and see you both soon.' She put the phone down and texted Yolanda a quick:

> Happy Xmas Day! All gone crazy here. Fill you in asap.

She'd just pressed send when the mobile buzzed. Hearing a pop of a cork and laughter coming from the bar, she murmured, 'My lovely customers, I love you all, but I'd really like to get my own Christmas Day started.' Seeing who it was she had no choice but to answer. 'Morning, Pete. Happy Christmas!'

'Morning, Livvy. Having a rare old time here. Even Skip's behaving. Just thought I'd ring to wish you Happy Christmas, like. Heard all about last night.'

'Already?' Livvy said, startled. 'News travels fast.'

'It do. Never trusted that Jason.'

Livvy could hear Pete sucking his teeth in derision and Skip's faint bark in the distance. 'We've all survived to fight another day but it was quite the drama.'

'And I missed it,' Pete said gloomily. 'Most exciting thing to have happened since Aggie forgot her knickers and flashed the vicar, and I wasn't there.'

Livvy giggled. 'And we missed you. We're keeping your chair warm.'

'Ar. Quite right too. When I gets back I'll sort out a fixtures list for next season's skittles matches.' Skip barked again, this time more loudly. 'I'm coming, boy.'

'About that, Pete,' Livvy began to say but was cut off. She stared thoughtfully at the phone. If she accepted her parents' offer and took over The Olde Gates, would the new owner of The George keep the skittle alley going? How could she let Old Pete down? She thought of all her friends who had made the effort to come to see her today. They hadn't just popped by in the car, they'd tramped through thick snow. Jason Lemmon had attempted to destroy her, but the community had rallied round, in their many different ways, to support her. She knew she couldn't have done it without them. They'd shown her the true meaning of Christmas. A wave of gratitude to them and to the little town of Lullbury Bay overwhelmed her. How could she leave it – and them?

Christmas lunch was a riot. Livvy managed not to mangle the food and the salmon en croute with hollandaise sauce and buttered spinach, while not traditional, were what she found in Fabio's stocks and knew how to heat up. They set up in the bar having put two tables together. With the lights on, the tree giving off warm pine scents and the wood burner lit, was cosy and atmospheric. Nats took charge of Aggie's old-fashioned record player. A medley of classic Christmas hits played in the background, but Frank Sinatra and Dean Martin were mostly drowned out by her indiscreet and hilarious stories about several famous actors.

'Ye gads, I've had the most marvellous Christmas Day,' sighed Simona. 'In fact, I'm being positively greedy. That's my second Christmas lunch this year! A snowball fight, delish food and enough champers to sink a battleship too. Still can't believe Brittany's commitment to that snowball fight. I had to rugby tackle her legs to get her down. Thank you all. Oh, and thank you, Mark,' she added as he brought in the coffee. 'Perfect. Oh goodie, biscotti too.'

Livvy poured the port and then sank back in her chair looking around at her friends. She was deeply content. Three short months ago she hadn't known any of them and now couldn't see herself without them in her life.

'Yes, thank you, Livvy,' Nats groaned. 'I can't believe I ate *three* of those chocolate brownies, and with clotted cream too. I'm going to have to diet from now until June.'

'Well, it wasn't turkey and all the trimmings but hopefully just as nice.'

'Better than nice, Livvy. I'm no fan of plum pudding,' Nats replied. 'And I can live without brandy butter sauce.' Shuddering, she drank down her port in one and held out her glass for a refill. 'I prefer my alcohol unadulterated. I can't believe Brittany, either, Simona. Unerring aim with a snowball. She got me twice right on the head. Certainly made me work up an appetite.'

'I've eaten far too much too,' Livvy said mournfully. 'And I had two breakfasts. Well, Angel ate the first lot of toast as we were,' she caught Mark's eye and blushed, 'otherwise engaged.'

Nats looked from her brother to Livvy. 'Aha!' she exclaimed, slamming her glass down as the penny dropped. 'About time you two got together. He's been banging on about you, Livvy, for the last three months. The lovelorn act has become very boring.'

'Nats,' Mark protested.

Livvy felt her face grow even hotter. 'I thought you didn't tell Nats anything about me?'

Mark didn't get a chance to answer as his sister butted in. 'Didn't tell me anything about you? He's not shut up about you! It's been Livvy this and Livvy that. Oh, she's so gorgeous but why would she have anything to do with an old, divorced bloke like me. On and on. Thank goodness he's finally made a move.'

Simona rescued them. Tottering to her feet, she announced, 'Darlings, I'm exceptionally delighted you've got together too. I can't imagine a better suited pair.' Toasting them, she said, 'Congratulations! And now, Natalie sweetie, I think it's time we left the lovebirds to catch up. It's been quite the hectic day and I'm sure they'd appreciate some alone time. You can come next door with me. I have a big old snuggly sofa, central heating, lots more champers, a bucketful of Hotel Chocolat and the latest Jonathan Bailey film.'

Nats managed to sit up. 'That's only just been released.' Heaving herself up, she added, 'You're on.' She kissed her brother sloppily on the cheek. 'Happy Christmas, bro.' Staggering round to Livvy she did the same. 'Thanks again. Don't wear him out too much,' she giggled, 'he's got to drive me to Yorkshire at some point.'

The women ambled in the direction of the kitchen, loudly discussing where they'd put their coats and scarves. Finally, Mark and Livvy heard the kitchen door slam and there was blessed silence.

CHAPTER 41

Vintage champagne – made with pinot noir, pinot meunier and Chardonnay grapes. The perfect way to celebrate a sparkling romantic occasion.

Livvy eyed the debris from the meal. 'Washing up?'

'Leave that. I'll do it later. Let's sit in front of the wood burner where it's slightly more comfortable.' Mark took her hand and led her to Pete's chair. Putting another next to it, he tucked a cushion behind Livvy's back and stretched out beside her.

When they were settled, Livvy wriggled her socked toes to soak up the heat. 'Quite envy Simona her central heating. This place is freezing when there are no customers. Next job, I suppose. Double glazing and a better boiler.' She sighed. 'This place eats money.' When Mark didn't respond, she asked, 'Are you all right? You've gone quiet. The snowball shenanigans this morning wear you out?' A sudden thought struck. 'Oh,' she said, horrified. 'You don't regret what happened? Last night, I mean?'

He shook his head, a smile playing about his lips. 'No. I don't regret that for one minute.' He fixed her with a look that was heartbreaking. 'How could I?' Getting up, he reached into the pocket of his jacket hanging on the chair at the table where they'd eaten. 'This is your Christmas present,' he said, rejoining her in front of the wood burner. 'It's not much. Nats would have scolded me for not getting you diamonds or perfume or something she deems a suitably expensive gift had I given it to you in front of her, but I thought you might like it.'

Livvy took it. It was a small book, old by the look of the battered maroon leather cover. 'Adela Dickson: A Life,' she read. 'Oh,' she said, surprised. 'It's a book about Adela. Have to confess, with all that's been going on, I'd forgotten all about her.'

'It's a biography. We were right. Adela had quite the life. Met her lover right here in The George, founded a Home for Gentlewomen and Infants in Distress, and a Scientific Institute for Girls, both of which she ran from her house in Lullbury Bay. The one which is now the museum.' Mark warmed to his theme. 'I've been emailing the research centre at Bindon House, that's the Dickson country seat over in the north of the county. They hold quite a lot of information about her.'

'Is it true she was involved in a carriage accident and an awful tragedy?'

'In a way. Adela used to meet a Henry Lovell and his sister Sarah here at The George. They regularly travelled from London to Exeter and would stop off here in Lullbury Bay. The three of them were great friends, and it's true they all moved in the same circles as Dickens and Ada Lovelace. All interested in the same things: science, philanthropy, literature. Christmas Eve 1828 there was a tremendous snow fall.' Pursing his lips, he added, 'A bit like last night's. The London to Exeter Arrow only just made it as far as Lullbury. Unfortunately, the leading horses' hooves slipped on the snow coming down the hill towards The George and crashed. Henry Lovell suffered catastrophic injuries. His sister survived. Sarah went on to live a long and fruitful life and she became Adela's companion.'

'Poor Adela. So we were right, she did suffer an awful tragedy. Poor, poor woman.'

'It was a blow to both women. Sarah lost her brother and Adela lost a friend. Nats drives me insane, but I can't imagine how I'd feel if something happened to her.'

As ever, Livvy was touched by the love Mark had for others. She squeezed his hand. 'Absolutely.' She paused, thinking. 'Henry was more than Adela's friend though, surely? He was her lover. The book of poetry Jonquil found in the chimney must have been Henry's. Although I don't see why it had to be hidden.'

Mark sat up, a gleam in his eye. 'Ah. There's a little more to it. It's fascinating. The research centre has been a mine of info. The general story is Adela lost the love of her life in the carriage crash when Henry Lovell died. The truth is rather more intriguing. Sarah Lovell wasn't just Adela's companion, *she* was her lover, not Henry. The women were conducting a love affair, but a clandestine one.'

'Oh my goodness.' Livvy's mouth dropped open. 'You mean they hid in plain sight? So the lovers didn't run away after all!'

'Only as far as Adela's house in town. They lived together until both were in their seventies and died within weeks of one another.' Mark smiled. 'I find it incredibly touching. Together they ran the home for women and babies and taught girls at their scientific institute which took in pupils from the town. Adela was a strong, independent woman who believed passionately in the power of community. She was just like you, Livvy.'

'What a story. Go Adela!' Livvy said, her eyes shining.

'You once said you didn't want The George to be associated with a tragedy. I think Adela's story and the role The George played in her life is something much more worthy of celebration. Something to display here. It's frustrating to not know why Sarah felt she had to hide her book of poetry. Don't think we'll ever find out the answer to that.' He smiled his love at her. 'Perhaps Adela and Sarah were so happy they simply forgot all about it.'

'I really hope they were. Oh, Mark, thank you. Thank you so much.' Livvy hugged the little book to her. 'This is a lovely Christmas present, one which I'll treasure. And what a thing to find out. You're right, this is The George's history I want to celebrate. I'll celebrate Adela and Sarah, and Henry too. What a story. Ooh!' she said, putting the book on her lap and clapping her hands together, making Angel wake up and grumble. 'I could name the letting bedrooms after them. The Adela Dickson Suite, how does that sound? And maybe make a display of this book and the poetry in a case. It would be wonderful, wouldn't it? I love the idea of connecting to The George's history and so will my customers.'

'I'm glad you like it.'

'Like it? I love it!' She drew him to her and kissed him. Drawing back, she added, 'It's worth far more to me than perfume or diamonds.'

'Will you be around to do all this? Get the themed rooms sorted, get the skittle alley refurbished?'

It dawned on her what he was thinking. 'You think I'm going to accept my parents' offer of The Olde Gates, don't you?'

He shrugged. 'It would be an amazing opportunity. You're ambitious. It's a bigger establishment. You could achieve extraordinary things with the opportunities it would afford.'

'That's all true. And I have to confess I've already got plans forming in my head.'

'Of course you have,' he said, smiling. He drew her hand to his mouth and kissed it.

'And, if I'm really honest, I'm not going to hang on to Fabio for all that long. Someone with his talent will want a bigger audience to perform for at some point. The George meets his needs at the moment, but it won't for ever. I can see him fitting right in at The Gates. But–'

'But?'

'Oh, Mark, I've worked so damned hard on The George. I love my team, I love the friends I've made.' She took his hand. 'I can't imagine being anywhere else. How could I leave?' She blew out a gusty breath. 'With everything that's been going on today, this is the first chance I've had to really think it all through.'

'You could,' Mark said carefully, 'run both.'

'Both?'

'Yes. The George and The Olde Gates.'

'Could I?'

'I think you could do anything you set your mind to.' He paused and then added, 'I could say the thought of you not being in Lullbury Bay, not being just down the road from me, tells me to say, don't do it. Stay in Lullbury Bay. Stay at The George. But I can't put my selfish needs in the way of your career, of your ambition. I can see you making a huge success of your new hotel. You're just like our friend Adela. Brave, independent, resourceful, hard-working, wanting to be at the heart of the community. I'm thinking all that,' he grinned, 'and what I really want to do is sweep you upstairs, take you to bed and order you to forget all about your career.'

'But you'd never dream of saying that.'

'Of course I wouldn't. I have too much respect for you as a person.'

'Bit too alpha male for you.'

He nodded. 'Agreed.'

Livvy wrinkled her nose. 'I quite liked the bit about you sweeping me upstairs and taking me to bed though.'

'I'll do that later, I promise.'

She reached out for his hand again. 'I love you, Mark Cavanagh. I really do.'

'Really? Thank all the Christmas fairies for that.' He sucked in a breath. Turning to her he said, 'And I love you. I have done for a very long time. What Nats said was right. I've been boring on about you for weeks. It's just that I kept overhearing you say you hadn't time for a love life, that you saw me as a friend.' He pulled a face. 'It's how most women see me. Friend material. And with you I thought I'd slipped into the friend zone. Again.'

'They really don't, you know. I think one thing I love about you most is you haven't a clue how sexy you are. With your gorgeous floppy hair and those muscles you hide away so successfully. Your lovely sense of humour and your kindness. I think you're drop dead sexy, and I know there are lots of other women who think the same.'

'Okay.' He tried not to look as if his ego had been massaged and failed. 'Well, that's good to hear. Thing is, I love you so much, Livvy. And loving you means I have to let you go to do whatever feels right. If that means taking over The Olde Gates, then so be it.'

'You won't have to.' She smiled at his confusion. 'I'm not going anywhere. How could I? I've poured my heart and soul into this place. It's got me in its grip. Lullbury Bay is such a special place and I want to be part of it. Oh, I'm accepting my parents' offer of The Olde Gates, it would be madness not to. But I'm not leaving The George. How could I leave Stewie and Eli, Lucie, Bee and Daisy. Austin and Aggie. Lovely Karl. Even Old Pete. Actually, *especially* Old Pete.' She paused. 'How could I leave you?'

'How's it going to work, then? Don't get me wrong, I think you're capable of achieving whatever you want. And I'll back you all the way.'

Livvy shot him a grateful look. 'I *will* run both. Last I knew of The Old Gates was it had extremely efficient management, with a reasonable kitchen team and a chef who's maybe not quite as cutting edge as Fabio, but who will be happy to stay.' She drew herself up, as if sucking in enough courage to convince herself she could do this. 'I think what I'm going to do is own The Olde Gates but leave it to the management to run it. That is, until I get The George properly established and then I'll have a rethink. It might mean me travelling up to the midlands every now and again but I think I can do it.'

'Of course you can do it.' He cupped the back of her neck and, bringing her near, kissed her soundly. 'You can absolutely do it. You can do anything. I love you, Livvy Smith. So much.'

'Oh, Mark. I love you too.' As Livvy responded to him the kiss deepened and became more passionate. It held the promise of trust and love, of now and forever.

A log splintering in the wood burner and falling, sending a shower of sparks had them breaking apart.

'Glad we've got that sorted,' Mark said, with a grin. 'Happy Christmas, my darling Livvy.' He glanced at his watch. 'It's just gone six. What would you like to do with the rest of your Christmas Day?'

'Happy Christmas, my lovely Mark. Is it still snowing outside?' Livvy cocked her head on one side coquettishly.

Mark's lips twitched. 'Hold on, I'll have a look.' He rose and, going to the window, pulled back the heavy brocade curtain. 'Oh dear,' he said, not sounding sorry at all. 'Fresh snow falling. At least another foot down. Don't think we'll be going anywhere tonight.'

'Oh no,' Livvy answered in mock concern. 'Does that mean we'll have to stay in?' She bit her lip, making her eyes go large. 'How are we to keep ourselves warm on this cold night?'

'I really don't know.' His eyes slid to the bar. 'Maybe another bottle of champagne?'

'I think that's a very good idea. And I don't know about you, but I really can't be bothered to go outside for more logs. So we might have to go to bed to keep warm. You know that bit when you said you wanted to sweep me upstairs?' She didn't get any further as he tugged her to her feet, wrapped his arms around her and silenced any more conversation with his kiss.

Livvy broke away, appalled. 'Mark! I've just realised I haven't got you anything for Christmas! After all you've done for me and that lovely book about Adela, which I promise you I will read–'

For the second time she was silenced by his kiss. 'You've given me the best Christmas present I could ever have, Livvy. You've given me yourself. Now shut up, woman. And get up those stairs.'

'Oh, Mark,' she giggled, 'you know, you can be quite alpha male when you want to be.'

'Trust me,' he said, pulling her to him again. 'You haven't seen anything yet…'

ACKNOWLEDGEMENTS

I've been fortunate to live in lots of different places and in each managed to find the hub of the community, a place to enjoy good food and to make friends – a great pub. The British Pub has had a tough time of it lately, with many closing. This is my love song to a wonderful institution. Long may they thrive.

As usual, I called upon the expertise of others to help me write the book. My thanks go to Nardia and Simon at The Plough who gave me the cherry picker story. (Sorry, Simon, I know dogs aren't allowed in commercial kitchens but let's hope no one else notices. By the way, we still miss your epic chips). And to Emma Shrubb, my thanks for giving Livvy tips on how to deal with undesirable customers, not that you ever have any in The Hind! To my long-suffering husband, thank you for the stories gleaned from your brief pub-owning experience. All mistakes are mine.

Thank you to the truly wonderful team at Bloodhound who continue to champion my books and are fabulous to work with.

And to my lovely readers, I hope you enjoy a trip back to Lullbury Bay. Thank you for the support. Much love. I owe you all a pint!